The Hedge, The Ribbon

The Hedge, The Ribbon

A Novel

Carol Orlock

Broken Moon Press • Seattle

Printed in the United States of America.

ISBN 0-913089-48-6
Library of Congress Catalog Card Number 92-75709

Cover image, *Grenipswitch,* copyright © 1991 by Sue D. Cook. Used
by permission. Author photo copyright © 1992 by Roger Schreiber.
Used by permission.

The publication of this book was supported, in part, by the
Western States Book Award for Fiction, 1993. The Western States
Book Awards are a project of the Western States Arts Federation.
The awards are supported by The Xerox Foundation, Crane
Duplicating Service, and the Witter Bynner Foundation for Poetry.
Additional funding is provided by The National Endowment for
the Arts.

Editor: Lesley Link
Copy editor: Audrey Thompson
Proofreader: Brandy K. Denisco

Broken Moon Press
Post Office Box 24585
Seattle, Washington 98124-0585 USA

For Jack

Contents

The Hedge, The Ribbon

Chapter One

I'll collect my thoughts, that's all. It's simply not what I expected. Of course I want to be here with you. What you ask takes a minute to think about, that's all.

The agency called to tell you I was coming, didn't they? They called this morning, that's good.

It is a fine program that the agency has, I agree. Most of the assignments they give us are temporary, a couple of weeks, a month at most. We go to the homes of those who are not feeling well, after surgery, or perhaps a long illness. Or, as you said, just feeling very old some days and it's such a struggle to get out of bed.

I understand that you feel that way sometimes. Don't worry, many feel just as you do. Of course I don't mind sitting in this chair while you lie down. I'm happy you're comfortable. Is the pillow just right?

There, push that pillow corner up. Much better? Good.

And you're warm enough, all tucked in? Good.

So, as I said, the agency sent me, and I thought I'd help with chores. I could dust mantels. Carry things upstairs perhaps? I'm happy to do that if you like.

Yes, you do have the chore people who come and help you with that. I'm not trained to give you medicine, whatever your needs may be, shots or pills, I don't know. I don't even know what illness keeps you here in bed, or in the chair, as you explained that you often sit there. It has a good view of the garden. Perhaps next time I visit you'd like to sit there. Not today, of course.

All right. I've tucked you in and made sure that you're

3

warm. On a day like this we should be careful. I'm comfortable, thank you. I've brought up the snack and the water you wanted from the kitchen. It's enough for your lunch, you say. I'd had mine already, so that was a treat. You're kind.

No, the agency did not say what I should do. Mostly cheer you up, I guess, though you seem happy. I'm not surprised, this lovely house, seventeen rooms, you say. I'm sure you had a wonderful family, children and all, big Christmases. Do they visit?

Of course. Everyone lives so far apart these days. It's good they come to visit sometimes, though.

No, it was very easy to locate this house. My supervisor at the agency said it was the biggest on the block, and it certainly is biggest. It would be a lot to keep up, a good three-storey brick house, with solid wood inside. A genuine antique through and through. As I came up from the kitchen I noticed the banister, the carved base of each post dusted and polished. And on the dining room shelves below, all the china figurines clean and shining.

A fine house, even if as you say, the wiring is old, insulated with gum wrappers possibly. The garden, I'm most impressed with the garden. It's too cold to see much now, but the dead heads of last summer's flowers are all picked off and the leaves raked. The empty bushes themselves tell me how it must be in spring. I like asters, yes, and chrysanthemums. The ornamental cherry, double-flowering? In the spring, the blossoms must look like big scoops of strawberry ice cream.

I imagine it just how you describe it, pinks bordering the walks, sunflowers out in back by the gate. The hedge would keep out a fair amount of the morning sun, but it's clever how you planted sweet violets along it. They catch reflections from the white pebbles on the walk.

So you won't want any chores done? Dusting, laundry perhaps? No? That's fine, of course. The agency just says we're to visit and do whatever is asked. I'll come once a month.

4

I do enjoy the work. Guess I'm a people-person.

That's true I must say, I've never before been asked to tell a story. It's a good idea you had, instead of us sitting around and talking about the weather. But a story, that's a new one.

No, I do like the idea. I only wanted to think a moment, to gather my thoughts before starting. I will get to the story. And already you've given me an idea of what it should be about. I admit, I was surprised when you told me I'd find our story idea in the dish on the dresser.

That little dish held a lot of things. The rose petals scattered on top still gave off a scent when I touched them. Under those, the business card of the plumbing service held the rose scent too. Is that the service you regularly use? Good. Just so you know I can make any phone calls you need made, plumbers, cleaners, whatever. It is handy to have a phone by the bed.

Frankly, I felt I was prying, looking through that old stuff in the dish. Except you asked me to. Postcards and paper clips, a graduation tassel—your daughter's you say—business cards, rubber bands that were broken. And the spring from a ballpoint. An address of someone. You say she's dead now. There was a lot of stuff in that dish.

I picked them up saying, "This one? This?" I kept wondering why you wanted my story to be about something I found in the dish. I picked each up, but not one was right until I came to the green ribbon. Don't they call that ribbon grosgrain? Long enough to wind twice around my wrist.

And that was it. You wanted me to make up a story and you said it would be about something I'd find in the china dish. And there it was, a length of ribbon. A pretty thing.

Yes, I'm ready to start our story now.

Who will it be about?

A little girl, I think. A story about a little girl, and her name might be Angela.

5

It Snows

Once upon a time there was a child who slept in a room in the attic of a house. She had a dormer window which looked out onto a neighbor's garden. This little girl had a brother who was taller than she was, two years older with blond hair and blue eyes and a voice that often confused her. Sometimes Johnny teased her and other times he was her friend. It seemed strange, he looked the same but his voice changed and he was different.

Angela was the girl's name. Her name was Angela, and her middle name was Mona. Or her name may have been Zoey, not that it matters. Anyway, the girl was small and dark, 'a gypsy child' her mother said when she was teasing, and Angela Mona Zoey lived in a place where it never snowed.

That was a lovely part of the country, sunny summers and mild winters. Maples were the only trees that changed color in November. As for spring, the people hardly knew it came, change came so naturally from faded leaves to new buds. Then it began to get warm and they knew.

Of snow, Angela knew what she had heard. People hated driving in it, kids loved playing in it for hours and built snowmen. Snow was like the frost in the refrigerator, cold; and like the fur on the cat, soft; and like the new baby brother or sister she was supposed to get the summer before. None of them ever came.

Snow, in short, was like many other things in Angela Mona Zoey's world. It seemed to her that much of the world was like a big deck of cards. The cards were the ones her parents played bridge with, except they never used a real bridge. Grown-ups knew what cards meant and said, "This one goes with that one" and, "That one's bigger because it has a picture." To Angela all the cards looked alike. She imagined a big hand, standing somewhere above her, gently tossing cards on a pile on the carpet. All the cards landed face down, but they actually had names like electricity, map, oboe. Until one particular morning, snow was just another card, its face hidden by the pile and a meaning she could not see.

That morning it snowed. More truthfully, it started to snow. Angela woke up in her bed, the head of which faced the dormer window. She looked out. Flecks of white were getting in the way of the old lady neighbor's garden. Angela looked again. The garden was not quite right this morning, not the way it looked yesterday. The fat bush by the lady's back door had lint on it, and the windowsill looked like the paint had come off, and farther down the street somebody had painted Mr. Pembroke's back windshield white.

Angela rubbed her eyes. She looked and saw more. The newspaper on the front walk had no headline. Down the middle of Pear Street, the white line looked wider. The yellow house across the street had coconut on its shingles. And all around, between houses and across the sky, in front of the stop sign and between her fingers if she looked through them, white flecks fell.

Angela turned cards over rapidly, this one and that. It took only a moment to find the one she wanted—snow. She closed her eyes and thought it and opened her eyes thinking that word. It was snowing harder.

Angela leapt out of bed. She ran toward the door, trailing a ribbon of sheets and blankets across the floor. She got caught and tripped until she untangled her foot and got to the door in only her nightgown.

She opened the door. "It's snowing," she shouted, running down the stairs. She smelled cooking from the kitchen. Her mother stood by the counter pulling bacon apart, and Angela ran up behind her. "It's snowing."

"You don't have your bathrobe on," her mother said when she saw her.

"But it's snowing. It is."

"What?"

"Look out the window, it is."

Her mother's hand pulled back the red kitchen curtain and sure enough, white flecks came down on that window too. "Why, you're right. That's amazing. But you still need your bathrobe."

Angela ran back up to the attic to get her robe and began running down again, but turned back to get her slippers. When she finally got to the kitchen her brother was there and he too had heard about the snow.

"I like it," he said. Angela burst through the doorway calling "Me too," and trying to button her robe at the same time. Then her father came in, still in his bathrobe because it was Saturday, and he said in his deep voice that went with his dark brown hair and brown eyes, "Snow. How do you like that?"

"I love it." Angela ran to the back door and got under the curtain to look out.

"It'll stop soon," her mother said over the sound of the bacon.

Her father's voice agreed, "Can't keep up around here."

Angela looked out the window and saw they were right. Even in the moment they spoke, fewer flecks hit the window. She looked over the yard and saw it happening everywhere, fewer white spots drifted down. To be snow, Angela decided, there had to be a lot of them.

The idea made her cheek burn against the cold pane. She felt sad inside and it hurt all over, like the time she burned her hand on the water faucet.

"No, it won't," she said quickly. "It won't stop."

Angela kept watching the snow. She could hear voices coming from the table and her brother's sounded best of all.

"That would be neat. Suppose it snowed and snowed, a

whole lot, and I could get a sled and go down Thurmond Street. That would be neat. Wouldn't that be neat? Suppose it did."

Angela watched and she noticed right away that her brother was right. If it snowed and snowed that would be wonderful. It would even be better than now, which was great because it was snowing harder again. It was snowing as hard as before.

Angela watched but the voices kept talking behind her. They distracted her because she wanted to think of the snow. It was such a big thing made up of all the many small white parts. They were moving around, chasing one another and dancing away, jumping on top of each other and soon she lost track of which one she was watching. The snow got busier for a minute and then lazy, as if it hardly cared, and then got wild again with its white bugs chasing each other to the ground.

"It won't keep up," her mother's voice said behind her.

"Probably melt before breakfast," her father agreed.

But her brother said, "Hey, if it did keep up, I mean really keep up, then we couldn't have school Monday. And Dad and I could go hunting, out in the snow. It would keep coming down. That'd be great," which was when Angela caught on.

Each time anybody said words about the snow stopping, it fell more lightly. Then when her brother said he wanted it to snow, it snowed again, faster, as if it were running a race.

Then her mother said, "It'll probably end while we're eating," and the snow slowed down. It acted like it wanted to leave.

Angela tried it. "It will keep up, it will." The snow fell harder. "Mom, don't say the snow's going to stop. You might be making it stop."

"Don't be silly, Angela."

"But maybe it's like that. It's like the little cat Mr. Pembroke got. Maybe it runs away unless you're nice to it. Try, please Mom, say you want the snow to keep going."

9

Her mother said, "Angela."

Angela said, "Would you?"

"Oh all right. Maybe it will keep snowing."

With that, the snow came harder.

By now Angela's brother had come up beside her. He pushed the curtain aside so he could see too. "Hey, she's right," he said. "Look at it go," but he was teasing. He started tickling her and making her bump into the door with the cold glass against her face.

"Stop it." She pushed back. "I am right. Look, you stopped thinking about it and look what happened. See over by the fence. There's no white snow coming at all."

Her brother looked. "Yeah, you're right. But I wish it would keep up." And it did.

Angela left the door and went over to the table where her father was sitting drinking coffee. She knew what she had to do. It took a lot of arguing, but Angela knew in her heart what was right. Everyone had to believe, and say so too, her father, her mother, Johnny and Angela herself too. If they kept believing, the snow would fall harder and harder. Perhaps it would never stop, except when they asked it to. She doubted that would ever happen. She made her mother say again, "Maybe it will keep snowing." She showed her father how it worked. At last he set down his blue coffee cup and pulled her onto his lap.

"Okay, Angela. I believe." His arms and the furry green bathrobe felt warm around her shoulders. "It will keep snowing and maybe even make drifts. It will cover up the front walk and I'll have to go buy a shovel. Then I'll have to ride a sled to work and we'll have reindeer in the garage. How do you like that?"

His arms felt warm but Angela slid out of them. She ran to the back window. She didn't have to answer his question because her father could see perfectly well how she liked it. The white flecks raced past the window harder than ever.

10

"Breakfast is ready," her mother said.

They sat down to eat, but first Angela insisted they pull all the red kitchen curtains so everyone could watch. "Keep believing," Angela said, and she watched it while she ate her scrambled eggs, a piece of toast, and some bacon.

That method worked for a while. Angela checked the windows and checked her family's faces so they kept on believing even while they talked of other things. If the race against the window pane slowed, she reminded them. In a way, as she soon saw, they liked it. Her father said reindeer could live on the vegetables left in the garden. Her mother said she would put extra wool blankets on the beds if the weather got a lot colder with so much snow around. Johnny helped most, talking about how he would have a regular sled, and a bobsled like they did in the Olympics, and a spinner dish, just for scooting in the yard.

Angela felt fine until, before long, she noticed a problem. Each time they stopped believing, the flakes got bigger and slower. Then she reminded them and they started believing again, getting smaller, faster flakes. Yet they never quite caught up to where it had been before. By the time Angela finished her toast and took her vitamin, they were losing ground. It was hardly snowing at all.

Her mother had noticed too. "Angela, want to play with your dolls today?" Her voice pretended nothing was wrong. "We could set up the doll house and put it up in your room."

"No, thanks." Angela swallowed her vitamin but still felt it stuck in her throat. She wanted to cry. They were all believing, she could tell, but it wasn't enough. The white curtain beyond the window was as thin as when she woke up and looked from the attic window. If the snow was stopping it was going just the way it had come. She got up from her chair and walked to the window.

"Dad," she said at last, "is it just snowing here, or other places? I mean all over the world?"

11

"Probably just in Millford," he answered. "Maybe out by the farmers, too."

"Could it be snowing only around here, between here and Johnny's school?"

"It's possible. Maybe it's just snowing in our neighborhood, why?"

"We have to tell them." Angela suddenly grasped it. "We have to go tell the neighbors not to think it's going to stop. Tell Mr. Emerson and Mrs. Roman and Mr. Pembroke. Everybody has to believe."

"Oh, no," her mother said, but Angela insisted.

Her father seemed to think it was a good idea. Angela could see he didn't believe as much as he pretended, but he said there was no harm, the kids should get out in the snow anyway. Johnny backed her up because he wanted to go and tell everybody it was snowing. He acted like he had caused it. His believing still helped, although not as much as before. The snow was getting lighter and lighter.

At last her mother agreed, but she insisted they both take a lot of time to get dressed with blue jeans and double sweaters, and their warmest coats. They had to wear hats. They had no mittens, so Johnny was made to promise not to make snowballs until Mom located some old gardening gloves. Then they went out, Angela and Johnny, in their rain boots and warm socks and thin socks under that. Angela stepped on the porch and snow covered the toe of her rain boot.

"She's such a dreamer," her mother said. "It's the only way she'll ever learn."

"Crunch," the snow said.

Angela's mother shut the door and waved at them through the window.

Outside, the snow-world had a whole new color. It was white everywhere, just as it was green everywhere in the summer. But this was white. The walk outside was white and the fence posts, the front of the mailbox had white on it, and even the rose bush had white taffy pulled over it. Johnny opened the gate and it creaked with a different noise.

Snow made different shapes. The rocks along the curb looked like a line of rabbits. The houses looked like sundaes, with chocolate roofs showing through. The cars were sleeping cats and their tires were circles of licorice, except on the bottom where the snow had eaten.

The air tasted different. It tasted like frosty wool and made clouds in front of their faces. Some snow landed on Angela's tongue and she licked her lips to get the rest of it. Walking on snow made her think of apples, and the taste was kind of like apples, very cold apples.

Best of all, snow still fell. It itched her cheeks like hair. It fell onto her hands and she closed and opened them, and it was gone. She reached out and caught more. Angela and Johnny stood outside the gate and Angela wanted to just stand there, turning around and around, but she knew she could not. The snow was faint, no more than speckles toward the end of the block. They had work to do.

The two children went to the end of the block and started along it. They worked down one side and up the other. They passed up their own house, plus the empty one across the street, but except for those, they left out only the old lady next door.

The first two houses were easy. People were home and they already knew it was snowing. Angela asked, "And you want it to keep snowing, don't you?" which they did. Snow fell harder.

Then they came to Mr. Pembroke's. They knocked and it took him a long time to come to the door. Mr. Pembroke was a nice man but cranky today, he said, because the mail had not come. He wanted to go see a remnant, he said, but could not leave until the mail came.

He was a tall, thin man Angela had never talked to, but she liked him at once. She asked if he wanted it to keep snow-

13

ing. He said snow was probably why the mailman was late. Angela asked him again. He agreed that snow was beautiful and fun. Nevertheless Angela was getting nowhere.

Johnny had to take over and explain how his sister believed everyone had to keep wanting the snow. Johnny acted like he was blaming the whole idea on Angela, but she didn't mind. Finally Mr. Pembroke said, "Oh all right, what am I supposed to say?"

"Say you like the snow," Johnny told him.

"Love the snow," Angela corrected.

"But I do," Mr. Pembroke said. Angela could see his eyes shining. "Yes, let's have snow for a long time." Then the flakes got smaller and faster.

There were more right away, and each time they got someone new to agree, it happened again. By the time they reached the end of the block and turned up the other side, Johnny started calling it a blizzard. It was coming down harder than ever. It made Angela think of times she got under her covers in bed and the light from the lamp was just pinholes. She wondered what would happen if she piled on more and more blankets, if it snowed even harder. It probably was a blizzard.

They knocked on doors at the first two houses on the other side of the street, but nobody was home at the Roman's house or the Bettlemans' either. They passed up their own house and the mean old lady's. It was snowing fiercely by now, whiting out their steps behind them, and Angela could hardly believe houses still hid beyond the white curtain. These flakes were little but so many more of them fell. Everybody believing made them fall and fall, a million bits of paper spilling into the street. Elsewhere, throughout the city, weathermen on all the radio stations said they couldn't believe it, snow in Millford, but there it was. It was happening right outside their own studio windows.

It was snowing by the high school. A listener who lived

14

right across the street from it called in and said so. It looked even heavier out toward the Buckram farm where foothills rose toward the mountains. Down south, by Millford Flats, overlooking the cemetery, snow fell in big lazy flakes and covered the level ground and the cemetery parking lot. Eastward toward the smaller city of East End, and northward again toward Ginnett, the flakes thinned out, but still were falling. Especially in downtown Millford, where the radio stations were located in taller buildings, snow fell like confetti at the annual summer parade. The broadcasters, looking out the windows, were amazed, particularly since snow had not been predicted.

"Wow," said Johnny Maxwell, standing on Pear Street.

"Wow," sounded good, but Angela could tell Johnny didn't believe her idea. She knew what was true. Snow was like sleep. It was like cats and like a ball that you threw that came back to you. Like most things, snow was magic, and she was making it happen. They had to hurry because it was getting colder, so they separated and hurried up the sidewalks to knock on the doors of the last two houses. Then they met at the sidewalk again. It was snowing even harder.

"Just one more," Angela said, pointing to the tall dark house next to their own. It was the house whose garden she saw from her window every morning and the house where the snow had started.

"Are you kidding?" Johnny stared. "That's old Mrs. Madden's, and she'd never talk to us. Come on, let's go home."

Angela followed Johnny as far as the hedge of the tall dark house, but then decided she couldn't go any further. "We have to have everyone," she said. "It won't work if even one person here isn't helping."

Already the sky showed that she was right. A minute earlier they could hardly see the houses across the street. Now the faces of those neighbors, who were all busy believing and helping by watching at their windows, were visible again. The neighbors looked out and tried to help, but already the snow fell a few flakes less.

"Now look," Johnny said, "I'm not going up there. It doesn't matter what you believe. It makes no difference. And that lady hates kids, she could kidnap us and take us inside and kill us."

Angela studied the house. This was the one she heard stories about. She had heard her brother talk of mean Mrs. Madden, and in another story this old lady kidnapped a boy and a girl and stuck the boy in the oven. This was the house.

It was a big house and it did look dark. It had three storeys painted dark brown, with light green shutters and one hanging on sideways. Looking at the garden from ground level she could see all the plants were dead, lying helpless under the snow. The old lady probably killed them. The front door was green, but dark green, and it had a big black knocker too high to reach.

Yet the snow seemed to fall in slower and slower motion. She reached out her hand to catch a flake, but had to leave it there to actually get one. Now she could see the curtains falling on the other side of the street. People walked away from the windows as they gave up believing. She had no choice.

"I have to go," she said and turned up the walk.

Her feet crunched in the snow as she went through the opening in the hedge and up the walk. The noise was loud enough she guessed the old lady could probably hear her and would be waiting. She knocked on the wood because the knocker was too high, but nobody came for a long time. Then the door opened a crack and a dark dress pushed up next to it.

Above the skirt was a belt of shiny leather. Over that, a white blouse showed the body of a lady. Above that was a mean lady's face, crinkly like something made out of clay.

"What do you want," a voice said. It sounded as if it were broken and should be fixed.

"Hi, I live next door," Angela said.

16

The clayey face looked down at her, bright black eyes behind glasses. The lady said nothing.

"And we want it to snow. Do you want it to snow?"

The voice sort of coughed, it didn't sound happy. Angela took a deep breath.

"See we want it to snow and everybody else has to too, or else it stops. I figured it out. Please want the snow, why don't you?"

"Why should I?" the old lady said, opening the door wider. Now it was wide enough for the lady to grab her and pull her in.

"Because, because..." Angela wanted to give up. She couldn't put it all into words in time before the lady grabbed her. The lady just had to understand, that was all. She started to cry.

The voice was just as hard as ever. "Because you want me to? Why would I do that? Just go away and leave me alone. Snow, no snow. What difference does it make? All right, I want it to snow. Now go away."

Angela looked back over her shoulder. Johnny stood by the hedge, leaning in to hear, ready to run. Between the porch and Johnny she watched it starting to happen. It was snowing, snowing harder. The big fat flakes seemed to break in mid-air and they turned into a million smaller ones. Johnny's face faded behind it.

"Thank you," she said, turning back, but she didn't see the lady. The door slammed.

By the time she and Johnny came up the walk to their house, Mom was standing on the porch in her coat. "I was coming to look for you," she said. "It's getting too bad to be out."

And it was. The sky had grown very dark and, across the street, lights came on in the houses. Faces looking out were only rose-colored spots through the snow. Angela and Johnny stood on the porch a minute, watching it cover their boots and

17

their coats. There were millions of tiny flakes and Angela could hear them whispering in the quiet air. Then Mom pulled her inside and took off her coat. Mom had made hot cocoa and Dad had a fire going in the living room.

After a while Angela took her cup of cocoa and went to sit by the window. Outside, it still fell, snow, snow. She was tired after the long walk and all the visits, but inside she still thanked them all, especially Mrs. Madden.

She watched through the window until softness covered her, wrapped her up in the snow and the happiness of everyone she knew believing in it. It put her to sleep. As she was falling asleep, she wondered if the snow would ever stop.

Chapter Two

I'm glad you liked it. You wanted a story, and I told one. And you liked it well enough. Of course you may be saying so only to be nice.

That's true, you have no particular reason to coddle me. It is tiring, being sick. The agency said you've been sick for a long time. Not exactly how long, no, but a long time. That's what they said. I never pry into the business of people I visit.

Oh, I visit different people. I make this visit today, another tomorrow. In some homes I do cleaning, in others I cook or pick up a bit. Some people just like to talk, so I listen. For most people I come once a month, but sometimes more frequently. It depends.

No, I'm not often asked to tell a story. Actually, I've never been asked before last time I was here. But it seemed to go all right.

How do you feel today? Well enough then. I could help you over to sit by the window. We could talk there.

Fine, especially since you're so comfortable in bed. Better to stay there. I'll look out the window and describe what I see for you. You relax on the pillows. You can hear me well enough from here.

It's an overcast day. Of course you can see that from the bed. The poppies are closing. They were open when I came through the hedge, red and pink flowers wide open to meet me. A few have lost their petals, not many. I expect they'll seed.

Does the hedge ever bloom? I'd love to see it. White blossoms, are they big? As big as my hand or yours? Yours is smaller and thin, yes, but you'll get better. Don't worry.

I would love to see the hedge bloom. Perhaps I will, the middle of next summer if I still visit. You? Of course you'll be here. So will I, if you want me. I've worked for the agency many years.

Enough of that, what shall we do today? Oh, the ribbon. Of course I remember it. That's where we got the idea for the story, from the ribbon we found in the dish. It's nice you kept it there by the bed.

If that's what you like, of course I could tell you another story. Should this one be about the ribbon too? Well, after all, why not? Let's try again.

Should I tell about Angela again, or someone else? Who? The older lady, of course. Then the older lady it is. I wonder what might happen in a story about her?

Of course, if that's what you'd like, it's no trouble. I promise to put the ribbon into the older lady's story.

Now that I think about it, I see her story is not exactly what you'd expect. You'll see.

Rites of Spring

Mrs. Madden who lived next door actually enjoyed children. Unfortunately, the morning she sat watching the soft focus of snow change the world, the flakes' continual fall took her back to the previous spring, to an incident that concerned daffodils. It was a bitter memory, and so when the little girl came to the door, Mrs. Madden answered in anger.

It had happened the first day of spring. The night before, springtime eve, Mrs. Madden cooked her dinner while listening to the radio news. Between reports of an electrical contractor going bankrupt and a late March storm in the mountains, the local announcer added an upbeat note. Tomorrow was the first day of spring. To celebrate, Amalgamated Florists, with flower dealers all over town, would give away daffodils downtown.

Mrs. Madden remembered the promotion, they did it every year. Each year she forgot, but tomorrow she would remember. She dished liver and onions onto her plate and settled down to dinner and the weather. The first day of spring would be fair and mild, a good day for shopping.

The next morning Mrs. Madden spent two hours in her garden. The foolhardy crocuses had already bloomed and gone, and tulips were beginning to poke pale noses through the dirt. She cleared winter's slow growth of weeds, doused known dandelion locations, then went inside and took a half-bath. Few ladies dressed specially to go into town these days, but Mrs. Madden remembered when she and her friends spent half the day dressing only to meet for lunch and go home. Most of her friends were dead now, or in homes. She herself had lost her husband ten years earlier, to a heart attack, but Mrs. Madden saw no reason to let go. She wore her wedding band and still kept the house they had owned for twenty years.

She and her husband had raised five children in it. Her children had moved, first out, then away, but she still hung on to the property she owned across Pear Street. She supposed one of the children's marriages might break up and they would want to move back, but deep in her heart her reasons were sentimental. She and Charles had lived in that big house before he died and she moved to this other one. She hated the thought of strangers changing it.

After her bath, Mrs. Madden put on powder and stepped into her white linen dress, pulling it up over the slip so as not to muss the collar. She decided on her blue cloth coat, the air still held a pinch of winter, but tied her pink and orange scarf at the neck. It was the first day of spring after all. She put on her tan felt hat, tucked loose ends of gray under the wide brim, checked her handbag for her bus pass and went out.

It was a busier day than usual downtown, and Mrs. Madden no sooner stepped from the bus than she saw, here and there in the lunchtime crowds, people holding daffodils. Most of them had only one flower but some held two or three. She had no errands to run, although she might pick up a new trivet if she passed the right store, so she paused and studied the crowd. Strangers coming from further north along Third Street usually had at least one daffodil. She set out walking in that direction.

The March sun reflected warm rectangles of light from plate-glass windows. Businessmen had taken off their jackets and tossed them over their arms, walking jauntily side by side discussing whatever businessmen laughed easily about. For three blocks the crowds flowed thicker and busier, and with each block more of those passing held yellow flowers. A few had tucked a daffodil into a pocket or the seam of a bag.

The flowers looked yellow and fresh. Daffodils always

22

made Mrs. Madden think of old telephones, though anyone who tried talking into one ended up sneezing. She threaded her way through the yellow-spotted crowd for three more blocks before the bustle quieted slightly.

Here, not so many held flowers. Those who did may have gone the other way first, then come back. She had somehow passed a distribution point, or should have turned and gone east. Mrs. Madden turned and doubled back three blocks, coming once again to the corner of Hoyt and Third, but the vendor must have moved. Hardly anybody had a flower now.

The stream of people moving toward her from further east on Hoyt Street, dotted with yellow flowers, confirmed her suspicion. Flowers danced in these people's hands, and she crossed the street into the stream. People smiled and waved to each other, holding green stems up to gesture, carrying on serious conversations but punctuating points with daffodils.

Mrs. Madden turned east and went a block on Hoyt, then turned again, north along Fourth, because at that point it was hard to tell which direction offered the most flowers. Yet when she reached Mulden, four blocks north, the flowery throng thinned again. She had missed her mark.

It was time to double back once more. Turning south, Mrs. Madden walked the three blocks to Woolworth's. She recalled that she needed safety pins and found that even inside the store, people carried daffodils. They walked along the aisles and leaned over the low racks, shifting flowers from hand to hand to reach for purchases. Mrs. Madden bought her pins and went back outside.

On Fourth Street again, she found disappointment. Hardly anyone passing held a flower. One daffodil lay tangled in a gutter grill, but it looked gritty with water and dirt, not worth picking up. Mrs. Madden stepped over it to cross Hoyt again.

How could she have missed them? Mrs. Madden stood on the corner of Hoyt and Fourth, and reflected that she must have walked right by one of the people giving away flowers. Supposedly scads of distributors were downtown, and there were certainly lots of flowers. She looked left and right, watching for a pot of the flowers or a display. Only rows and rows of strangers came toward her from each direction, few of them now carrying daffodils.

Several older women in the crowd, retirees like herself, had whole clumps of the bright yellow flowers stuffed into shopping bags and large purses. These women had collected handfuls, half-dozens, and full bouquets. Mrs. Madden knew their type. Whenever anything was given away free downtown, cigarette give-aways or cereal samples, they got an early start and made the rounds stocking up. They knew how to make a penny squeal. For a moment Mrs. Madden felt like one of those, a miserly old woman working the downtown streets for a handout, then she reassured herself. She was no such person. She only wanted one daffodil, a sign of spring to set in a vase by the window. She would get only one and go home.

More determined, Mrs. Madden waited and watched the flowery crowd. At last a friendly looking young woman crossed toward her. She wore a yellow cape and carried a lunch sack, probably hurrying back to the office after lunch, but she paused when Mrs. Madden caught her eye and said, "Excuse me, Miss."

The young woman smiled.

"Can I ask where you got your daffodil?" The young woman carried a single stem.

"This? Over there." She gestured over her shoulder. "But they're all over the place. I had four more but gave them away. They're giving them out everywhere."

"Why, thank you." Mrs. Madden watched the yellow cape move away through the crowd.

She decided to go west this time. She took a turn west along Brooke, heading into the mall of small ladies' shops and quality men's wear. The flowers flourished here too, and after

24

two blocks most of the crowd carried them. Two blocks more and the old women passed holding clutches and bundles of daffodils.

Mrs. Madden inspected the blossoms nearby. They did look fresher. That must mean the source lay close. She checked her hair in a plate-glass window, shifted her bag to her other arm, took a deep breath and kept going. She concentrated, looking down the side streets and at likely corners, scanning the bobbing crowd of flowers and faces for someone who stood surrounded by flowers.

It was useless. Three blocks further, the crowd thinned. Anxious faces, hands empty of daffodils, hurried by, office workers rushing because it was well past lunch. Broken glass littered doorways, and when she looked up to get her bearings Mrs. Madden saw a disheveled man, probably drunk, lurching toward her with his hand out. With a sudden chill she realized she had wandered into the seedier part of downtown, the Tenderloin as some called it. The pocket of the man's pants, which were nearly falling, held a daffodil.

Gripping her handbag to her chest, Mrs. Madden ducked around a corner, ran down the block, turned another corner and then leaned against a cold wall gasping. How had it happened? She had taken a wrong turn, overlooked a clue, made a mistake. She knew where she was, but there were long blocks to cross before she got into downtown proper again.

She didn't relish walking them. Her back hurt and her shoes were beginning to pinch. For a moment, she considered calling a cab and going home. She could buy daffodils from a florist if she wanted them. Yet buying flowers missed the point.

She had come downtown to go home with a free daffodil. She would put a clean cloth on the kitchen table, put her daffodil in the opaque white glass vase. She would set it by the window overlooking the garden. The whole arrangement would give a promise of spring, of things freely given, of how

25

the world would look in just a few short weeks. She could not go home without that.

Mrs. Madden collected her thoughts. She was going about this whole thing all wrong, she knew that now. She acknowledged it and set out, with a firmer step, toward downtown again, ignoring the cluttered doorways and knots of strangers who stared at her.

She tried to think. If I were a daffodil, she asked, where would I be? The answer was simple, she would be in her own hand and on her way to an evening at home. If I were a flower vendor, then, where would I be? Of course, she realized, flower vendors would be around wealthier people. They would set up in the business district around stock brokers, lawyers and insurance salesmen who could afford their wares. They would avoid the stores where secretaries and shop girls and housewives shopped. Those types seldom bought flowers. At Second Street, Mrs. Madden turned toward the business district, her handbag at her side once more. She walked with slow determination toward towering building blocks of glass and steel.

In front of Milton-Biggs, she thanked herself for the insight. Milton-Biggs was the largest brokerage house in the city and proud enough to say so with marble steps and a colonnaded fountain that spouted shimmers of shining water. Around it, healthy-looking, tan men passed in fine suits and beige top coats. They carried newspapers and briefcases, and were handsome and intent upon doorways. Among them, attractive young women darted, sleek in high heels, maroon and sharp navy suits, their hair trimmed in less than feminine but professional styles. Both the men and the women carried daffodils, clutched along the grips of their briefcases or folded into their newspapers. Even the policeman who also served as Milton-Biggs' doorman had one silly looking yellow flower tucked into the lapel of his blue uniform.

Mrs. Madden sighed and sat down on the edge of the fountain. From her earlier adventure she knew the flower

26

vendors moved from place to place. They never stopped long enough to be spotted. This place was an obvious target, she would wait. Besides, it felt good to sit. She checked the Milton-Biggs' clock, a flashing band of digital minutes and the stock report. It said 3:15. If no flowers came by 3:30, she would go home.

At 3:45, Mrs. Madden pushed herself to her feet. She had watched the comfortable faces pass for half an hour, watched them nodding and talking together, seen many greet each other with the lift of a flower. The stream of daffodils had been steady, never more than a dozen at any one time. They disappeared around corners to be replenished by blossoms held by those stepping from doorways or coming around another corner. The flowers came from no fixed direction, they never got thicker along any one avenue. They simply came, daffodils. Daffodils tied together with ribbon and daffodils in florist's tape or with moist paper towel wrappers around their bases to keep them fresh. Daffodils stuffed in tiny baby pots, obviously on sale somewhere, and daffodils held raw, in the hand or at the elbow.

At one point it had occurred to her that, with their money, these people could buy the flowers. Florists would not give away what they could motivate the rich to buy. She had stopped a middle-aged man coming out of Milton-Biggs holding a leather case and a clutch of daffodils.

"They're given away free," he said. "You should get some."

"And where would that be," Mrs. Madden asked.

"All over the place, they're everywhere. Here, take one of mine."

Mrs. Madden shook her head. He made the offer as if he had millions to share, here was this poor lonely woman sitting on the edge of the gold fountain without a daffodil.

"I'm allergic," she lied and was glad when he sauntered away.

At least now I feel refreshed, Mrs. Madden thought as she

27

headed back toward the downtown stores. Her step felt brisk, her back was only beginning to hurt again. She must get back to Third and Pollard to catch her bus, and she intended to, but as she approached the broad plate-glass windows again the crowds thickened.

Almost everyone in them had at least one daffodil. Most had three or four. Even a blind man gripped two alongside his white cane. The passing faces looked as joyful as they had earlier. More joyful possibly, reflecting the flowers' golden glow in sun which shone full like a summer day. People carried their coats, some walked along eating ice cream cones, others nibbled cookies as mid-afternoon snacks, and they all, all had flowers. Mrs. Madden could hardly bear it, being the only one in the crowd without that crazy yellow look on.

In another block, it was unanimous. Yellow trumpeted to the right and the left and all around. At the corner by Marshall and Morton Department Store the throng fairly roared with flowers, their heads laughing and turning this way and that with the swirl of the crowd. Every single shopper had at least one. Teenaged kids in patchy denims had them, wealthy ladies in furs had them, and even a tall bleached blonde in a sequined vest who looked like a streetwalker had one—everyone did. The crowd elbowed one another aside, tangling stems and pushing Mrs. Madden along. She nearly fell into the bouquet held by a plain-looking woman in a green coat.

"Excuse me," the woman laughed, the bouquet bouncing against her coat.

"It's all right. But please, tell me where did you get the daffodils?" Mrs. Madden said.

"They're everywhere," the woman replied, giggling now. Her white teeth were banded by scarlet lipstick. "Absolutely everywhere. Walk down any street. Absolutely free. Plus they're free with a purchase at Marshall and Morton. But who'd need that, they're absolutely everywhere."

A surge of the crowd pulled the woman away, pushing

Mrs. Madden toward the building. She turned and found herself facing plate-glass doors and the M&M insignia. She hurried through them.

She could not face the street again without a flower. She knew that now. She would get a flower, if only to defend herself.

Inside, the store was cool and quiet. The hushed carpeted aisles gleamed with showcases and hardly any customers. Mrs. Madden spotted a young girl in a yellow smock along one aisle. The girl stood beside a green plastic florist's pot giving away daffodils.

Mrs. Madden hesitated. The girl had seen her come in and was no doubt instructed to give flowers only to customers. Mrs. Madden turned past the jewelry counter and headed for the elevators.

She stepped from the elevator on the sixth floor—linens, silver and foundations—with her mind made up. She needed a trivet and Marshall and Morton sold them, but it was not the same to spend money to get a daffodil. A flower traded for was not a complimentary bud, an open trumpet freely given. She turned left into the silver department and, spotting another girl in a yellow smock, approached her confidently.

The girl gave two tightly closed buds to a well-dressed man.

"Oh, daffodils." Mrs. Madden glanced toward the pots piled up in the display as if she had only just seen them.

The salesgirl gave Mrs. Madden's empty hands a quick look. "Sorry, they're only given with purchases."

Mrs. Madden turned toward the elevator to hide her burning cheeks.

The doors opened almost at once, she was glad, and the car was empty. That incident absolutely frosted it. She would go home without a flower. She would not spend her money in a store so rude. It was the principle, taking advantage of this day when people came downtown for a breath and a gift of spring, and then making them pay. She gripped her hands around her handbag's clasp and stared down at the floor, nearly trembling.

An empty paper bag lay on the elevator floor. It was a small pink and gray bag with the M&M insignia on its side, apparently tossed away from whatever blackmailed purchase it had contained. Mrs. Madden stooped quickly. Before the doors could open, she gathered the paper top in her fist and lifted it to her lips. She blew until the sack looked reasonably full. The elevator carried her smoothly toward the first floor, and when the doors opened, Mrs. Madden pulled the bag to her side.

The young girl in yellow stood by the fragrance counter now. Mrs. Madden approached her.

"Oh, I just bought something and forgot to pick up my daffodil," she said.

The girl glanced down. "Here you go." With too sweet a smile, she handed Mrs. Madden a big, broad-billed blossom.

The rest was easy. Getting out of the store with her back turned to the girl and the package riding in front of her was a snap. She reached the street and dropped the M&M bag in a trash can, then pulled the flower to her waist for defense as she hurried along toward the bus stop.

The flower was needed too. It was rush hour. Everyone else held daffodils at the ready. Mrs. Madden smiled and nodded, glancing from their flowers to hers. Others had more or bigger flowers, but it didn't matter. She was going home. She would put the flower directly in water. It would brighten her kitchen. It would look friendly in the morning. She had gone through some rough times to get it, but now it was hers.

On the bus the crowd was lighthearted with laughter and the feelings of spring. Many in the seats held bouquets among their packages, others sat stroking a single stem. It was standing room only, but an attractive man stood up and Mrs. Madden settled on an aisle seat, sighing with relief.

All at once she felt a pang of shame. They held legitimate daffodils. She had gotten hers by a trick. What right did she have to smile and nod, sharing this glorious frivolousness? Then she forgave herself. What she'd done, after all, was a desperate act. She thought of her husband and knew that if he was looking down he'd forgive her too. She studied the blossom, turned and twirled it in her hand, then made her decision. She'd never be able to enjoy the ill-gotten flower as she'd planned to enjoy the free one. It was the first day of spring, just the loveliness of it mattered. All the crowds had been glad and boisterous and for a moment she felt part of it too. When the bus pulled to her stop, she showed her pass and then handed the stem to the driver.

"Why thank you." He grinned and tucked the big, broad-billed flower beside his seat where, as Mrs. Madden now saw, he had a whole pile of the yellow fares.

Mrs. Madden got off the bus first, but the stop at the end of the block was a busy one, so she led a crowd up the block. She stepped firmly toward the gate in her hedge. She felt sad about the outcome of the day, but after all the true idea was more than a flower. With a smile, she opened her gate.

Daffodils lay everywhere. Daffodils were tossed near and far across the grass and the sidewalk, crosswise on her steps and her front porch. Yellow buds piled atop each other like pick-up sticks, tens and dozens and possibly hundreds of them, littered from her gate to her house in tangled heaps. Apparently someone had tossed one over the hedge. Several were caught on hedge branches. Then the other people kept on. She would have done the same thing if she had seen such a lawn. Daffodil heads hung upside down willy-nilly on the rose bushes, several dangled from the windowsills, but most lay tumbled three and four deep on the lawn in glad, yellow, crazy pinwheels.

Mrs. Madden pulled the gate shut and started up the walk. Stems were crunching under her feet when the first flower hit

31

her back. She heard a cry of lighthearted laughter. She broke into a run. Stems whistled through the air and the soft slap of blossoms hit her shoulders and back. Raising both arms against the hail pelting onto her hat, she ran for the steps and stumbled up them. She managed the door and closed it behind her, leaning against it.

At her back, the soft swish of stems hit the door. She did not know how long it could keep up. She would call someone tomorrow to come and clean. Next November she would plant bulbs. In the mirror over the mantel a big yellow blossom curled over the brim of her hat. She pulled it off and let it drop.

Chapter Three

It was too bad about Mrs. Madden. I agree. I understand why she wanted a flower, but it turned out sad. She seemed such a nice person.

You are looking better today. Maybe the pinch of autumn put that bloom in your cheeks. You have more energy too. I was surprised to come up the stairs and see the bed empty. Frightened? Of course not. I was pleased to find you already in the chair, in time for an afternoon snack.

I brought special cookies. I helped myself in the kitchen, I hope you don't mind, and put them on this plate. It makes a pretty setting, doesn't it, lemon wedges for the tea and your pretty cups steaming. Thank you, I will.

Looking out the window, you know, it reminds me. Your hedge is growing, or grew a good bit last summer. I can tell. Can you see? Look over there, several leaves sprout from the gate. The hedge grew into the metal wire. Yes, it is sad to see flowers gone brown. You'll want to mulch the dahlia before the month is up. I mean your gardener will do it.

Can I make up the bed fresh while you sit?

No, just thought I might. Of course, the cleaning people do that.

We'll sit and watch the wind in the cherry tree. Maybe play a game, guess which leaves will come down if it blows through them.

Yes, that's sad to think about leaves dying and falling. All right, a story. That's no trouble. These stories do seem a good way to make my visits useful.

And, look, you've brought the ribbon over to the window

with you. It coils prettily in your hand. I should have known when I saw the ribbon that you planned for me to tell you a story. Truthfully, I did hope you wanted one.

Of course other people live in the town of Millford, lots of people, interesting people too. Have I mentioned Angela's brother, Johnny? Yes, he was mean to Angela sometimes, but there's a story about him too. Here's how it goes.

Why No Daffodils Grow
in Mrs. Madden's Garden

Daffodils never grew in Mrs. Madden's garden. She planted two dozen of the gnarly bulbs, six inches down in loosened soil with a teaspoon of bloodmeal for each. She put them on the east side of her house by the lupine rows. She planted them correctly, by the package, but not one bulb sprouted. Johnny Maxwell killed them by a foolish mistake on a cold night when he was trying to save his soul.

During that same spring when Mrs. Madden came home to find too many daffodils on her lawn, Johnny got a baseball glove. It was a WorldSport rawhide outfielder's glove, World-Sport item number 48651. It came in a black and red box which Johnny stored on the top shelf of his bedroom closet. The day they picked out the glove his dad said a glove wasn't really yours until you looked after it for a season.

There were things Johnny's father said that he knew were true, like the time they went hunting and Dad said never aim a gun at anything unless you really meant to kill it. There were other things, unfortunately, like, 'Your mother wants us to stay home this evening,' that were not solid. They had no weight like a gun or a glove, so Johnny pretended not to hear them.

From April to August Johnny treated the glove once a week with glove softener to keep it as smooth and supple as inner tube rubber. When he practiced and played, the glove was a weight around his fingers when the ball thwacked into it, taking up the sting and closing like a clamshell. It had done best one afternoon early in June when his dad hit flies to him in the front yard. Now, on an evening late in August, Johnny sat in his room vowing the glove would do as well again tonight.

After what his father said about not coming to the game, Johnny didn't feel like being downstairs with the family. Twenty minutes remained before Johnny planned to leave for the school field. His room was on the second floor of the house on Pear Street and his sister had the room in the attic overhead. He actually liked the attic better, but his sister wanted this room, so he said he liked it better.

He had his own desk, beside the dresser, and the desk drawer had an old metal lock which sometimes worked. He had no trophies or game balls yet, so he kept his favorite trading cards—Joe DiMaggio and Boog Powell and a couple others who he changed from time to time—lined up on the back of the desk.

His window, which Mom had put red plaid curtains on, looked out on the back yard. Sometimes he lay on the bed just watching lights go on and off in other people's houses. Even better, if it was still light, he could lie with his head propped up on the sill and watch squirrels in the back yard jump from tree to tree. Their brown bodies raced from one side of the yard to another, bounced to the bases of trees and scrambled up them. They could stop dead in the middle of the trunk then disappear instantly into the branches. He enjoyed seeing the dark shapes of the squirrels grow larger with shadows until he could only watch the way the trees moved in the dark and imagine squirrels leaping from bough to bough. Tonight he already had his gold and white uniform on, it would get messed up lying on the bed, so he sat at the desk reading over his list of New Year's Resolutions.

Thanks to the first on the list—READ THESE RESOLUTIONS ONCE A MONTH—he practically knew them by heart. He had kept the first resolution, except in May when practice started and he got so busy he forgot. On the next two resolutions he figured he broke even. GET A GLOVE AND SOFTEN THE GLOVE EVERY WEEK. He had done that. LIFT WEIGHTS EVERY DAY fell apart because Mark Millings, whose dad bought him the weights, wouldn't let Johnny come over every day.

The next three resolutions he could not control. It was too soon to tell if Dad would take him hunting again in November. They had gone last year, for the first time, and Johnny had not shot anything. Dad shot a white bird. Johnny ran to pick it up and then dropped it again. How he felt that time, holding it, was wrong, was not the way you were supposed to feel when you held a dead bird. But when he got to go again this year, when November came, he would feel differently.

As for the next resolution, GET DAD TO COME TO GAMES, that was a loss. Dad came to one game early in the season, but now they were in the play-offs and Dad wasn't coming. Mom said the team could come over after the game tonight, which was all right. But all right was just all right, tonight's game had to be perfect.

Johnny read the last resolution and pushed the list back into his desk. He locked the drawer and the lock worked for once. The last resolution gave him the most trouble: GET BETTER AT BASEBALL. He'd hated it the minute he wrote it down. All the others you either did or didn't do, but with GET BETTER AT BASEBALL you never knew. He picked up his glove and headed downstairs.

When he got to the park, the green wooden bleachers were already filling with other kids' parents and friends. Since Millford Junior High was in the state play-offs, people from town came too. Millford had closed out the season 11 and 3, and since Ginnett lost to them twice, Millford was up against the best in the state. Johnny walked over to where Coach Sobella crouched by the field house. Staring up at the bleachers, Johnny thought about the best part of all. Mark Millings' father had said his son couldn't go on all the bus trips for the play-offs, so Johnny got to play the whole series. Coach Sobella thought it made them more of a team to have the same players every time.

"Looking for someone?" Coach crouched checking out the equipment. Johnny had been just standing there, staring at the bleachers. Now Coach was watching him.

"Sorry. Just looking for someone."

Sobella glanced at the crowd, then shoved another bat into the bat bag. He waited for the boy to snap back from somewhere, wherever Johnny went when he stood with that slouch, both hands working his glove like it was some kind of magic lamp. The kid was mostly all right, he guessed, but a little strange. Sobella hoped he'd made the right choice for outfield, this one drifting off like he had a nonstop ticket to another galaxy.

"Help me with this stuff," Sobella said. Mostly the kid was all right, he supposed. Johnny worked hard, too hard in fact, and he went after grounders like he was hungry enough to eat them.

Johnny picked up the bat bag in one hand and the catcher's pads in the other, and followed Coach toward the dugout. Most of the team had already arrived, and they stood around joking and tossing practice pitches.

"Coach Sobella." Half-way to the dugout Johnny stopped and leaned the bat bag against his leg. He'd remembered what he wanted to ask and guessed he'd better say it away from the others.

Coach balanced the box of balls on the shoulder of his gold jacket. "Yeah?"

"I wanted to ask, I mean I made a New Year's resolution. Okay? I said, get better at baseball. Now I practice and all, but is there a way to do that, get better at baseball, all at once. Sort of?"

Johnny had let the catcher's pads go and was working his glove, his eyes fixed like he was tracking a high fly. The boy was serious. Sobella shifted the box to his other shoulder.

"When I was in the Canadians, a kid did that. Overnight, like he was struck by lightning."

38

"What'd he do?"

"Caught, hit, fielded, ran, bunted, you name it."

"But how'd he do it I mean?"

"Can't say absolutely, the way you want me to. Plus he traded out pretty soon after that. But I asked him. Said he thought about animals, can you believe it? Like he was a dog and the base was a rabbit or something and he was out to get it. Southern kid, lived in the woods before he came up. Looked like you, like when you go after grounders."

"Yeah?" That was the one thing he'd improved, Johnny thought. These days he could really close in on a grounder.

"You look just like a squirrel going after a nut."

"That's it, see I watch squirrels. We get them in our back yard. That's what I feel like, you know?"

"Could be, it never worked for me. Hit hard, throw hard, that's what I believe. Teamwork and a gotta-have-it attitude."

"Sure."

The boy wasn't listening. He'd taken off for that galaxy again, nonstop, so Sobella picked up the catcher's pads and waited until Johnny followed him with the bats.

During the early innings of the game, Johnny thought about what Sobella had said. He didn't have much occasion to use it, nobody hit much of anything. This was the final game, and with the series tied 2–2, both teams were nervous. For his own two ups, Johnny hit a grounder and made it to second, but got called in when the next guy struck out. The second up, he struck out. He was glad it was the last of the inning. He didn't have to face the team in the dugout.

Finally, in the bottom of the ninth, things started heating up. Millford was ahead, 4–3, but looking at two runners on base and only one out. Johnny stood in left field watching the fog start to roll halos around the field lamps. He tried to remember what he knew of the line-up. The guy in the batter's box already had two strikes and was probably good for a third. That would make one out to go. Toby Jenkins was next in the

39

line-up. Toby Jenkins, the Toby Jenkins. Toby was practically famous for grounders.

Johnny snugged his left hand tighter into his glove and used his other to flex the rawhide fingers. He tried to keep the glove warm and soft in the cold air, as ready to move as a real hand. The fog was paling the lights and the full moon, which had glowed like an extra field light when it rose, now looked like a dull nickel dropped on the fog. Johnny thought about what that kid in the Canadians had said and he thought about squirrels.

Squirrels ran back and forth around the yard, finding nuts, burying them, digging them up again. Their long bodies stretched as they ran, but they pounced to a stop on a nut, like a snapshot froze them. Johnny always imagined them still out there after nightfall doing the same thing, doing what he would have to do soon. And he would have to do it almost in the dark, like them.

Toby Jenkins, carrying his own bat, took up position at the plate. Johnny watched the wind-up and hoped this would be the one. He felt ready, like one of those squirrels, tensed to race and pounce on a nut as it rolled into the outfield. The ball whizzed toward the plate and seemed to dip and disappear into the haze of the fog. Toby must have thought so too because he swung and whirled off balance, turning full around to face the umpire's signal. One strike.

Johnny crouched and imagined the way it would come. He would hear the sound first, that sturdy smack, a lower sound than the high crack of a foul or a fly. Jenkins always hit the ball hard, hard and fast, which was why infielders dove and missed. Johnny would have to know where it would come, trust his instincts and his eye which had seen the pitch and the angle of the bat.

Next would come the whiz of its bounce over the baseline. By then, his body would already stretch full-length in a run, in the perfect direction, his glove open and angled to scoop up that nut. Johnny crouched deeper and rested his elbows lightly on his knees, his glove ahead of him like a magnet to attract the hit.

The next pitch was a ball, and Jenkins hit two fouls after that, his swing once too hard and then an instant too slow. As the fifth pitch wound up, Johnny felt a tingle in his thighs and adjusted his stance to keep it loose and ready. The ball sped toward the plate and he listened for the deep smack of a solid grounder, a signal in the darkness telling which way it came.

He heard a high crack. It was a fly. On the lower edge of his vision he saw figures stumbling backward from the infield, their faces staring up to the lights. He heard a voice calling his name. Johnny searched the sky too, trying to locate the white glow the bat-sound said must be moving toward him.

There were too many balls. There was a ball in the glow of the moon and more balls in the field lights where the fog displaced them. Twenty, thirty balls shimmered and danced above him, white circles moving toward him through the haze. He raised his arms and tried to forget about squirrels. Squirrels were no use now. Voices were yelling his name, but he tried to think of an animal. But what animal stood on the ground and waited for food to fall on him? No, the ball was a bird. The ball was a high-flying bird, lifting off from the plate, was a falcon, was a sparrow, was a hawk. If he just held out his hand with food in it, the bird would want to land there. The bird was tame. It watched him as it flew.

A bird took shape in the fog. It was small and white, and it seemed to take its time deciding. At last it lofted gracefully downward. Johnny could not remember later what his arms and legs had done, but he remembered asking please, please. He heard his own voice beg the bird to land.

Then it did. The whole team was screaming and running toward him. They pounded his shoulders and pushed into each other, leaping and pointing down at his glove. He had caught it, they had won. They were the champions. Johnny

41

held onto the ball as they pounded his head and back, repeating his name over and over. When the crowd parted slightly he could see even Coach Sobella coming across the infield in a galumphing run. Johnny opened his glove to see for himself.

The bird lay dead. It was white and about the size of a sparrow, its wings tucked close as if pulling covers around its body. Johnny touched the feathers. They were still warm, but the body did not move. He closed his glove quickly so the others would not see.

"That's right, kid. You keep that ball." Coach Sobella finally came up puffing. "It's all yours. That ball won the series."

Johnny held his glove toward Sobella and opened it. He held out the bird, hoping Coach would take it.

"It's all yours. Your championship ball, Maxwell." Coach had always called him Johnny before, but now that he held a dead bird, he was Maxwell.

How could the others not know? It seemed they did not. They all stared at the glove while he kept it open, and they pretended not to notice. He closed his hand again and ran alongside the others toward the dugout. He hung on to it and tucked it under his arm when they piled into Coach Sobella's car for the ride to Johnny's house. He got to sit in the front seat because he had won the game.

When they got to his house, everybody told his mom and dad and sister about the catch. He had to open the glove and show the bird again. It lay as still and quiet as ever. No one reached to pick it up, but his sister threw a fit asking to play with the ball. He told his sister no, it was his. For once his mother stuck up for him, but it was clear that everyone else thought it was only a ball in the glove.

While his mom was pouring sodas for the team, and Dad took Coach Sobella in the kitchen for a beer, Johnny quietly waited until everyone was busy talking. Then he slipped upstairs. He took the red and black box down from the top shelf

42

of his closet and eased the glove into it, the dead bird cradled in the palm. Then he put the box back on the top shelf and went downstairs to pretend to enjoy the party.

The glove stayed on the top shelf for four months. Johnny never moved it or took the box down to look and find out if the bird was still there. He knew that it was. He left it up in the closet throughout September when school started, and into November when Dad did not take him hunting (that same November when Mrs. Madden planted daffodil bulbs), and into December when he got a new glove for Christmas because he had told his dad he was saving the old one for only play-off games.

He didn't much care about the new glove. Coach Sobella was more friendly to him these days, but Johnny had no plans to play in the spring. He did save the ribbon and wrapping paper from the new glove and take them upstairs. The paper and ribbon stayed locked in the drawer of his desk over the days between Christmas and New Year's.

Johnny had decided on only one New Year's Resolution. It was a thing he guessed he'd better do right away, as soon as the new year started. On New Year's Eve he fought back sleep and kept himself awake until the sound of cars passing had died down long after midnight. The clock said 2 A.M. He could hardly believe he was seeing its bright face glowing in the dark with an hour he had never seen before, an hour when the house was finally silent. It was like this every night but he had never known it before.

Because he had crouched by the open window to keep awake, his body was cold and tight when he slipped from the bed. He kept his p.j.'s on and pulled his clothes over them. He took the wrapping paper from the desk drawer in the dark, lifted his desk chair and carried it over to the closet to get up to the top shelf. He took down the box without a sound.

He walked downstairs on the edges of the steps to keep the stairs from creaking, and managed to get out into the back yard without a sound. The garden tools clanked when he felt his way through them, and he had to set down the box to find a spade. The one he finally found had a broken handle.

It didn't matter. He had picked out a spot where the ground was partly dug and that would make the digging easier. Everywhere else the ground was frozen and packed down hard for the winter. The spot was in Mrs. Madden's garden, which was better too, since his parents might see a dug up place in his own yard.

Johnny slipped through the thin spot in the hedge and felt his way along the ground until he found the softened spot. It was by the side of the house. The ground was icy under his knees when he knelt, and the broken spade handle dug into his palm when he started digging. After five minutes his fingers hurt and felt cut up by the dirt. He wanted to quit, but knew he could not.

Before long he discovered two things. For one, this soil had dark solid chunks that felt like wood worked in it. He picked the solid chunks out and set them aside. For another thing, he'd be digging until morning if he wanted to include the box, so he opened it up and took out the glove. He put the chunks of wood in the box so he wouldn't have to bury them again. He dug the hole deep enough for the glove before he rested.

Johnny wished he could just drop the glove in the hole and shove the dirt back, but he knew that would be wrong. He picked up the glove and took it over under the light Mrs. Madden kept on over her back porch. He hoped no one would see him. He held up the glove and eased its thumb and leather fingers apart.

In his dreams the white bird had rotted and turned into bones, but here it lay, perfect as the day he caught it. Its wings curled close to its chest, and its feet looked like small cup hooks tucked up under its belly. The feathers were soft and smooth under his fingers, their color so white they made

44

Johnny think of snow. He said goodbye and closed the glove. He took it back, wrapped it up in the paper and ribbon and buried it. Then he carried the box of wood chunks two blocks away to put it in some stranger's trash can where no one would find it.

That spring, and for many years to come afterward, Mrs. Madden's lupine rows were wonderfully fertilized. They grew tall as the swords of ancient kings.

Chapter Four

Mrs. Madden did have difficulty with flowers, no one would argue with you there. But then things were never easy for Johnny either.

Why did the story go that way? I don't know. I'm sorry you disliked it. It's only that right after I came through the hedge that day—the gate is broken by the way, did you know that?—that day I saw your lupines' stalks sticking out. You've cut them back and now they're just a frozen tangle. You could see them if we sat by the window.

It's chilly, of course. I'll sit by the bed with you.

Anyway, I saw lupines and so that's how the story went. It's like this bit of ribbon from the dish on the dresser. Grosgrain, yes. Tangle it into my fingers and it goes this way, that way. Here, you play with it.

The cold air makes your fingers stiff, but they'll loosen up. I could go make another warm snack.

The story, of course.

Today you're tired. Well, maybe a little cranky, if you want that word, but I say only tired. I'll go on with the story, but only if you like. Twist the ribbon, there you go. Then what about Mr. Pembroke? Do you remember the nice old man Angela met the day it snowed? Mr. Pembroke lived up the street. Twist once more, that's good.

A Difficult Day for Mr. Pembroke

The day that it snowed was a difficult day for Mr. Pembroke. He liked to leave for Buckram's Farm and Art Gallery after the mail arrived, but the snow made the mailman late. It was a Saturday, making it even more important that Mr. Pembroke get there since Buckram's was closed on Sunday. If he missed Rembrandt's daughter today, he would not see her again until Monday, a thought which frightened him and made him sad.

Lamar Pembroke fried two eggs for breakfast, and ate from his wife's favorite yellow plate. He did the dishes and dried them by hand because they spotted in the drying rack. Then the Maxwell children knocked on the door, asking if he wanted more snow. That annoyed him. Usually the mail came while he was eating and now these children wanted more snow. The little girl asked politely, so he said he would wish for more snow. He did and the snow kept on falling, but he had nothing to do with that.

Lamar Pennington Pembroke was retired, seventy-three years old, a pharmacist all his life. He had graduated from Millford State College and worked at Foster's Drug and Home for forty years. A tall pencil of a man, he had married the year he was thirty, and lost both parents the year he turned fifty. Dora, his wife, bore him one child, a lovely eight-pound girl, but the child was weak. None of his own pharmaceutical preparations, nor friendship with Millford's best children's doctor had been able to help her, and she died the night before she was to be baptized. After that Dora said she wanted no children, and they had led a quiet life, the name of their daughter buried in a silence only a quarter century of marriage can make so deep. Neither of them blamed the other, yet each

48

feared the other did, and when Dora's weak heart took her away, two years after his parents' death, Lamar settled into a life that, on the surface at least, changed little. He did his own dishes now, and kept the house neat, went to work until the year he retired, and in the evening read magazines alone instead of with Dora beside him. He missed Dora, but he could not have said how, anymore than he could have explained the shock that hit him the day he entered the Buckram Gallery and met Rembrandt's daughter.

On this Saturday, when the snow finally stopped falling, the mail still had not come. Lamar left without waiting, taking the keys to his blue two-door Chevrolet. It was fifteen years old but kept up so it ran like a top, and these days he used it only to drive out to Buckram's six days a week. Each round trip added thirty miles to the odometer. He brushed the snow from the windshield and checked the street for children, then backed from the drive and slid onto Pear Street.

While waiting for the mailman, Lamar had read the drivers' manual and now this was it. Weaving up Pear Street, trying to dance a metal elephant across ice, was far more difficult than the pages about driving in snow described. He began to have doubts about reaching Buckram's, but decided he must try. Going without Rembrandt's daughter for one day was bad enough, he refused to face her absence two days in a row. He would get there as long as he kept moving and whether he moved forward, backward or broadside meant inconvenience and delay but little difference. The Chevy spun the turn onto West Brooke, wobbled back into line, and made its uncertain way toward the Elmwood turn-off. At Elmwood, it spun again. Lamar righted the hood toward the road, and kept going.

As he drove, Lamar thought about Rembrandt's daughter. He and Dora used to drive out to the Buckram's Farm and Art Gallery on summer Saturday afternoons, and since his wife's death, Lamar kept the tradition, taking a spin through town and out to the farm once or twice a year because it was good for the car to go the distance. Then one afternoon a year and a half ago, he recalled it as a clear summer day, he walked through Buckram's front door to be confronted, directly above the silver tray where wealthy patrons left calling cards, by a dark resinous piece of canvas with a glow of light in its middle. The glow, a young woman's face, stopped Lamar in his steps.

Lamar left the door open and approached the canvas on tiptoe. He drew near and pushed his face close, blocked by the small table with the silver tray. He simply stared. At his back a gust of wind swung the door shut with a thwack, but Lamar heard no sound.

It was a painting of love. Blue eyes told of sorrow and laughter. Porcelain cheekbones crested in shadows. Peach skin drifted off into golden hair that curled like surf in rings down to where her shoulders sloped, draped in a shawl. Her mouth was small and plain, set in pleasant patience through what must have been hours of sitting. Her hands folded together on her lap, still and white, but they lifted and reached to curve around Lamar's cheeks and press them.

"I see you've found our little masterpiece."

Lamar Pembroke whirled. Howard Buckram, alerted by the door's slam, had come downstairs and stood behind him. Howard wore, as usual, an ash gray morning coat and matching pants, their parallel creases at right angles toward the floor and sharp enough to give paper cuts.

"Good morning," Lamar said to the man in the morning suit.

"Good afternoon, and may I personally welcome you to Millford," Howard Buckram replied. "What brings you to our lovely little town today?"

"I live here," Lamar blurted out.

That guaranteed, after a few more pleasantries, that Howard Buckram returned upstairs to finish making his calls and

50

left Lamar Pembroke alone.

That a gallery offering a Rembrandt, and other old masters for occasional resale, could be found in Millford was no less strange than an ash gray morning coat on a cobalt blue Saturday afternoon. Howard Buckram, the gallery owner, had made his success up north and, as everyone understood it, returned to the outskirts of Millford to care for his mother. He set up business, temporarily he thought, but by the time his mother died he'd found patrons who liked driving 200 miles to turn off on a country lane. They enjoyed pulling up in a rutted driveway and being welcomed by their impeccably dressed friend, a middle-aged man who ushered them into parlors perfectly appointed to show them remarkable treasures they would never have expected to find here. In short, for selling art, setting is everything, and the rustic setting of Millford made artwork of quality all that much more astonishing. Howard Buckram kept up contacts in nearby cities, they told their friends, so that when estates were sold, Buckram got to take the best pieces on consignment. That was where the little Rembrandt had come from. Buckram had hung it in the front hall hoping that it would move quickly out the door.

Lamar turned to stare at the painting. The young girl's gaze pulled him in. He swirled underwater inside it, lost in blue liquid that felt warm on his skin. He remembered his wife's back against him when he woke up in the night, and knew it had been that warm.

After a long time, when his knees already hurt from shaking, Lamar managed to pry his gaze loose and look at the painting's frame. It was wood with ornate raised curlicues like lockets on Greek statues' heads, painted in goldleaf and worn away on the raised portions. At the base of the frame, set into the wood, a small gold plaque about the width of his thumb said, *Rembrandt's Daughter ~ Rembrandt van Rijn.*

Lamar touched it to make sure it was real. His thumb left a print so he took out his handkerchief and rubbed the smear away. Then, because he felt bold in the glow of this young woman's love, he pulled one of the two chairs from alongside the table, set it front and center for the painting, and sat down. He let time drift while his eyes moved over the canvas and caressed it.

Lamar Pembroke had fallen in love, though he could not have said so. He questioned the stunned, awful silence inside him, and could only suppose what everyone said about art was true. He sensed that this gentle adolescent was Rembrandt's only child and that Rembrandt had loved this child more than, as ministers liked to say, God loved the world. All that love shone inside a one-foot-square piece of canvas. It had lasted Lamar did not know how many years, and here it stood. Lamar leaned back on Howard Buckram's formal chair and let himself drift away from the life he had known. For a time he was Rembrandt, overwhelmed by the beauty and purity of this child.

Lamar sat for several hours the first day. A wealthy couple finally arrived in response to one of Buckram's calls, and in the hub-bub of the patron's arrival, Lamar replaced the chair and slipped away. On the drive back into Millford he prayed the wealthy people would not buy the painting, that it would still be there on Monday.

Lamar had repeated the prayer many times in the past year and a half and it had always been answered. In that time, Rembrandt's daughter had moved from the front hall to the parlor, then to the rear parlor and finally upstairs to one of the former bedrooms. The light changed in each room, but the painting's glow remained pure and evident. Lamar Pembroke came every day, and got used to taking up residence in the various rooms and spending hours in each of them. Howard Buckram also got used to Lamar Pembroke, and he hardly minded the local fellow stopping by. One day Lamar asked the price of the piece, but he seldom bothered Buckram after that.

All of which explained why, on the day of the big snow, Lamar Pembroke sagged like a towel draped over the steering wheel when he reached the edge of town. He had skidded and slid all the way through Millford and come back out the western side where snow lay even deeper on country roads. The sun was beginning to set. He'd never get out to Buckram's in time, or if he got there, it would be only for a minute, a fleeting glance, before Howard Buckram shooed him out the door.

He bumped along Highway 12, rolling into ruts and spinning the tires to lurch out of them. For the past year and a half he'd been meaning to take an afternoon off from Buckram's and go to the library. He wanted to fill in a few details to the completed life of Rembrandt he'd already imagined. It occurred to Lamar now that any biography of Rembrandt surely would have a photograph of so fine a painting, and at least that way he would get to visit with a photograph of Rembrandt's daughter. He edged the reluctant car onto the gravel, ground the wheels until they got purchase enough to turn the car, and headed back into town.

Three hours later Lamar let himself back into his house and turned on the lights against the dark and cold. He left the heat off but ran hot water into the tub and sat down in it. He felt despondent.

Granted, Millford's library was a small one, little bigger than the starting Carnegie collection, but it offered five works on the life of Rembrandt van Rijn, two of them lavish books with color plates of all the major works and black and white photos of many others. Lamar had looked at portraits of burghers and doctors and military men. He had seen portraits of the wealthy and of the poor and numerous portraits Rembrandt did of himself.

Lamar had read other works of art history too. He nearly emptied a shelf of the Dewey Decimal 740s and combed the books' indexes and lists of plates. Not one photograph, nor any of those in the other books, nor a single line of print, nor even a word in the indexes gave a clue about Rembrandt's portrait of his daughter. Nowhere did he find mention of *Rembrandt's Daughter,* a work done in oil presumably between 1630 and 1670. Nor did any of the many pictures he saw bear a hint of resemblance to the face his mind envisioned so dearly. Only one muddy reproduction, in the paperback *Lives of All the Major Artists Throughout History,* vaguely resembled the face of the young woman Lamar loved. It turned out to be a detail from a Spanish fresco.

At 5:15, when the librarian turned out all but the green exit light over the door, Lamar left two tables littered with stacks of volumes and scribbled slips of paper. He carried one piece of paper home. In a thick volume he had found an address of a museum in Amsterdam which had published a dozen catalogs of all Rembrandt van Rijn's work. The words of the address were foreign so he had taken pains to copy them correctly.

After his bath, Lamar fixed himself a light supper and ate it quickly and without joy. At last the dishes were done and put away, and he turned on the light over his desk and settled down to work. He could not guess at what the catalogs might cost, so it appeared he would have to write at least twice before he held them in his hand. He used the smallest, most common words he knew to ask the catalog's price and only hoped someone at the Amsterdam museum could read English. When the letter was done he signed and addressed it carefully. The following Monday, he bought two International Coupons at the post office, enclosed them for a reply, and mailed the letter off.

Six weeks passed. Lamar used the time to learn more about Rembrandt. He went regularly to see the painting and found himself falling, if possible, even more deeply in love. He learned to look beyond the face and appreciate nuances of the background hardly visible before. There were deep grays and browns behind the young woman's figure, and he now knew that light came from a distant window. It played over her left shoulder and glossed a mirror on a dresser at her back. The room was carpeted, as the mirror reflection showed, and the carpet's braided pattern made curls like those in the young woman's hair. The room seemed warm, perhaps a fireplace gave the rose tinge to her right cheek. When he looked at that cheek, Lamar could almost smell wood burning in the fireplace. In the distance, a kitchen gave smells of ale and of mutton cooking. He could detail the mounds of rich bread rising in the long hours of afternoon while the portrait was painted.

He also knew a great deal more about Rembrandt's life. Each morning before going out to Buckram's, Lamar hurried to make a stop at the library. He exchanged the books he had read for others pulled from the shelf. He read them all, in the order in which they were shelved—five biographies of Rembrandt's life, two lives of the Dutch masters, and a dozen or so histories of art. Reading helped him wait for the reply from Amsterdam.

He knew now that Rembrandt had painted literally hundreds of paintings, and so he was not surprised, when the letter arrived, at the costs of the catalogs. He also knew that this Rembrandt, the father of the woman Lamar loved, had as a young man been influenced by someone named Caravaggio. After marriage and the birth of his only son, Rembrandt was said to have matured into a style all his own. So far the books made no mention of a daughter, but he'd only gotten three-quarters of the way along the shelf so he hoped she might turn up soon.

Thoughtfully, the letter from Amsterdam was written in English. From it, Lamar gathered that he could either buy all the catalogs separately, or one large volume which compiled and included them all. The complete catalog promised representations of all known paintings by the Dutch master. Lamar weighed the costs, exorbitant either way, and decided to send the equivalent of a month's pension for the larger work. He went to the bank and mailed off a money order for an amazing

55

number of guilders.

Eight long weeks passed. Lamar finished the last quarter-shelf of the 740s and made regular visits to Buckram's. Howard Buckram and the crowded rooms of the old farmhouse had not been kind to Rembrandt's daughter. After lingering for a month in a third-storey bedroom, nearly hidden by a drape, she had been moved to an inconvenient hall location right off the bathroom. For a time Lamar feared she might move into the bath and he'd have to spend long hours studying her face at the side of the shower curtain, but Buckram would not risk work by Rembrandt in moist quarters, so she stayed in the hall.

Buckram had spent a fortune on phone calls trying to move her out the door. She simply would not sell. He had a professional photographer take her picture and sent copies around the world to addresses of patrons which his patrons provided. He sent notices to museums, including the Amsterdam, without getting so much as a nibble. As Buckram saw it, Rembrandt had painted too much. The market was flooded with the stuff, and anything short of *The Night Watch* would have to stand in line for a wall-space. At least, Howard consoled himself, the local fellow kept coming to visit the piece. Sooner or later he might say something to someone, and as unexpectedly as that, the painting would move out the door.

Lamar, for his part, hated climbing the three flights of steps to the third floor, but he came to like the upper hallway location. The light was gentler here, letting the portrait glow with its own light rather than flash in the glare of a cup spot. He had returned from the contemplation of the background to appreciate the face once more. He saw the individual brush strokes, the mauves and pinked whites in her skin, the persimmon highlights in her lips as if her tongue had just wetted them. In the oceanic blue depths of her eyes, a glint of laughter or tears, depending on the weather, made her eyes shine. As he drove to the farm each day, watching winter turn into

56

spring, he saw colors he had never before seen in the land-scape. Purple lay concealed in the gray crevices of clouds, blue hid in the green of budding leaves, and dandelion golds, like those in her beautiful hair, flashed from the ribbon of weeds along the side of the road. Wherever he turned, his field of view seemed one foot square and he could imagine it all as a painting. He would have preferred a world made of brush strokes, those delicate feathers touching each inch of the world with tenderness.

By the time the catalog arrived, Lamar was re-reading the *Life of Rembrandt* he had read first. He had finished every conceivably relevant book on the shelf and now returned to this one in a state of stunned curiosity. Nowhere in any of the books had he found mention of the great Dutch painter having a daughter. Now, on page forty-five of Marlborough's work of 1937, he encountered the fateful sentence which laid the situation bare: "Rembrandt Harmenszoon van Rijn, spelled Ryn in court records, married Saskia van Uylenburgh who died ten years later after the birth of Titus, their only son who survived." Lamar read the sentence again. Rembrandt had only one son. The couple had had no other children. It seemed impossible and Lamar read the sentence once more. As he finished the third reading, the one which sealed it, he heard the thump of a package dropped into his mailbox. Lamar knew what it would contain, and also what it would not.

In the months that followed, as Lamar made his drive out to Buckram's, he gained deeper appreciation for the painter who had done the works in the catalog. As he drove, he envisioned hundreds of paintings, and saw how perfectly the great master's style had been copied to capture the soul of that young woman. He had written a third letter to Amsterdam, and received a reply. The curator's English was poor, but sufficient to convey the truth, "... by Dr. Rudolph de Bourges it was said, this overmake of 1642 etching, by a Rembrandt student could be done possibly." Lamar gathered that the painting had surfaced several times in art history. Each time all who knew Rembrandt had disavowed it as a forgery.

For Lamar's purposes, it did not matter. The father's name made no difference to a man in love, and he had no reason to speak the truth to Howard Buckram. Love in all of its fullness had finally come to Lamar Pennington Pembroke. He knew a completeness he had never encountered before. Now he knew the pain of its absence in college and in work, in marriage and in all the years of his widowerhood. He could catch a remembered glimpse of it in the early days of courting Dora. They had enjoyed many happy times together, especially their quiet, wordless evenings, but since the child's death life had never blossomed like this. As he read magazines in the evening, or as he worked in the garden Sunday afternoons, he guided his thoughts by the beauty of *Rembrandt's Daughter*. If he turned a page, he let it go gently so as not to disturb her repose. When he picked strawberries in the garden, he washed them to gleaming red so she could appreciate their glory.

One summer morning, after a breakfast of strawberries, bathed in cream the color of her skin, Lamar arrived at Buckram's Farm and Art Gallery as usual. Because his legs often tired with the long hours of standing, he took a chair from the first floor and carried it slowly up to the third. He arrived at the end of the dim hall, set the chair down and sat, only to find himself face to face with a still life of thistles and grapes. Lamar looked around.

Rembrandt's daughter was not on the third floor, not in the hall nor the bathroom nor any of the three bedrooms. Lamar checked the second floor, carrying the chair along. He had often reconnoitered like this when his friend had been moved, but this time she was not on the second floor. At last he toured the rooms away from the office and through the main galleries. Then Lamar set the chair back where it belonged and walked into Howard Buckram's office.

Howard Buckram sat, in his gray morning coat, writing

58

on embossed Buckram's Farm and Art Gallery stationery.

"Where is she now?" Lamar demanded.

"Pfuut!" Howard said, looking up. He gestured widely with a gold pen, then went back to his writing.

"You sold her?" Lamar supposed he could find the buyer and burglarize the house.

"It was a fake." Howard glared back and replaced the cap on his pen. "One of the museums finally wrote to me. No wonder my patrons wouldn't touch it."

Lamar waited for more, but Buckram merely smiled. "So where did the painting go?" Lamar finally asked.

"Burned, of course. The estate agreed, naturally. I won't have that sort of thing in my gallery. Imagine what people would think?" He gave a quizzical glance, and then looked toward the enameled brick fireplace.

Lamar looked down. A pile of tangled, ashy twine lay on the grate. He stooped and picked up a small blackened strip of metal and turned it over. It said *Rembrandt's Daughter ~ Rembrandt van Rijn.*

Lamar stumbled out of the gallery before Howard Buckram could see what was happening to his face. A scream gripped him as he slammed the door of the car. He turned the key, the engine roared to life, and he managed to back out of the drive before sobs clobbered his chest. His sight bleared, but he did not need sight to drive this road. He wiped his cheeks against the tears and his wet fingers made the steering wheel slick. He hung on, his chest leaping and contracting, and kept on driving. When he got to the edge of town he turned left up Brooke Street instead of taking Myrtle to the Thurmond turn-off. He parked in the loading zone in front of the library, and half-stumbled, half-ran into the office supply store next door.

The office supply store also provided for the art hobbyists of Millford, and Lamar found all his needs on the shelves at the back of the store. He gripped the edge of the counter while he waited at the register, fighting the storm raging inside him. His body felt like it wanted to twitch and flap like a wind sock. At last the clerk dumped brushes and pigments and canvas into a sack, and Lamar carried it out to the car.

It is no secret what Lamar did the rest of that afternoon and evening. It is all in the painting. Those who saw it after Lamar Pennington Pembroke died, when his will donated it to the library, read his thoughts in that face. It is a portrait painted not from memory but from life, this rendering of a young girl. She might be thirteen or twenty or thirty-two, might be a child of the library patron's own time or of some ancient ancestry. She calmly looks over the card catalog, her expression one of infinite patience at the time it is taking for her father to give her life.

Howard Buckram saw it once. He was old then, and nearly blind, but he examined it with opera glasses and said he could have sworn he had burned that painting. He guessed now he had not. Buckram's young assistant compared it to a photograph from the gallery files, and she testified, for library insurance purposes, that this was in fact the original fake. The insurance calls it the Pembroke Painting, but everyone knows it as *Rembrandt's Daughter*. In the winter time, when all the windows are closed, the library always smells slightly of mutton.

Chapter Five

Well I'm glad that cheered you up. You didn't like the last one so well. It is too bad he died at the end. Of course, he was very old. Much older than you, yes.

I promise I will, another story. And about young people this time if you like. That's no problem, but first, I hope you won't mind, I must give a bit of advice.

Thank you, I do try to keep my nose out of the business of the people I visit. The agency encourages that, and it's nice of you to notice.

It's about your hedge. The gate has broken, I think I mentioned that. It's a month at least now. Anyway, the hedge vines sort of caught hold of it. First it was loose, then a hinge broke, now it's fallen. I'm surprised your gardener hasn't mentioned it.

Well he should. It should be fixed.

I had to step over vines coming in today. How a hedge grows so much in December I'll never know.

Your yard is still nice, of course. It's been a while since you've been out of bed, hasn't it? No, I don't think we should sit by the window, the air is cold. To tell the truth you're looking pale.

Yes, I've said that, it's enough advice from me. Only do get it fixed, I hope you will. Who knows but the hedge won't cover the whole opening? Then where would we be?

All right, the story. Now give me the ribbon. It's good you keep it on the edge of the bed now. The story has to be about the ribbon, of course. I will get to that.

The Man with Cornflower Blue Eyes

Two months after her fifteenth birthday, Angela Mona Zoey Maxwell decided to change her name. Her mother still called her by Angela, and so did her father. Her brother called her unkind names when he spoke to her at all. Teachers at school called her Angela too, but her two best friends, Pam and Josephine, quickly agreed to begin introducing her as "Angie" to the boys they met outside Hamburgette's. They went there for ice cream after the movies on Saturday afternoons.

Pam, Josephine and Angie usually stopped somewhere on the way to freshen up and pick popcorn husks out of their hair. The boys sat in the back of the movie and threw things. When they arrived at Hamburgette's the boys would be crowded outside, sipping sodas and pretending to admire the cars parked in the lot. The girls knew the boys were really watching, standing back and nudging elbows to let them pass, and the boys always burst into laughter when Hamburgette's plate-glass door swung closed behind them.

After her usual sundae, Angie fingered the sets of initials carved into the battered wood table. They said: Eddie Loves Ruth, J.C. + C.O., Charles and Elinor Forever. She and her friends always talked while drawing heart designs in the soup left by the ice cream in the bottom of their glasses. Eventually, Angie followed her friends outside to be prevented from going straight home, which they always said they had to do, by boys who got in their way and bumped into them. The boys said "Oops, sorry" or "Oh, it's you," and then stuck their fists in their pockets and turned away to collide with some other girl to keep her from leaving. The boys could see the girls coming through the plate-glass door and a crowd usually gathered ahead of Angie, Pam and Josephine. Angie and Pam agreed, although never telling their friend, that Josephine drew the crowd. She'd gotten big up-top first, and though she pretended to eat her ice cream carefully, a wet drip usually shone through her blouse when they came out the door.

A few of the boys outside were cute. Angie agreed with Pam and Josephine about this. Especially cute were the ones who went to other schools and drove in from nearby towns for Saturday afternoons. The cutest boys, as Pam and Josephine insisted and Angie agreed, were already inside Hamburgette's. They sat with girls they had taken to the movie and bought their sundaes. Everybody wanted those already-taken boys, boys who had cars and nice clothes.

Pam and Josephine agreed on this, and Angie went along. Those boys inside, plus a few cute ones out front, were the type a girl could fall in love with some Saturday afternoon. The movies had love in them usually. All the songs on the jukebox were about it. Love was what was supposed to happen next, to Pam, to Josephine, to Angie, to all the other girls except the ugly ones. Everyone understood about that.

Except Angie wished she understood better about love. It was a Saturday afternoon late in winter, when they had seen a double bill of Cliff Conway movies, and they had come to Hamburgette's. Angie was feeling odd, so she ordered only a soda. Then, feeling somehow sad, she decided against even finishing it. Josephine had not dripped ice cream on her sweater yet. Pam was saying that one of the boys outside seemed to be watching Angie. Then, suddenly and for no reason she could put her finger on, Angie wanted to leave.

She glanced through the front window. The boy who had been watching her looked away quickly. Angie had seen his face before, or boys' faces like his, and she knew what he'd say when he ran into her. If he had a car, he would point it out. If not, he would suggest a walk over to the culvert which carried Millford water out to the farms.

Angie did not want to talk to this boy. Today she did not even want to hear Pam or Josephine say how cute he was. He was slightly cute. She wanted to be alone, or maybe better than alone. At the end of both movies today, Cliff Conway had fallen in love. Angie wanted that. The boy outside would probably just be like other boys, but she wanted to be in love.

"Do you know if there's a back door, out into the alley?" she asked Josephine suddenly.

"Sure, how come? Anyway, you have to pass the Boy's Room to get to it."

"I want to leave that way."

Josephine raised her eyebrows. Pam stared at Angie too.

"I got something on the back of my skirt," Angie said quickly. The easy lie dawned in Pam and Josephine's eyes. "I think, you know, it just started."

Pam and Josephine understood. Angie threw her coat over her shoulders to make it hang down in back. She headed for Hamburgette's back hall.

The hallway was dim, lit by only one bulb. She passed the door marked MEN where, mercifully, no boys emerged. A black door stood at the end of the hall. She pushed the crash bar and stepped into the alley, which was wonderfully empty, and she headed left to avoid the route everyone else took.

It was mid-afternoon, the last Saturday in February. Ice still glazed puddles in the gutters and the trees lining these streets were bare. A flat plate of clouds slid along the sky, moving in the sharp, chill wind.

Angie decided to pretend she was lost. She knew pretty well where she was, but it felt good to imagine she was lost. Walking and thinking, she took every alley and street that looked unfamiliar as long as it tended toward home. Twenty minutes later, with the sight of the tall downtown buildings over her shoulder, she knew she must be near her own neighborhood.

She had thought about her new name—Angie. It was a

good name as long as she married someone with a strong last name. Sometimes Pam and Josephine, she felt absolutely sure, said boys were cute only because they had good last names. Cliff Conway was already married, although Angie Conway sounded good. Or a Mr. Strong, to make her Angie Strong. Or even Angie Maxwell. Maybe she would never marry.

Angie drew her hands up in her sleeves to warm them. She crossed the street and turned down a block she pretended she had never seen before. It curved away from the direction she was taking, veering off toward a long hill. The sign said Thurmond Street. Angie Thurmond, she thought. It sounded like a bad marriage.

Getting a new last name, she reminded herself, was only a detail of marriage. She tried to focus on love, but wondered if perhaps she should have walked the other direction, over toward the culvert. She had always imagined herself sitting by the culvert to think out love completely, to sort it through. Love had something to do with water. In movies the ocean was huge and sometimes crazy. Lakes were calm as milk. Water simply felt like love. Maybe because water came and went. Water was blue and deep, which was like love too.

Most of all, she thought as she crossed from Thurmond Street, she wanted to be someone she had never been before. She turned down an alley that looked vaguely familiar. She'd be home soon. Then she corrected herself, she did not want to go home. She was lost, walking in a strange city far from being Angela Mona Zoey Maxwell or knowing Pamela Anderson or Josephine Gimetta. She was on her own, someone, a grown-up person with a real life to lead instead of just wishing all the time. That was the hard part, being inside and always wanting. She hoped to change her name and make it different, but today it all felt the same.

She longed be able to take a deep breath, say a few words in magic, presto—she'd be a person, a someone. Parents were someones, teachers too. Even strangers in stores looked exactly like perfect someones. Even Pam and Josephine, even ugly girls and plain boys she could never imagine kissing, and people who worked in her father's office, everyone looked like someone from the outside. Being inside, for her at least, felt like being no one at all.

Angie stopped halfway down the alley and studied a puddle. The ice had melted and the reflection showed the wide bottom of her coat. Then her familiar shape narrowed upward toward this small round face and dark curly hair. A breeze chilled her ankles and the picture wavered. Behind her own shape, the top storeys of a white house showed in the puddle too. They seemed to move like ghosts around her shoulders. Then the picture jerked sideways as Angela leapt. She heard a loud thwack.

The back door of a big white house beside her swung wide in the wind. It hit the wall of the house and snapped back to close. It shut with another thwack. It rebounded and the wind caught it, swinging it open, thwack, closed, thwack, open again. Angie guessed someone would come and close it soon. A someone would come and close it, a grown-up probably. She could watch and study them and maybe learn how this simple act, Being Someone Closing A Door, was done. She decided to wait.

The door took two more loud thwacks back and forth. Angie crouched by a bush nearby, careful not to let the hem of her coat dip in the puddle. Dark clouds dimmed the sky and the wind was cold, so she pulled her knee socks up and closed her coat around her ankles. Gusts of wind swayed the bush, nudging it into the rickety back steps of the house. The steps shook as the bush thumped into them.

The back door of the big house continued to swing, thwack and thwack. It was wide and made of wood, and Angie began to worry that the glass in its small top window would break. The door swung open, hit the side of the house, and then, in air momentarily stilled, eased slowly closed. The wind

66

caught it and threw it open again, thwack.

Angie glanced down the alley. Except for gray weeds tossing by a fence, nothing stirred. Lights shone from a house toward the other end, but those people probably did not hear the pounding. She strained forward to catch a glimpse inside the door. No lights burned in there. An old white stove stood against the far wall, and a broad wooden table sat nearby. The edge of the yellow tablecloth tossed in the wind.

Angie felt sure no one was home. She wondered if this was the house she had heard about. Someone said a house around here was haunted because an old man died in it. It was probably a different house.

She glanced along the alley once more, then mounted the rough board steps. She timed her reach to the moment when the wind let go and the door glided toward her. She would be a nice person to whoever lived here. She would simply close it, then she would run down the steps, take the other side of the alley, and run home.

The wind held the door just out of reach, making it swing slowly beyond her hand. Then a sudden gust hit the door broadside, slapping it at the wall. The door thwacked, ricocheted, and whooshed backward. Angie leapt before it caught her, her ankle hitting the doorsill, and fell inward. She tumbled across a slippery wooden floor, dimly aware that now the lights were on in this room. She heard a boom as the door closed. She also heard her own cry.

Her hip thudded into the thick leg of a table. Her ankle hurt. She watched the door for a moment, hoping it would open so she could run for it. The door stayed shut. At last, when the throbbing in her ankle softened, she pulled herself up by the edge of the table. She felt scared to be sitting on the floor if someone came in.

The door, she now discovered when she pushed against it, was tightly closed. That last violent thwack sprung the latch somehow. The kitchen felt warm for having had the wind rushing through it moments ago, but she listened and heard only a ticking sound on the back window pane. Rain had started.

Another tall door stood on the far side of the room and Angie crossed to it. When she leaned, it opened a crack, a swinging door. The next room was a dining room, a fine, lovely and old one. A yellow lace cloth covered a long dining table and an old chandelier hung from the ceiling. The chandelier's tiny lights were burning. She eased the door open wider and saw a cabinet on the far wall. It gleamed with rows of glasses and plates, each piece of crystal shining separately on the glowing maple shelves. At the far end of the room, a doorway led to another room.

Light was on there too. If people were home, they probably sat in there.

"Hello?" Angie called.

No sound.

"Hello," she called again. "I closed your back door and got stuck inside."

Angie waited and listened.

"I hope you don't mind," she called at last. "I'm in your house now. I'll just go out the front."

She pushed slowly on the swinging door and stepped into the dining room. Then she froze.

"That's fine, come on in." A deep voice spoke from the far room. "Thank you for closing the door. I couldn't get up to do it myself."

It sounded like an old man's voice. He sounded tired but not particularly mean. Taking a deep breath for courage, Angie let the swinging door go and skirted the edge of the lace tablecloth to ease her way across the dining room.

"Hello?"

She peeked around the doorway.

It was dim in there. Shadows outlined a couch with a dark curvy bracket along the top of it. Chairs stood on either side, tall straight-backed chairs with skinny slatted backs that let ribbons of light from the front window shine through. Thick net curtains covered the window, and from that side of the room came scratching sounds of wind whipping rain against glass.

"It's dark in here, isn't it?" The deep voice came from the grayest corner. It was to the left of a big, dark, square mouth—a fireplace. "Let me turn on the light."

Instantly, shadows moved and took new positions. Soft orange light glowed from beneath a cloth shade to the right of a big antique chair. The chair was bigger and older than any Angie had ever seen and sitting in it was a man, an old man, a man smaller and older than any Angie had ever seen.

"Is that better?"

The old man's bright eyes were blue and looked straight at her. Angie nodded. She eased around the side of the doorway, uncertain what to do.

The big chair where the man sat was immense, with a scalloped top and green velvet covering it. The man in it was awfully small, but he reminded Angie of her grandfather. She had met Josephine's grandparents too, and those of other friends, but this man looked older and smaller than any of them. His one hand moved back from the switch on the lamp to fold with his other in his lap. Together the hands looked like the pile of chicken bones left after a chicken dinner. His face was a small white spot in the middle of the green velvet. His forehead looked as wrinkled as an old map, and his hair, flowing away from his temples to trail over his ears, was as white as typing paper. His cheeks sagged below his eyes and hung down like the wattles on turkeys. When he spoke, the skin there wiggled, but Angie decided his voice sounded younger than he looked.

"Angela Mona Zoey Maxwell," he said. "Nicknamed Angie, I believe. A girl who left Swenson's Soda Fountain early today to come see me."

"It's Hamburget..." Angie started, then stopped. "How do you know my name?"

"That's right. We used to call it Swenson's," the old man studied her. "And I knew your name because, because," his voice trailed off and his eyes looked straight through Angie. "I met you once, yes. You were little and don't remember."

"I have to go home," Angie said.

In that instant the old man's hair flashed whiter than fresh white paint. A strobe of light lit the room, instantly everything was visible. Before thunder rumbled its drum, Angie saw rows of photographs set up on a cloth on the mantel, flowered wallpaper on the walls—pink roses with tiny green leaves laced around them—worn spots on the arms of chairs, a rippling pink and gray pattern in the carpet and the threadbare carpet path leading straight from the old man's chair to the door where she stood.

"I have to go home," she had said just before the lightning hit.

The old man looked as white and astonished as she was. Yet while the thunder clomped away, he spoke as if he had not heard her. "Sit down. Come sit beside me and wait out the storm." His chicken-bone hand moved toward his wife's chair, a matching green velvet on the other side of a thin-legged table.

That was odd, Angie thought. She knew the chair belonged to his wife even if he had not said so. She knew it before he spoke. Now he was speaking again.

"You were looking for something, I think. And then you closed the back door for me." He paused as if trying to remember. "That's right, you wanted to figure out love. And how one goes about being somebody."

Another stroke of lightning threw white fire around the room. It surprised Angie less than the man's words, and his cornflower blue eyes. Those eyes studied her as she swayed there, gripping the door jamb. His eyes seemed to plead for her to come and sit down. In the white light of the lightning and now the vague orange haze from the lamp, she could find no meanness in those eyes. Thunder rumbled away. She crossed the room slowly and sat.

Sheets of rain whipped over the windows across the room from the two chairs. The old chair was comfortable, although its seat was too big to sit all the way back and keep her feet on the floor. From the skinny-legged table between the chairs, the broad orange lamp threw a circle of light around them.

"I made myself a cup of tea," the man beside her said. "Quite a while ago. Perhaps it's still warm. You can have it if you like."

"No, thank you. I never had tea," Angie answered.

Up close, the old man's face looked like papier-mâché. Little scraps of skin seemed stuck together to make it. He spread his bony hand to point out the china cup on the table. His white skin had blue lines, the same colors as the pattern on the china teacup.

"I don't get up much anymore. My tea gets cold. I've had a stroke, you understand. Moving around is too much trouble."

"That's too bad," Angie said.

"Depends on where you want to get to," the man answered softly. "You, for example, want to get to answers to all of your questions."

"Well, I, sort of." Angie decided to drink the tea after all. She looked at him to make sure it was still offered, the old man nodded. The cup felt light, and the liquid on her tongue was bitter. She swallowed a cold sip. "How did you know what I was thinking?"

"That one, of course. You'll know that eventually. I know your name is Angela and you have other names too, good names I think. This business about love, that's what troubles you isn't it? And being somebody, like all the others."

Angie nodded and breathed into the cup. She wished her hands and breath could warm the cold tea.

71

"Well then. I should explain." The old man locked his pale fingers together on his lap. "Some people say you're only somebody when you love. They say it makes you feel important like that, a somebody. Others say you can't do both at once, be somebody and love somebody. One cancels out the other, so to speak, like water putting out fire."

"I think love is like water," Angie said. The idea sort of seemed to the point, if there was one.

"That's good. Water knows about love. And about being somebody too." The old man glanced down at the cup. "You're holding water in your hands, but it's tea. Water falling outside is rain. In an ocean, water is the ocean. Water follows the moon, and tries to go up to the sun. Then it rains."

He paused. Or a roll of thunder drowned out what he was saying, Angie could not be sure. She tried watching his lips, but she could hardly tell when they were moving. Even when his lips looked still, she heard him speak.

"But then maybe you already know all that about water. It's hard to know where to start." He paused. "But it is nice to be warm and dry in here," he said, suddenly reminded. "I think of this house as love."

"Are you married?"

Angie guessed all old people had to be married, but it was a better question than the others flying through her head.

"Oh, yes. Of course," he said. "I'm waiting here for my wife. She'll be along someday."

"You mean she doesn't live here?" The question blurted itself out. Angie wished it wasn't so personal.

"Not exactly. Not for a long time anyway."

Angie guessed he must want his wife to come back. His wife probably wrote him letters.

"No, no letters, and I'm not in a hurry," the old man said. He leaned over to look down into the teacup. Angie saw she had finished all but a small pool in the bottom, and decided to leave that. It was probably polite.

72

"Look around you," the old man said as Angie set the cup back in its blue and white saucer. "My wife's love is all around here. Those are our grandchildren up on the mantel."

Angie's eyes had adjusted to the dim light, and she could see the pictures now. They showed children, five of them, and then one picture with all the children together with the oldest one, maybe a third grader, holding a baby in a sleep suit.

"They're all grown up now, of course. Our oldest, that third grader you see, has three girls of his own."

Angie nodded because he seemed about to say more. The old man paused and shook his head. Soft white hairs fanned out and then settled. He turned away from the pictures.

"Telling about my grandchildren, and great-grandchildren, won't help." He looked disappointed and met her eye. "Suffice to say they're all grown up now and have cups of tea of their own."

"I beg your pardon?" Angie hoped not to be impolite, but after all.

"Teacups." The old man's papery face brightened. He reached out and let the tip of his long, ribbed fingernail barely scrape the rim of the saucer beside her. "Pick up the teacup again, I'll tell you about that."

Angie obeyed. The cup felt light and delicate again in her hands. Its curved handle, no wider than a piece of spaghetti, had a tiny chip at the top.

"I'll get to that chip in a minute, but it's always best to begin at the beginning. I was thirty-six then, which means nothing to you, but suppose you were my child and I got a new job and our family moved into this house. Which was new then."

Angie looked around. For the first time she noticed that a layer of dust lay over everything, a pale glaze covering the room like the sheen of ice on puddles. It was hard to imagine all of this new, but Angie tried.

"My dear wife always wanted good china. We had only dime store stuff in those days. So I gave her money and we went miles away, into Ginnett City, because Millford was smaller then, and Elinor picked out her china." He paused, his blue and white eyes studying the blue and white cup in Angie's hands. "Elinor, that's her name."

"Elinor," Angie repeated. She wished she knew the old man's name, especially his last, but it would be rude to interrupt for that.

"We brought a big box home. Thirty-six pieces of English china, including saucers and teacups, four of each piece in all. Exactly the kind she always wanted."

Angie remembered the yellow lace tablecloth on the dining table. She thought of blue and white plates and bowls and cups and saucers. It would look nice.

"Our children were small then. The first night, because of course my wife washed it right away and we had to use every piece for dinner, the first night my son dropped his milk glass on his plate and broke it. A new china plate."

Angie glanced at the photographs on the mantel. She wondered which son broke the plate.

"One never remembers which son. Anyway, my wife stared at it and bit her lip. She wanted to cry, I could tell. That night when we went to bed I promised to go into Ginnett City and buy her a new plate. Which I did."

At least the story might end happily, Angie decided, even if it was a bit boring.

"I won't bore you with the accounts of all thirty-six pieces. A lot happened to each of them. There's just that cup you have now. One other left like it, out in the kitchen."

Angie had wondered if it was the only one left. She was relieved to know about the other.

"The first few years we used that teacup, and all the other pieces of china of course, only for special. Neighbors visited at Christmas, we served them tea in that cup. On anniversaries we put the children to bed early, gave the oldest a ticket to a concert or movie in Millford, and ate dinners for two. After

74

dinner Elinor drank hot chocolate from that cup. My oldest daughter had three friends over one evening shortly after her high school graduation. They looked at pictures in our album and one friend, a chubby girl named Jo, drank mulled cider out of that cup."

"Was her real name Josephine?" Angie asked, sure of the answer.

"Right you are, she was a Josephine alright. A thorough somebody now, living in Boxford these days, I believe." The old man smiled and Angie could see that his face, despite all wrinkles, was soft and friendly.

"That same cup," he repeated slowly, "the very one you are holding now." He paused to stare at it before going on. "Then, of course, after our children got homes of their own, Elinor used that cup every day. And the rest of the china too, what was left of it after the girls' apologies and the boys' big slippery fingers. Oh, but I promised to leave the other thirty-five pieces out of it, didn't I?"

The old man paused and refolded his hands. "My wife Elinor," he began again, "probably washed that particular teacup over a thousand times. Elinor held that cup in her hands. Elinor always asked me to put it up in the closet. Even though we used those dishes every day by then," he added pointedly, "they still stayed on the top closet shelf."

Angie supposed she should know what he meant. She liked her own mother's good china, but they used it only for company.

"Then one day I broke a plate. I had been building a bookshelf and came into the kitchen holding a hammer. The plate was on the counter. But never mind, we promised to leave the plates out of this, didn't we? Anyway, it was the next to last one. We would never again eat from the china together, just the two of us."

Angie nodded. The old man was no longer even looking at her. His eyes gazed away, toward the window where rain tapped steadily, though not so loudly now. His eyes stayed open, but he sat so quietly for a time he might have been dreaming. Angie watched, guessing he might be asleep, but if she got up to leave that would wake him. Finally, to distract herself, she studied the rest of the room.

The velvet covering on the mantel was red and had a torn edge on the side that hung down. The frayed piece trailed almost to the top of the fireplace. A dusty wooden bookshelf hung over the mantel, only a long piece of wood with square ends on it. She guessed the old man had probably built it himself. Black spots singed the pink and gray ripples in the carpet in front of the fireplace, but to the left, beneath a chair, the light from the window made the pattern look new. The carpet must have been beautiful once, Angie guessed, and she liked the pink glass vase on the nearby table too. The dead blossoms of two roses trailed over its lip now.

"But you're forgetting the cup," the old man spoke at last. "Possibly my fault. Never mind, let's get back to it." His eyes looked clear and blue again, and they fixed her with an intelligent glance as if he'd known all along what she was thinking. Angie closed her fingers more firmly around the cup, which at last felt warm from her touch. "After we picked up the broken pieces, I told Elinor I'd buy her another set. A better one, you couldn't get that pattern anymore. But Elinor was right. The children were grown and gone. There were only the two of us."

"Do you still have the last plate?"

"Oh, naturally. I happen to know Elinor ate lunch from it some days when I still went to work. She forgot to put it away one day you see."

The old man fell silent again, but Angie was glad of the pausing. The oddest feeling was trickling into her. It felt sort of like the rain, which would tap once hard on the glass then go away, but tap again in a minute to let them know it was still listening. Angie could not exactly say what the feeling was. It

76

made her think of the rain, filling up an ocean someplace. She thought of rain filling flowerbeds and gutters and lakes and dropped paper cups. It felt comfortable somehow.

She studied the pink rose vase again. How long had the dead roses nodded there, she wondered. Had Elinor put them in the vase? Or maybe one of her sons brought her a bouquet for Mother's Day, and the roses lived longest. Last year, or the year before. The roses looked quite dead.

"I could tell you about roses," the old man's voice seemed to come from all around her. "But better I stay with cups, don't you think?"

Angie considered the question. She had to decide he was right. Beyond the roses there would be the vase itself, and all of the other flowers it held. And the table that held the vase. And the times Elinor polished its legs, which were intricately carved. This could go on forever. "Okay," she said, and rotated the cup half a turn in her hands. The chip on the handle, from this direction, looked like a small, dark stain.

"I promised to get to that chip. For many years the handle had no chip. I can remember those years quite well—tables and carpets and roses and cabinets. Quite a bit of that, until I had my first stroke. The second one was the big one, you understand. The first one brings us back to our topic." The old man reached a blue bony hand across the table to graze the rim of the china. Angie could see now that the pattern had worn slightly along the edge.

"Elinor brought my tea upstairs to the bedroom every afternoon while I recovered from that first stroke. I took naps, and tea was just right after those. Then one day I was moved downstairs, into this room. I usually napped in my chair then. But she still brought me tea every day. I remember it was a Tuesday. She had joined me with a cup of her own, and she was just taking the tray to the kitchen. She was about to touch the swinging door, an old door, I oiled its hinges many times, when she heard me cry out her name in my frightened voice."

77

The old man's eyes dimmed. He seemed to be listening for a sound. "I know the sound frightened her. I didn't see it happen, but the tray dropped. That cup you're holding there hit the leg of the dining room table. We bought that table second-hand, big enough to seat all of us. And that's when the chip happened. Poor Elinor."

"The big stroke?"

"She moved across the street a few months afterward. But left everything just as it was. The day the children came to help her move she was finishing up a cup of tea. She left it here on the table."

Angie looked down into her hands. The teacup was half-full again. Holding with both hands so as not to let it slip, she moved it over to the table and set it in the circle on the saucer. The dark liquid jiggled for a moment and then lay still.

Silence crept over the room after the clink of china touching china. The corners were dim, and memories hovered there. Fingers of light moved like children playing hide-and-seek around the shadow-shapes of objects. Voices called and murmured and fought and spoke clearly in the cool air. Children's voices and those of grown-ups. Angie listened, unafraid, but sure they would not hear if she tried talking with them.

"Are you somebody now?" she said at last, and the voices folded back into the silence.

The old man nodded.

"I was all along of course. Only now I know it. And you are too. Think of all the things you touch. Think of all those stories. No, better not. When you're like me you'll have time to enjoy them."

The rain had tapped only a few times lately. Angie wondered if time had passed. "I better go."

"Fine. Pam or Jo, I mean Josephine, might call you up when one of them gets home. That should be fairly soon now." The old man smiled and his eyes reflected lights moving in the corner behind him. "You got the part about love, I hope."

Angie reached toward the cup, but did not let her fingers touch it. She took a long last look at the mantel, its worn velvet cloth, the pretty vase with its dusty roses looking down at the table. Her eyes followed the path on the carpet toward the dining room door. In there, shelves were filled. And the drawers in the hutch too, probably, with tablecloths and old photograph albums and maybe a pocket watch the old man's wife had given him but it broke and never happened to get fixed.

"I think so," Angie said. She hoped he would not ask her to explain it, like some answer in geometry.

"Fine." The old man's face looked paler than before. Angie guessed he was tired, if those who had already died could get tired. "You'll have no trouble getting home," he added softly, closing his eyes. "The Maxwell house is right across the street."

And he began to snore.

Angie tiptoed to the front door. She opened it and looked out. A house stood across the street all right. She imagined how a stranger would see it—a two-storey house, painted white with gray trimming, an attic bedroom window way up at the very top by the chimney.

She could not see the door mat, but she knew the letters WEL had all worn away. It only faintly said COME. The lights were on and through the windows she could see figures. They moved. It looked like a place where a family lived, a mother, a father, a brother and a fifteen-year-old girl, a girl named Angela. Someone closed the broad door at her back and she went home.

Chapter Six

*Y*es, that was our Angela, always inventing things. An imaginative child, inventing things. But then she herself is only pretend, we know. A lovely child nonetheless.

You have the ribbon in your hand, that's nice. Of course I will, if you like, but tell me first how you feel today.

That's too bad, did the doctor say more about it? No, I don't mean to pry, just thought maybe some new medication. Well, if it's age, I can understand. Not that you're so old, of course.

Another muffin? I've had two already, reached my limit. I'll wrap them up and leave them here beside the bed. Perhaps this evening before bedtime. My pleasure.

What do I do when I'm not visiting? The usual things, shopping, laundry, go to a movie. There were good movies last month, but this time of year nothing much. People stay at home I imagine, bad weather.

I wore my wool coat. It's downstairs drying out. It got so wet in the rain I was afraid it would drip on the steps coming up. It's a dark time of year and from here you can see the lights in the house across the street. Yes, new people live there now. Always changing. That's the one thing you can count on, I say.

I'd be happy to tell you that story. Yes, it happened that same day. And a day a lot like this one, nice in the morning, then an afternoon storm. It was lovely in the morning.

Mrs. Madden Rides the Bus

Earlier that morning, Saturday looked like a perfect day to go downtown. It was cool and crisp, finally late winter and the frost on the garden melted by mid-morning. The maple tree in the back was beginning to bud, and it made grand gestures in the sunlight that spilled between clouds.

Elinor Madden looked out her kitchen window and noted that there was a bit of wind. She would wear her bright green wool hat to warm her head. She had often noted how people wore colors to match the way the landscape changed each season. She looked forward to spring when the world would turn green again.

Doctor Winthrop had said she should not spend her strength getting chills and fighting off colds, so she had not gone downtown since Christmas, and then only for an hour or two. The months of weakness wore on her, one head cold after another since September. A woman over eighty ought to be able to go out, if she dressed properly. She had no cold at the moment. The spot where her partial plate rubbed was even healed, since she wore it seldom lately, and the swelling had gone down so it fit comfortably.

Or so it seemed, a perfect Saturday to go downtown shopping. And when she got there, despite a chilly wind, she felt happy she had come. It was February and stores put calendars on sale. Early in the afternoon she felt pleased when she found a beautiful one in Marshall and Morton. It had pictures of flowers representing the various seasons. There were tulips and asters and poinsettias. The pages were ragged from handling, but she could tape the edges after she tore the pictures out. The pictures would replace those from last year, already yellow from sitting on the sill of her kitchen window.

Now Mrs. Madden stood waiting for a bus to take her home. Any bus would do she decided. She accepted the sadness of having visited only one store, but the calendar had taken a long time to select, standing in front of the long row of bins, stepping back to let others look and trying not to get in the way. It was especially tiring today. Marshall and Morton had a lovely coffee shop on the eighth floor, attractive young men and women in pink and gray to wait on her and be very kind. It had Millford's best blueberry muffins, which did not exactly go with the hot chocolate, but she had wanted to taste both those things today. It had been so long since either. Now her mouth hurt again, and she guessed she had a touch of indigestion.

Practically all Millford's westbound buses passed within a block or two of Mrs. Madden's house, but they ran less frequently on Saturdays. A few minutes earlier the Maximillian Theatre had let out and teenaged children poured into the street, shouting against the wind that whipped their clothes and hairstyles. An anvil of thunderclouds rose behind the office buildings to the east, making the horizon look like one wide gray-blue bruise when sunbreaks wheeled light across it. All at once the cry of a siren joined the children's shouts and the wind made it two sirens, three. Red lights swiveled over the neon lights several blocks east. There had been a traffic accident.

So many lights suggested it might be a bad one, although Mrs. Madden hoped it was not. It did mean no buses could come up Pollard. Then the 83 Sweetview turned the corner, coming east on Pollard. It ran the wrong way but if Mrs. Madden remembered her buses correctly the Sweetview took a jog out to East End, turned and came back downtown. When the light changed, she crossed the street. She would nap on the Sweetview until it turned and came back through town. Then it would take her home.

Some time later Mrs. Madden awoke refreshed, if suddenly. She had chosen a seat toward the back. She had been dreaming, or more or less remembering, a circus her father had taken her to when she was a child. The tent was dark and the fire-eater's shape danced in the center ring in the flames. As he lifted a stake, a sudden flare lit the entire tent. That must have been lightning, she realized now. Circus drums of thunder echoed around the bus. Rain was seeping around the rubber edge of the window beside her and forming a puddle near the window on the seat. At the next stop she moved forward and found a place on one of the long sideways seats near the front door.

They were passing Marshall and Morton again, going the right way this time. Mrs. Madden checked her handbag and her packages—the calendar, a pink and gray M&M box with two blueberry muffins for tomorrow's breakfast. Her stomach felt better now. Everything was okay except for a damp spot on the bottom of her handbag.

Raindrops made ribbons and rivulets across the front windshield, but it was warm here. The heater blew warm air around her feet, and the steady thwack-weep of the windshield wipers made the inside of the bus feel peaceful and safe. The bus made a few stops downtown, but it seemed hardly anyone wanted to take it. The dozen or so passengers scattered here and there in the seats looked comfy and warm. They looked like a nice group of people, all in all. Mrs. Madden looked again after her first glance because, in fact, they looked like an exceptionally nice group of people.

A mother, a baby wrapped in her arms in a green blanket, occupied a seat toward the middle. The woman looked old for her age, a cap of gray hair ringing her face and the rest brunette. Her face was lined and pale, and she looked tried by long patience, though not in a hurry now. She kept glancing at the other passengers, then down at the child. Her hazel eyes met Mrs. Madden's for an instant, a questioning glance, then turned away. The child was snuggled into her shoulder and looked no more than a few months old. It looked like a good baby, nice and quiet on the bus, and Mrs. Madden could not understand why the woman worried.

Ahead of the mother sat a big red-faced man. He looked overweight, but comfortable with it, though he probably drank too much. He was nearly bald and beneath his shining forehead watery blue eyes scanned the page of a newspaper. Mrs. Madden caught the headline, a prediction for the economy. She had not seen that paper on the racks earlier, a weekly sold on corners everywhere. From what she could read of the date, it looked like next week's edition. Perhaps they put them out earlier downtown these days. Or perhaps it was a whole year old. Headlines like that came out all the time.

Toward the back sat another widow, or a woman old enough to be a widow. She wore too little make-up and her skin looked sallow. Perhaps she had been sick and was coming home from the doctor. At least she wore a bright green hat, probably wool to keep her warm, but it added a spot of color, and she too had a Marshall and Morton bakery box on her lap. Despite her sallow skin, her lips were pressed together in a small smile. She wore no glasses, must have good eyes because she moved her head like a small bird to catch glimpses of the views passing outside.

The bus was on the outskirts of downtown now, a sporting supply store passing on the left as they turned onto avenues where lawns gleamed with a fresh coat of rain. The drops on the windshield were growing smaller, and the wipers squealed against the glass. Looking the length of the bus and out the back window, Mrs. Madden saw where dark clouds shredded off into pale gray slate. They had a couple miles to go before she could ring the bell and get off. She turned her attention back to the passengers.

On the left, two-thirds up toward the front, a teenaged boy held a motorcycle helmet in his lap. His skin was broken out, boys did at that age, and over the helmet the boy was thumbing a magazine with a shiny red car on the front of it. His eyes held wonder, a fascination making them almost too bright. He wore a worn leather jacket and the knuckles on his left hand looked swollen like small flowers—a fresh abrasion. He turned a page, and she saw that a sleeve of the jacket was torn, an exploded fringe at the elbow. He probably drove his motorcycle too carelessly and too fast, like that accident earlier. Nonetheless the young man looked like a good boy. He just needed to grow out of his problems.

Mrs. Madden startled herself with that thought. It was odd how today everyone on the bus looked nice, a pleasant group of people she might come to know. In the years of living alone, she had grown to prefer her own company, enjoying other people less and less. Now the bus stopped, letting an elderly foreign gentleman mount the steps. She smiled at him. He returned the smile, settling in at the other end of the long seat. She did not mind sharing the seat with him.

By now, since several people had gotten on once the bus left downtown, its seats were more crowded. A middle-aged black couple shared the seat diagonally across. The man, who was tall and older-looking than his pregnant wife, talked to her in urgent, low tones. His wife seemed unperturbed by whatever was worrying him. Two seats behind them, an older man, probably retired, moved his lips as if counting to himself. To adjust something, he lifted a hand, liver-spotted, the skin crepe-like with age. He was saying a rosary.

That was nice, Mrs. Madden decided. Very nice. She had never understood Catholic ways, but a Methodist heart could have room for one. These were good people, every one of them. The thought made her heart expand, and she surveyed the faces and let the sensation wash over her. Good people, every one, to move her so much. This affection for them felt like warm water, perfusing her skin. It was odd, the affection she felt. She actually liked them all, particularly the frightened mother with her baby in her arms; it ought to cry and it was too quiet. She also liked the puffy man reading his newspaper, and then he looked away out the window as if none of it mattered to him. She liked the woman in the bright green wool hat, her treasured pink and gray Marshall and Morton packages cradled on her lap, and the boy who loved motorcycles and fast cars. She liked the black man and his wife, that woman too thin to be as far along in her pregnancy as she appeared, and liked the pensioner saying Catholic prayers. The old man on her right was a slender fellow, East Indian maybe. Under his coat he wore what looked like pajamas. She liked him too. It all felt strange and delightful.

Suddenly an even odder thought struck Mrs. Madden. While the bus had stopped from time to time, admitting new passengers, no one had gotten off. She thought back and tried to remember if anyone had left. None had, as well as she could recollect. The side windows had grown hazy with steam, but through the windshield where the wipers waved goodbye, goodbye, back and forth, she could see where the bus was moving. In four or five blocks she would have to ring the bell. She pictured it, being first to get off, and her heart, which had swollen larger to encompass them all, suddenly contracted.

She could not be the first. That was easy enough to decide. She could ride to the end of the line this way, taking this bus back, or perhaps some other bus eventually. It did not matter, but she knew her heart would break to lose this wonderful group of people all at once, to go away from them. She would stay on.

The afternoon was waning, but not yet dusk. Only the rain made it dim. She would be late getting home, but home would be there if she still wanted it. How strange that was, not to care. But then getting home only meant fixing dinner, and she was not particularly hungry. In fact, she thought, turning sideways toward the foreign man on her right, "Would you like a blueberry muffin?"

87

"Why yes. Thank you very much." He spoke like an East Indian, each sound accented, and his smile drew bronze skin back from perfect white teeth. He was old though, his hand shook accepting the muffin, and the lines of his face tightened with concentration as he worked to remove the paper wrapper. She would have liked to help him, but she would not, herself, have liked to be helped.

The view from the front window showed familiar homes and yards. In two more blocks they would reach her own stop. She studied the rain-washed houses and lawns. The bus paused at Pear Street to take on a new passenger. Mrs. Madden looked up the street to her own house, dark but a few houses in the neighborhood had lights on. She saw the Emerson and Roman and Pembroke houses. The lights from the Maxwells' seemed to reflect on the house across the street. A figure was crossing the street toward them. It looked like that neighborhood girl, Angela or Mona or Zoey, whatever her name was. Then the street flickered past and the bus turned up a winding avenue.

The new passenger had just gotten on. It was a blind man. He had a black Labrador dog in a harness that rested lightly in his hand. The dog looked old, white around the muzzle, and once the man sat on the opposite long seat, the dog relaxed to the floor like a pillow losing its fluff. Mrs. Madden guessed she liked the blind man, but she liked the dog even better. The dog was overweight, probably spoiled with treats, and it looked sad. Its name was Jude, Mrs. Madden thought. She recognized it suddenly. Yes, Jude. The dog sighed.

"Would you like to play a game?" The East Indian was speaking to her. He had finally freed the muffin from its wrapper, and now he held it in both hands, taking small bites from time to time and chewing slowly.

"That would be nice," she said, but he remained silent. He stared at her. Apparently he could not think of a game.

"Suppose we guess who'll get off the bus before either

of us," she suggested quietly. It would not do for the others to hear.

"That is a good game," he said at once. "As long as we do not make too much fun of it. Only to pass the time. Do you say it like that?"

"Yes, to pass the time. That's right. And we must not make too much fun. That would not be right."

The bronze head nodded, and Mrs. Madden saw that the man wore a small squared-off white hat. "That one," the man said, nodding again. She followed his gaze down the aisle to where the mother and child sat.

"You mean two."

"Only one."

"Of course," Mrs. Madden said. Of course the child would stay.

"You say now." The East Indian's eyes were soft and warm, like sweet dark chocolate liqueur. His fingers shook, lifting for another bite of the muffin. She turned to study the faces.

The black man sat beside his wife, but he was no longer talking. His wife seemed content, her tan hands templed over the rise of her belly, but her husband slouched sullenly on the seat, his features scowling. She studied them for a moment, then turned back.

"Do you think?" she asked. The East Indian man had followed her gaze. He nodded.

"An unfortunate thing," he said. "Perhaps the children will keep him company at home."

Mrs. Madden hoped so too. The black woman, Madelaine, was too weak to bear this child. And the child itself, conceived too late, was not healthy inside her. Mrs. Madden looked out the window to keep from thinking about it.

She had read in the newspaper about new roads built out this way, but not been out here in years. When she and Charles used to drive this way to go into Ginnett, this land had been mostly forest. Now houses dotted the hillsides, and rows of

89

streetlamps led up into the foothills. The bus slowed to joggle over railroad tracks, and she caught sight of a tall long-needled pine, a pine by the name of Evelyn. It leaned with the wind into the glow of a streetlamp. Almost all the trees out here had women's names, Mrs. Madden noticed, Marion Pine and Laurice Juniper, and a willow called Elinor, which hardly suited it at all. But the shrubs were Jonathan and Mark and Clark and Charles. One oak went by the name of José, though he looked more like a George.

Suddenly the sound of the bell brought Mrs. Madden's attention back. She turned to watch the young mother slowly stand and lift her baby. The baby's face only showed as a pale bluish spot in middle of the green blanket. Pausing in the aisle, the woman scanned the faces of the passengers.

At last, when the bus had already slowed and was pulling over toward the curb, the woman carried the child two seats back to stand by the man with the rosary. The mother spoke a few words and the man nodded. He took the child and made sure its blanket was closed. The woman thanked him. The bus had stopped so she stepped sideways toward the rear door, which was nearer, looking back once. There were tears in her eyes. She went out.

Then the back door closed and the front door with it. They rode several miles in silence before Mrs. Madden turned to the man on her right again. The bus was climbing the roads of the foothills, grinding gears as it crept up inclines and slowing occasionally to go left or right among the winding trees. It was wonderful, Mrs. Madden decided, knowing a personal name for each one of the trees. And she had discovered unfamiliar names now too, strange-sounding ones like words in the language Naren must speak, East Indian sounds and exotic murmurings that meant the names of animals and stones and bacteria in the soil. She decided to test her new knowledge.

"Naren," she said to him, "we forgot your last choice."

90

"That is true, Elinor," Naren answered. "It is good that the man is blind and knows the path to his house so well. Do you agree?"

"Yes."

Then the dog would stay with them. They had passed a small country store a few miles back and the black man had left them there. He stood tall and straight when he went out the door. He was angry about this.

The game was over now. Elinor occupied her thoughts thinking about Naren, about his life and the lives of all the others on the bus. The baby was content and warm, sitting toward the back in the Catholic man's arms. The baby was chewing quietly on the rosary, whose beads the man jiggled and clicked for the child's amusement. Elinor looked at each face and her thoughts could enter each mind except the blind man's. It was a relief when that one finally rang the bell. About Naren she knew that he was a wealthy man who had traveled from India to teach a favorite student to dance. The dance was ancient, an Indian antiquity, and the doyen had failed to successfully teach as the master he was. 'It must belong to all the movements around it,' she heard him think to himself earlier that day in the student's small studio. 'To dance is the meaning of life, yes, but an old life is passing.' He had taught the student a few gestures today, scraps of style the boy could use, then he had gone home to sleep.

The bell rang again while she once more listened to this conversation. She liked to hear all the nuances in Naren's voice and study the steps the student made, imitating the movements but unable to breathe to the right rhythm. Now the bus was shifting toward the side of the road again. When it had completely stopped, the blind man stepped with care over the fallen black pillow of the dog. He held a rail and leaned over to stroke the salt and pepper hair on the dog's muzzle.

Jude's thick black tail rose and fell, thumping half-way up, like the end of a rope being shaken. The blind man got off and Elinor watched him work his way along a path in the dark, touching trees. A house lay a few yards from the road.

There was no game left to play as the bus pulled back onto the road. There was only the catalog to enjoy, all the true names of all the animals and plants and people and chips of wood and spots of metal ore in the hills and other things. After a while, the white circles of the headlight beams seemed to widen and grow bigger, as if reflecting from snow. The bus slowed down, driving more carefully.

Then the man with the newspaper held it up. He looked at the others and said, "Say now," to get everyone's attention. He did drink too much, but everyone liked him by now. They turned and smiled.

"Feathers." The man pointed to a place at the top of the front page. "They said a feather front was moving in tonight."

"So it is as you say." Naren was closest to the front window and could see best. "A very large storm of them, it appears."

Feathers fell outside all the windows, obviously feathers. It was clear when the bus slowed down further. The bus finally came to a stop, illuminating a simmering wall of falling light feathers in front of the headlights. Everybody got off and played in the feathers a while. They scooped feathers up in their arms and threw handfuls over each other. The Labrador ran and barked playfully, chasing after clumps of feathers they threw for him.

After a time of this, though, they grew tired, and one by one got back on the bus. Some napped and others sat together in the front, repeating the names of all they passed. Naren did a dance for them.

Elinor enjoyed it so much she overlooked the moment when the bus left the road and burrowed softly in through the trees.

Chapter Seven

*Y*es, Mrs. Madden died at eighty-three. But she had a good life—wonderful years with Charles in the house across the street, then peaceful widowhood in her second home. She left everything just as it was after Charles died and she moved out. Her son finally sold it. The daughter took charge of the second house, after Elinor died on the bus. But that's another story, isn't it? I agree.

But she was eighty-three and you are, I can't exactly guess your age. Be mysterious if you want, that's your prerogative. I won't pry. But you are looking fit today. A good day to sit by the window, even if wind does rattle the pane. It's certainly blustery all right. And everything still wet from that shower.

I came through the garden, through the hedge actually, troublesome thing. I use it like a gate these days, since you won't have the real gate replaced. Or since you haven't, none of my business.

No, I couldn't see any new shoots, too soon for that. Next month we'll see crocuses. Daffodils not long afterward, if you planted daffodils. But of course you would.

That reminds me of Johnny, and Mrs. Madden again, her poor daffodils. You have the ribbon? Turn it over. About Johnny then, whatever happened to him? A lot of the usual things, of course, plus some others. I'll explain those.

Lost and Found

When he was two months shy of seventeen, Johnny Maxwell got a job at a photo processing service. He was a rangy red-headed kid with freckles, pale in the winter and sunburned in the summer, except for his freckled forehead which was pale year-round because he always wore a baseball cap. Johnny had not played baseball since junior high school, but he liked the game. He was a B and C student, well-liked by his friends. Beginning in February he spent less time with those friends because he went to Sudby's Photo Service after school. Saving his pay, he could eventually buy a car. With a car he could spend time with Nancy Gibson, once he got to know her better.

After school each day, Johnny biked down alleyways, his cap pulled low over his eyes, taking the back route so Nancy would not see him wearing his work clothes—green pajamas with the SPS insignia sewn on the pocket. He punched in at 3:45 and walked alone down the long central hall to the unfinished room at its end.

Passing along that hall made him feel crazy inside. On either side lay huge white hangars cut up into cubicles by stacks of white cardboard boxes. Under pink fluorescent lights, stretching bank after bank toward distant walls, clerks sorted and filed red and gold SPS photo packages, one clerk to each jigsaw-piece cubicle. The clerks wore green pajamas too and their faces looked pale. Phones rang constantly, making the room sound like the inside of a pinball machine. Once in a while Johnny heard a snatch of conversation, which he preferred to ignore. As far as he could tell the other workers were outer space beings, brought in by an arrangement SPS had with another galaxy. It was like the Jupiterian plastics factory he had read about in *Tales of Wonder*. Only interplanetary slavery could explain creatures fixed in a room like this day after day, doing the same boring work and never going crazy.

Darkrooms and chemical labs lay off to the right, but only once had a small steel door opened to give a glimpse inside. He saw shadowy figures leaning over tables and trays in darkness lit by a red bulb. He liked the solitude of Room B-26, and he felt more secure when its gray door, with the sign saying "Lost and Found," closed at his back. The man who hired Johnny had said three kids had quit already that year. Mr. Nelson guessed it was no fun working alone. Johnny disagreed, but he kept silent about it.

A stack of mail always waited on the floor below the mail slot.

Dear SPS people,
I sent two rolls of film last August and the prints from one came back okay but I got somebody else's pictures for the other. Here are those pictures. Please send me mine.

Another might say:

Dear Manager in the Photo Lab,
I wrote you before saying I didn't want any pictures of an Irish setter and an office building. Now you send me pictures of rocks beside a beach, plus one shot that looks like something died on the rocks. I told you we went to Connecticut. My husband and my son and Aunt Val were there, she'll be the easy one to spot because she was really overweight then, a fat lady. We were on a beach, that's right, but in Connecticut. This looks like California my son says. There's a yellow beach umbrella with a hole in the side that I patched up with black electric tape. That shouldn't be too hard.

For another, Johnny would have to search back into the files:

I don't know these people and my wife swears we never took their pictures for any reason. Anyway, the camera must have

95

had a good lens on it because the focus is better than ours. You made a mistake and I bet somebody else got our pictures of the new swimming pool and my last party. Make the switch and send mine, okay?

Johnny pinned the letters on the Search Board, then turned to the prints the customers usually enclosed. He held them up to the board, checking requests from recent weeks. Occasionally he had good luck, the yellow beach umbrella gave a match-up, for example. More often he cataloged the extra pictures, dealing them out to bins on the twelve broad tables around the mail slot.

Each table had its subject painted on its side: FAMILIES, LANDSCAPES, VEHICLES, ANIMALS, FURNITURE, and others. The bins on the tables broke subjects down more narrowly: FAMILIES—Caucasian, Asian, Black; ANIMALS—Wild, Domestic. Then there were finer gradations: ANIMALS—Wild—In Motion, Still; or ANIMALS—Domestic—Still—Eating, Sleeping, Looking Left, Looking Right.

The room held thousands of pictures. The number stayed about the same, give or take a dozen match-ups each day. One slow day, Johnny started counting, but gave up around five thousand and multiplied for a total.

The bins helped with the job, but decisions were often difficult. What about a happy-looking group that had several ages and more than one race. Was it a family, not a family? And what about dogs posing at dog shows—were they still or in motion? Johnny made judgments and tossed snapshots into bins to await better descriptions. He averaged 30 match-ups to every 212 letters. Mr. Nelson said that wasn't bad, better than the last kid, in fact.

While he worked, Johnny thought about the car. It was a green Ford he passed on his way to work each day, a 370 with a dent in the right door. "But good rubber all around," the dealer said, "and real pick-up." The dealer said a kid his age liked that. Johnny preferred to imagine the car sitting still, out by the culvert near Buckram's Farm or parked a few miles south of Cliff's Roadhouse. He and Nancy Gibson would be snuggled into the front seat. That was what he liked best about the Ford, it had comfortable seats, soft, plushy short couches where Nancy could lean back toward the door with her eyes closed. When he thought about this he would first reconstruct what they had done earlier that evening. It seemed more respectful to Nancy to think back through the whole evening before he got to what they were doing in the car. Besides, he felt less guilty thinking backward than forward.

But those thoughts, as always, made Johnny think about money. He would need money to get them out to a movie at the Maximillian Theatre, not to mention gas, and popcorn, plus a beautiful scarf or something Nancy would see in a store window and say she liked. He would run right in and buy it for her. Even if he were old enough to take Nancy to the Roadhouse and buy her a cocktail, he would need money. By then he would have money, being grown-up, but Nancy might be married.

Thinking backward about money was easiest anyway, Johnny decided after he had worked for three months and was a good way toward the price of the car. It was easier than thinking all the way back to the first step before all those other steps that would bring them together in the dark in the car. That first step meant he had to say something besides, "Hi, how's it going?" to Nancy Gibson when they met in school on the way to third period. He had probably said, "Hi, how's it going?" twelve times already. She was probably getting sick of it.

One day Johnny was sorting snapshots, trying to think of what to say, and a particular picture caught his eye. His fingers almost let it fall into the bin marked LANDSCAPES— Foreign Places, when he pulled back. A fancy stone castle rose on a hilltop overlooking a lake and three people stood in the foreground. The man and the woman looked like tourists, a camera strap hung over the man's arm, and a young man stood to their right.

He had red hair. He was tall and thin, about Johnny's age, but his sharp adam's apple made his neck look like a man's. He was looking up at the castle. Johnny had never seen himself at that half-angle, except in clothing store mirrors, but he guessed this was how he would look if only his freckles would fade, if only his chest grew larger. The young man appeared sure of himself, handsome, wearing a dark brown corduroy coat and tweedy slacks with brown penny loafers. Loafers were definitely out at Millford High, but Johnny guessed he wouldn't mind, in a couple of years, looking like this. He would be visiting castles, but not with his parents. The tourists were probably the boy's parents. He might be out visiting castles with Nancy.

Johnny dropped the picture into LANDSCAPES—Foreign Places, and finished sorting the others. They were mostly of the tourist parents in front of rivers and waterfalls. The young man did not reappear, and after a few days Johnny forgot about him.

The following Tuesday, Johnny said, "Hi, how's your Biology?" to Nancy Gibson in the hall before third period. She looked at him like the question was strange, but she did almost smile. He pointed to his book to remind her that they had third period Biology together, Mr. Meakins. Nancy said, "Oh, right." She pushed open the door of the Girl's Room. The minute she was gone Johnny thought about the strange smile she had given. "How's your biology," he whispered to himself and, hearing it, knowing she was on her way into the Girl's Room, he died.

Until the following Monday Johnny forgot about the picture in LANDSCAPES—Foreign Places. Then in the middle of his busiest time, another photo caught his eye. The batch of pictures must have been taken by the same people, but then been mailed out to someone else, because here were those parents again, same camera strap, holding hands in front of a statue. Another picture showed them carrying packages in a market filled with foreign-looking people, and, in another, carrying suitcases down a corridor. The young man with red hair showed up in the last picture, waving goodbye. The young man's freckles were visible in the bright light of the corridor, probably in a train station or airport. His hair and clothes were mussed, maybe from helping the old guy carry a suitcase. He wore tennis shoes instead of loafers and he looked younger in this picture than he had by the castle. In fact he looked a lot more like Johnny himself. Johnny didn't own a blue striped shirt and tan slacks like the guy in the picture was wearing, but he wished he did. He filed the photos with the earlier batch and shifted them all to VACATIONS—Abroad, before opening the next letter.

Johnny had sorted almost all of that day's photos, and made match-ups with two letters, when another batch stopped him. It was two minutes to six, almost time to punch out, but he left the last few packets unopened to pore over these prints. The young man was in all of them, but his tourist parents were gone. Instead, he stood beside a new set of tourists, three old women, each of them holding up a flowery cloth bag with its price tag still attached.

The women were standing outside a department store, gold lettering on the window said HARRODS. The young man was wearing the blue pinstriped shirt from the last picture, but gray pants this time and penny loafers. Johnny sorted back to the earlier set for comparison. These were the same penny loafers he had worn to the castle. The young man looked a lot more like Johnny now, his adam's apple had just looked bigger because his head was turned in that first shot. From the way he stood beside the old ladies, Johnny guessed he was bored stiff. Johnny too would have felt bored going shopping with those three.

The other pictures showed more of the three old tourists,

99

but not the young man. Johnny gave the pictures titles in his mind—Three Old Ladies Take A Boat Trip, Two Old Ladies Wear New Hats, Old Lady Wears Clip-on Sunglasses. He checked the background for the familiar face and red hair, but found no one. He studied the pictures and decided he'd probably look good in a blue pinstriped shirt. Maybe he ought to buy one. Then he put away all the pictures, in VACATIONS—Abroad, and punched out.

Several weeks elapsed before Johnny ran across that face again. By then he had made several decisions. He had counted how much money he had, including bank account, wallet, pockets, and an estimate of what his sister Angela owed on bets she usually lost. If he kept saving, he could pay for the car in August, by which time school would be out and Nancy gone away somewhere with her parents. Besides, as he saw clearly now, having a car was pointless if he had no nice clothes to make Nancy like him and no money to take her anywhere. If he spent a few dollars on clothes now, he could still afford the car in September.

In March, Johnny spent two Saturdays searching for a coat like the one the young man wore in the picture. He found a similar brown corduroy and tried it on, turning his head to see how his adam's apple looked in the three-way mirror. Each time he looked back, his neck relaxed, so it was hard to tell. He bought the coat anyway and put it away in his closet. Next year when he was a senior and built more like the guy in the pictures, it would look right. He liked wearing it alone in his room at night. Wearing the coat, he would lean on the dresser and study his reflection in the mirror. "Hi, I'm Max," he tried saying a couple of times. He had chosen that name for the young man in the pictures, a rich sounding name, short for Maximillian, like the name of Millford's movie theatre. He remembered Max in the pictures as tanned, but the reflection in the mirror was pale. Johnny hung his baseball cap on the corner of the mirror and left it there after that.

Toward the end of March, photos of Max began pouring in. Two packets in one week brought news of him. One showed Max beside a tour bus with foreign lettering on its side. Another showed Max holding a bottle of wine and a half-full glass. Max was trying to appear happy, but he looked like he was forcing it. By now Johnny had become accustomed to discovering his own face in the pictures. He and Max did look incredibly alike. Yet when he uncovered the next photo, the shock of recognition hit him hard.

Max leaned against a wall in the background of a blurry print. He wore khaki slacks exactly like those Johnny's mother had bought for him last autumn. Max's red plaid shirt was faded around the collar, just like Johnny's own red plaid shirt. Max held his left foot out for balance, and below the pant cuff Johnny saw black socks with red stripes. He looked down at his ankles. He was wearing his black socks with red stripes today. He wore them only when they were last in the drawer. One toe had a hole.

Johnny wanted to tell somebody. He dug back through VACATIONS—Abroad, and carefully lined the other photos down the length of the table. The stack had grown to a couple dozen, but Max never appeared with the same people in more than two or three shots. Max stood with arms draped around shoulders in the middle of cozy groups. Max leaned over the sea wall on a bridge and waved down at a passing boat. Max extended his left arm and shielded his eyes with his right, pointing out a distant tower for whoever was shooting the picture.

In this picture Johnny noticed a detail he had missed. Max wore different shoes. Instead of penny loafers or tennis shoes, his feet stood on wet pavement in beige bucks, their toes darkened by dampness. Johnny had not worn his beige bucks today—the shoestring on the left one was broken—but he hurried to the desk and took out the magnifying glass. Even with magnification he could not be sure of the detail. He thought he saw it. A dark smudge, like a knot with frayed ends, showed in the exact middle of the lace on Max's left shoe.

Johnny took a deep breath to slow his heartbeat. He looked again. It might be a knot, or a water spot. He wished he could get a blow-up of the picture, but he had no legitimate reason to ask for one. He checked the other pictures again, slowly, magnifying detail by detail. Except for the khaki slacks, the plaid shirt and the broken shoelace, none of Max's other clothes looked familiar. But these did, Johnny reminded himself. Not only familiar, they were exactly the same. Max wore the same clothes and looked incredibly like him—Johnny's height, his weight, his features. In several shots the resemblance was perfect.

"And he's got my clothes," Johnny whispered in the stillness of the small room. "He's got my clothes. Maybe he's wearing them right now."

It reminded him of a story he read once in *Strange! Magazine.* Two wars were being fought in parallel universes and both the universes blew each other up. Finding Max was like that. If only he could find out who had taken these pictures. But then what would he do? Maybe find out where Max lived. He could send Max a letter with some pictures of himself in it. Of course that was assuming Max lived in the same universe. All the other people in the pictures were tourists, dumb, dumpy-looking American tourists. Could there be the same exact kind in a parallel universe?

Johnny corrected himself. Parallel universes were parallel, perfect duplicates. Then again, he thought, Max's world might not be parallel, might be right here on earth. Johnny tried to figure out what to do.

A thought struck him. Suppose he told his manager, Mr. Nelson, that he must find out about these pictures in case they came from a parallel universe. Johnny started to laugh. Mr. Nelson would stare at him. Mr. Nelson would think he was crazy. Laughing all alone like this felt crazy enough. Hot tears welled up in his eyes. He was laughing so hard he might cry. Johnny choked back the laugh, coughed and took a deep breath. He wanted to cry but he wouldn't. In a way, he wished Nancy Gibson were here to hold him.

When he calmed down, Johnny collected the pictures of Max. He slipped them into an envelope and carried them home that Friday night. He had to tell someone. Maybe over the weekend he would get an idea.

During the next two days, Saturday and Sunday, Johnny kept the pictures locked in his desk drawer. He hoped the drawer's lock would hold if his sister got nosy and started snooping. He thought about telling Mom or Dad, but decided it was out of the question. They didn't like the idea of him working after school and would think too much work was making him crazy. Saturday afternoon he went with Tony Jones and Rob Wilton for a ride in Mark Millings' new car. He thought of telling them, but could not face telling all three together. Then he got home and decided against calling Tony or Rob or Mark. Explaining over the phone, without showing the pictures, would sound dumb.

In the evenings, before going to bed, Johnny took the photos out and lined them up along the back of his desk. He had read in a story once where two characters, an animal from Jupiter and one from Earth, met by using thought transference during sleep. The Jupiterian Worf and Earth Possum had dreams and could talk to each other. By Monday morning Johnny concluded it only worked in stories, or for animals, because he awoke that day disappointed after three dreamless nights.

The Spring Dance was coming up at school. It was three weeks away, and Johnny had sworn he would at least give it a try with Nancy. After second period Math he stationed himself near her locker on the way to third period. When she appeared, he took the position he'd planned. She'd have to look right at him when she opened her locker.

"Hi, I'm Johnny Maxwell, remember?" Johnny held up his biology book so she'd make the connection.

"Sure. Hi."

"How's it going?"

"Not bad." Nancy opened her locker and took out her Biology book. Johnny stood silently staring at her. She closed her locker door. She turned carrying her Biology book and walked down the hall to Mr. Meakins' classroom. Johnny followed her, without a word, through the door.

Around 3:30, riding his bike fiercely toward Sudby's, Johnny vowed to stop blaming himself. Nancy might have said, "Yes." Or she might have said, "No." Instead, she had said "Not bad." Halfway through Biology class he had realized that he had asked, "How's it going?" instead of "Want to go to the Spring Dance?" It could happen to anybody.

Today he carried the borrowed photos of Max back to Room B-26. When he was safe there, he lined them out on the edge of the table. He would leave them for the afternoon, in case any match-ups came. Then he would put them away.

By 5:30, he could see that there would be letters left from today's mail. Many people had taken pictures over Easter vacation and gotten the wrong prints back. He reached for another envelope and slit it open. A loose pile of photos fell to the floor.

Max appeared in every one of them. Max stood next to a brand-new Mercedes Benz in the picture on top. He smiled and waved happily to the person holding the camera. In the next photo, Max sat in the driver's seat of the Mercedes. To his right, her face shadowed by the sun visor, a woman looked out. Her hand covered Max's hand on the steering wheel. Two more shots showed Max dancing with the woman, fast dancing at a nightclub where the light was poor. Max looked a couple years older, his clothes were new. His face was so tanned Johnny could hardly see his freckles, but it was Max all right.

104

Johnny shuffled the photos to pick up a location or tourist he recognized. At the middle of the pile a print flipped over and Johnny's heart smacked to his stomach like a fly ball hitting a wide mitt.

Max stood next to the young woman. They held hands, her small braceleted wrist visible above the tanned back of Max's hand. The young woman was beautiful, dressed up in a shiny white skirt and deep blue blouse that looked soft—only her skin could be softer. The woman was Nancy Gibson.

Her breasts tented the front of her blouse slightly more than, by the locker today, Nancy's breasts poked under her sweater. Her hair was long, dark brown and pulled back from her neck by a ribbon trailing over her shoulder. Her wide brown eyes, every bit as beautiful as Nancy's when she said, "Not bad," by the locker today, looked up toward Max. Her eyes held love. The woman looked a couple years older than Nancy did today, but it was her all right.

Johnny flipped rapidly through the shots he had already seen. He recognized Nancy in them now. Her face peered out from the beneath the sun visor of the Mercedes. Her shoulder turned away as she danced with Max at the night club. In the remaining photos, Nancy and Max stood in front of a merry-go-round. They sat on a green park bench and ate popcorn. Nancy held a bouquet of flowers Max had obviously picked for her. Max, tanned and broader shouldered than Johnny had ever been, poised to dive into a sunlit swimming pool. Nancy watched from a lawn chair. She wore a bikini.

Johnny picked up the envelope that lay at his feet. The pictures had come from a town named Boxford, and the envelope's postmark was two days old. He extracted a letter. The people who got the pictures, it said, sent film showing lots west of Boxford they hoped to purchase.

"Wrong pictures. Try again," the letter ended. Mark and Virginia Melden had signed it.

Johnny picked up the magnifying glass and moved it over

105

the shots. Of the clothes Max wore, he recognized only the gray neck scarf worn in a shot on a boat deck, a duplicate of his own winter muffler. He studied the pictures more closely. He wanted to memorize every detail—the shopping bags Max carried, buildings and street signs Max and Nancy stood beside, the three outfits Nancy wore in the pictures, and last of all her jewelry. On the third finger of her hand, which Johnny figured had to be her left hand, she wore a gold ring with a bright stone at its center. It appeared in the picture where Max held Nancy's right hand, where she smiled up at him. Max and Nancy were engaged.

"Impossible," Johnny whispered under his breath. "Impossible."

Yet scientists thought parallel universes possible. Now he had found one, a parallel universe where he and Nancy fell in love and got engaged. Max had a car, and lots of money. He and Nancy went to famous places together. They were engaged to be married.

"You going to work all night?"

Mr. Nelson's pale pock-marked face leaned through the doorway. Johnny nearly dropped the magnifying glass.

"Sorry, I, no. Just finishing up a couple things," Johnny managed.

"How many'd you get last week?" Mr. Nelson asked.

At first Johnny counted backwards for pictures he had found of Max. Then he remembered, on Mondays Mr. Nelson took his match-up count.

"Twenty-five, thirty. I'll count back, if you want."

"Don't sweat it." Nelson stood in the doorway. He wrote a number on his clipboard. "Time to go."

Johnny could not resist asking. "Mr. Nelson," he paused, unsure how to word the question. "Do you believe in parallel universes?"

"Parallel whats?"

"Parallel universes. Oh, nothing. Never mind."

The man's figure disappeared from the doorway. "Keep going to school, kid," Nelson muttered as he walked away. "Then you'll understand all that stuff."

The month of June arrived, and with it came the Spring Dance. The dance absorbed all his friends' attention, but Johnny lied and said he had to work that night. In a way, he was working. By then Johnny worked many more hours than Mr. Nelson paid him for.

Before he left work on the Friday night of the dance, Johnny emptied a bin of photos into the red canvas bag he now carried. Max held one like it in three shots Johnny had recently discovered. He carried the prints home and spent the hours that night spreading them out on his bedroom carpet and sorting through them. He had bought his own magnifying glass—he guessed Max owned one too—and with careful inspection, not rushing, he managed 350 prints Friday evening and another 350 on Saturday. That matched his average from recent weeks—700 prints every weekend.

Johnny studied faces and backgrounds. He examined details of clothing, jewelry, interiors and landscapes. He memorized animals in motion and domestic pets, and he paid special attention to the features of the pets' masters. He penetrated the lives of the people in these pictures, the strangers, whoever they were. To keep himself going slowly he imagined their lives—what they said and how they felt right before the camera clicked, what they did right after. He tried to know each intimately, these creatures who lived in the same world he did or in a parallel one.

He looked for Max. Occasionally he found him, but the people themselves were fascinating too. Any one of them might know his own parallel self, might hold a clue to what would become of him, to his past and his future with Nancy.

On weekday evenings, Johnny carried home piles of letters. He went over them time after time, questioning each line for the faintest hint, any clue that might match a picture or tell more about Max. A few weeks before the Spring Dance, a letter yielded a clue. The boy in the pictures had taken Mrs. Ellisten and her two friends, Elizabeth and Kathleen, shopping for shoulder bags at HARRODS. He was their tour guide. His name was John.

The caption matched that whole set of pictures—the three old ladies on the boat, old ladies wearing hats, one old lady in sunglasses. Johnny set the letter aside. He would not return these pictures just yet. Recently, with all the extra time he was putting in, his match-up average had leapt to sixty per week. There was no need to add these pictures to his total to impress Mr. Nelson.

Johnny returned to his task. He worked through that weekend and through the following weekend and the one after that. He worked through the Spring Dance. When school let out in June, Johnny began putting in more hours at Sudby's. He upped his average of match-ups to eighty per week, winning a small raise from Mr. Nelson. He could have turned in more, but throughout that long summer Johnny set aside a small collection of photos and letters. These he would not return yet.

The tour guide's name was John. Johnny Maxwell knew that by now. This tour guide, as Johnny learned before late August, had been born to nice-looking parents. For a baby, he had not been too ugly. His mother held him for his crib pictures. John, the tour guide, went to school in what looked like a small town. He had two best friends and he liked to play baseball.

This first set of pictures unraveled seventeen years of a young man's life. Johnny Maxwell knew it made no sense—the dates on the pictures' backs covered the span of only one year—yet there it was. In the last of the set, developed only six months before, John the tour guide wore his high school graduation gown.

Around that time the backgrounds of the pictures

changed. Maybe Johnny's parents died, or sent him away to a school in Switzerland, because the shots showed him skiing in what looked like the Swiss Alps. Then dates for two months were missing from the backs of pictures before John's face showed up again. He was a tour guide now. John, the tour guide, pointed out castles and monuments. He stood beside smiling strangers who held cameras and flowered bags from HARRODS.

The young man's story, thus far, was told in fifty-three pictures. To these Johnny Maxwell added a dozen more, culled from LANDSCAPES—Foreign Places. He had been so busy looking for his own face, Johnny had missed these pictures of Nancy. She had been hiding in the photographs all along.

At first, Nancy showed up as part of a tour group. Her face appeared among the faces of a crowd which listened to John, the tour guide, as he spoke in front of a church. Soon Nancy appeared in pictures without Johnny, leading her own tours. The tour guide and the beautiful young woman must have met while working for the same company. They probably got to know each other and fell in love. They were engaged. These were Johnny's favorite pictures to date. He treasured the shots of the two of them dancing together in the night club and holding hands. He especially liked the one where Nancy smiled up at Johnny. In the last picture, dated in March, Nancy wore the diamond ring.

The complete set of pictures, showing John growing up, his fiancée, and John and Nancy together, numbered seventy-two. According to the dates on the backs of these seventy-two photos, the young man's birth, schooling, employment and engagement occurred in less than a year. That was certainly odd, but acceptable.

No more pictures arrived during the summer months. Johnny completed his review of all fifteen thousand from the Lost and Found. He kept seventy-two photos at home, along with the letters that referred to them. The others he returned to the Lost and Found, and to their owners if he found them. As the long months of summer passed, months without seeing Nancy, Johnny studied every new photo that arrived. No more news came from Europe.

At last September arrived. The week before school started Johnny bought a car. It was not the car he had wanted, the Ford with the long plush seats had been sold, but the seats of this four-door Chevy were comfortable when Johnny took off the plastic the former owner had put on them. Because he'd forgotten to figure in tax and licenses, the Chevy cost more than he anticipated, but Johnny had hardly spent money over the summer and he had plenty left.

Before school started, Johnny drove the car downtown and went shopping. Spending half of what he had left, he came home with two shirts, identical to those in the pictures he carried, a sweater he felt sure John already owned, and a pair of loafers. The salesman said loafers were going to be in this year in Millford. The first Monday of school Johnny wore one of the new shirts, his beige slacks, the corduroy jacket, loafers and his red and black striped socks.

In Home Room he sat listening to announcements, fingering photographs in his pocket. Johnny looked over the class. This year he and Nancy Gibson had been assigned the same Home Room, and she sat in the row by the window.

Nancy had grown more beautiful over the summer. Her skin was tanned as if she had been away at some beach resort, her long dark hair fell in soft folds away from the ribbon which gathered it at her neck. Johnny watched her until the bell rang, and resolved clearly in his mind what he would do the next morning.

At work that afternoon, Johnny found a big yellow note pinned to the door of Room B-26. Mr. Nelson had signed it. TIME TO SHRED PICTURES MORE THAN ONE YEAR OLD. SPEND YOUR TIME TODAY DOING THAT.

Johnny sorted photos from the bottoms of the bins and

carried several hundred to the shredder. He fed them through, watching the lives he had not been able to identify cut thinner and thinner. He held out seventy-two photos, thirty-five of which he knew belonged in the stack. That worried him slightly, but he put fear of getting caught out of his mind. He watched dogs and children and patios with barbecue pits sliced at odd angles to fine lines. By six o'clock, when all those lives had been reduced to a tangle of colorful twine, he knew exactly how it would go the next day.

The following morning Johnny drove his car to school and parked directly outside the window of Home Room. He had worn a different new shirt today and pushed his chest hairs up carefully to trail over the edge of the collar. In Home Room Nancy sat by the window. Her hair shone in the sunlight streaming through it, sunlight probably reflected from his very own windshield, Johnny thought. The bell rang and Johnny, his books at his hip, was the first to push open the door to the hall. He paused to stand beside it.

"Hi, remember me?" He slipped into step beside her as she came through the door. She was pulling a thick blue notebook to the top of her books. She paused and smiled slightly.

"Sure, you're..."

"John, John Maxwell. We had Biology together. Meakins' class."

They had reached the staircase, and Johnny stepped aside to make way for her. Yesterday she had gone to Rossiter's Home-Ec class on the second floor. He had timed it out. He would pop the question on the second floor landing.

"Biology, sure. I got a C, how'd you do?"

"Oh, okay." Two steps up to the landing. One step, now the easy smile. "Say, since we probably won't have homework yet this weekend, let's go to a movie. What do you say?"

Johnny heard his own voice echoing back from the high walls and tall ceiling of the landing. He sounded exactly like the voice he could imagine from those pictures.

"Sure," she said. Easy as that. "What kind of movies do you like?"

Johnny tried to keep the amazement from his voice, but it did crack once. "Sci-fi, how about *The Mound From X-32*? It's in town."

They had reached the second floor. Nancy Gibson was frowning. The door to Rossiter's Home-Ec classroom lay halfway down the hall.

"I sort of wanted to see *Misty River*," Nancy said, then she paused. "But if you'd rather..."

"That's great. I want to see that too." Johnny's voice cracked again, but he managed to deepen it. "See you tomorrow to work out the details." Nancy waved lightly over her shoulder. She passed through the door of Mrs. Rossiter's room.

That afternoon Johnny lined up seventy-two photos, slightly worn around the edges, down the longest table in Room B-26. He looked at each for a last time, then matched up letters and addresses for those he knew. He got that lot ready to mail in red and gold SPS packages. He stacked the rest in a neat pile. His hand trembling with fear and joy, he fed the photos into the slot and watched the faces and landscapes and waterfalls cut and cut again to clean shiny strings. Once they were shredded, compressed into a bale and tenderly eased down the chute toward the incinerator, Johnny turned to the day's mail.

At a quarter to six, around the middle of the pile, Johnny found the photos he was looking for. The letter writer wanted her baby pictures back.

We have twins, boy and a girl. We put them in matching wicker baskets. The camera moved a couple times, so the pictures might be blurry. These wedding pictures aren't ours, and the couple that's in them must want them back. Sorry for the trouble.

112

Johnny studied the pictures of the red-haired groom and his beautiful dark-eyed bride. A crumb of wedding cake made an extra freckle on the groom's chin. The bride's eyes shone more brightly than the gold pitcher on the gift table. Johnny prayed that no letter would come describing these prints, not ever.

Chapter Eight

Of course Johnny married Nancy, exactly like the story said. They both had jobs in Europe after high school. That was where they truly fell in love. They came back for the wedding, Angela was the bridesmaid. She caught the bouquet even though she was standing far away. The ribbons spread their wings and carried it. But of course you'd know that.

A nice story, thank you. And good cookies today too. I'm sorry you're feeling weak, but at least we eat cookies and drink tea together. We have pleasant talk.

The crocuses are up, have you seen them? Oh, I am sorry. I understand how hard it must be to get to the window. It's just you're looking so well today. I assumed you felt stronger.

Certainly I'll go the window. Let's see, yellow and purple crocuses, mostly yellow, like Easter eggs hiding under the hedge. It's grown a lot over them, I hope they get enough light. Crocuses, foolhardy flowers, don't you think? One late frost will nip them. But away they go, rushing up from the ground. I bet if they talked they'd have high squeaky voices like this, they'd talk about flower gossipy things.

Oh dear, no. I won't go on. When you laugh it makes you cough. I was just being silly. What else shall we talk about?

Other things went on in Millford, of course, lots of things. You remember Howard Buckram, and his art gallery out by the culvert? Mr. Pembroke fell in love with the Rembrandt there. And Nancy and Johnny liked to park by the apple orchard on summer nights. Now let's see what happened to Mr. Buckram.

Yes, cough until your throat's clear, that's good.

Here we go.

Out of Sight, Into Mind

Howard Buckram was going blind. His mother had lost her sight in middle-age and that was why Howard returned from the city to care for her, back in the days when he first opened Buckram's Farm and Art Gallery in Millford. Howard's mother was dead twenty years now, reduced from a weekly visit to the Foster Cemetery, overlooking Millford Flats, to twice yearly visits, on her birthday and his. Howard thought about his mother more often than that, of course, and in the autumn of that year, when night arrived earlier than the clocks said it ought to, Howard began to understand how she felt when she asked him to come home.

The individual apples in the apple orchard disappeared first. Then the trees themselves. They remained out there, Howard knew, but the empty November branches faded from distinct lines to blue shadows that hunched beside the pump house. Howard had never cared for apples, never harvested them or pruned the trees anyway, so he ignored the disordered blobs out there and six months passed.

In February he mistook a Murillo for a Cézanne at an auction. An easy mistake, he told himself, judged at a distance and in poor light. Nevertheless, the overbid cost him dearly on resale and he resolved to carry opera glasses in the future. In June he missed a step at a charity function. He tripped and nearly threw Mrs. Winnellton into the canapés because he had not noticed the table they were dancing toward. He pulled a stud near his collar and had to leave and miss the raffle. The following morning he called Dr. Winthrop.

Despite the status of his trade, Howard was not a wealthy man. When old Winthrop pronounced his condition, a name longer than those of several Italian painters, Howard knew he could not afford to seek out specialists who, after all that, could probably only pronounce the Latin better. The prescription, filled at Foster's Drug, helped temporarily, as Winthrop said it would, but Howard got in the habit of keeping several sets of opera glasses throughout the house, convenient to be picked up on occasion when the patron was not looking.

By now the apple orchard had disappeared completely, even at noon light, so one Sunday afternoon Howard walked out that way to make sure it had not somehow been stolen. He smelled the scent of summer stronger there, a round smell, as full and rich as good claret. He passed from the gravel onto grass and heard the silk talk of leaves overhead. He carried a set of opera glasses as a precaution, but hesitated to lift them in case a neighbor saw, so before long he ran into a tree.

He had been moving gently, careful to avoid tripping over roots, so the blow was a glancing one. Yet as he picked himself up and dusted off, he felt pain in his shoulder and, in his mind, a strange wonder. Groping unsteadily across the grass, he found the broad trunk again, the one he had hit. It was firm and rough, imperfectly round and knotty, knobbed with uneven nodules. His fingers probed and tested, counting nicks and circles, discovering a knothole that felt soft as a bellybutton. Howard knelt on the grass for a full minute, until a car approached along the road. He investigated what fingertips had to offer and felt, for whatever reason, his own pulse as well, a fluid channeling through his body like water rising up the tree. Howard pulled himself to his feet and felt his way back to the gravel. He had lost his best opera glasses and guessed the gardener would mow over them.

Being blind and owning an art gallery was more than inconvenient. As months had passed and his bill for opera glasses grew—Howard wrote away to the city for them, to an address he knew by heart—he had considered the consequences. As for appreciating art, he never felt great love for it. Paintings came and went, or if they did not go they were shipped to a volume house. Yet like state and federal taxes, patrons' money and good will ought to go on forever. He supposed it possible to hire an assistant and delegate carefully to run the gallery, but the patrons would surely catch on sooner or later. There went the farm and the invitations. The evening following the moment in the apple orchard, Howard finished his brandy before bed, settled his mind, and lay confidently down to sleep. He would make a clean breast of it. He would hire an assistant, re-do his stationery and calling cards, change the ad in *Proportion Magazine* and become a specialist in sculpture. The freight was worse but mark-up could recover it. Besides, Howard concluded as he drifted toward deeper darkness, what happened with that tree felt intriguing.

The transformation was art history six months later, and was the subject of an article written up in *Proportion*. Workmen reinforced the floors of the old house so they'd withstand the strain of bronze and marble. Decorators installed pale cream-colored wallpaper, off-white Miramaseen draperies and clean white sculpture stands. Howard memorized the floor plan and used raised lettering to print up the price list. The invitations went out. The ribbon-cutting weekend was stunning. Patrons were loyal beyond the call, in part because Buckram knew family secrets, and Howard's new assistant ran out of red SOLD tags even before the liquor ran dry.

His new assistant was a local girl, not very knowledgeable about art but with a dreamy college girl voice that could effuse at the exactly right pitch to warm a sale. Howard had taught Angela Maxwell the essential words—Composition, Proportion, Force, and Making A Statement—and trained her not to use any one of them with the same patron more than three times. The exhibit of Fanzetti bronzes and marbles sold remarkably.

That night before going to sleep Howard toasted himself

with Drambuie. His face felt fixed in a smile of greeting and delight and he had to massage it to make it relax. He was pleased about the near sell-out, though it meant he would have to bring in new works and memorize a new floorplan. Nevertheless Howard felt disappointment. Again and again throughout the evening, each time Angela told him that one or another piece had been sold, disappointment had come over him.

His hands had come to know these works. They were friends, as familiar and in these days as comforting as the friendly touch of pots and pans in the kitchen. Howard never saw the works, not exactly, but he trusted himself to spot a replica of any one of them, no matter how good, just by training a finger along its curving surface. He was sorry to see them go, those cool, smooth bronzes and those cold, more pure marbles, torsos which would never know his fingers' heat again. They would probably be put out in some garden for birds to comment on.

Several months passed. Howard's new assistant, a sharp girl if occasionally dreamy, learned more about the art business. Howard became adjusted to his blindness, and his remaining four senses heightened until he could tell which Bentley or Mercedes was turning into the drive. He even caught Mrs. Winnellton out one day, remarking that, from the sounds of the engine and the scent of aftershave, she must have hired a younger chauffeur.

The figure of the blind gallery owner became a curiosity among his patrons. Howard played to that. He held ladies' hands and ushered them through the gallery's rooms. He guided gentlemen at the elbow with a firm touch that, thanks to his height and his healthy looks, Howard used to intimidate them into purchasing. Howard wore dark glasses, even to social events, and soon became a garden party favorite because he was easy to keep track of. A few gentlemen copied his taste, others had their reading glasses tinted. As the young

Winnellton girl confided to Angela one day, while her mother was shopping, "They like Howard better blind, he's just that bitty dram more collectible."

For his part, Howard kept track of the cash flow and looked forward to evenings alone. In those hours, after Angela turned out the lights and left to go home, when the alarm wires hummed quietly along the windowsills and the furnace vents blew warm air around his ankles, Howard wandered the art-filled rooms in darkness. He wore his silk bathrobe. He liked having as little as possible between himself and the sculptures. He soon found it easier to leave the cord untied, pushing the soft skin of his chest and belly—so sensitive it felt preternatural—over wood and stone and polished metal.

Certain textures, certain surfaces resonated, like one string of a Stradivarius stirred in a hushed concert hall. Other surfaces moaned softly, ebony and silver did this, and certain thicknesses of alabaster. Mahogany thrummed like a well-oiled diesel, rosewood lilted medieval choir melodies. And those were only the sounds.

Howard could smell the different patinas of bronze, could guess the humidity in the house from those scents alone. He would touch his fingers to bone and then lift to taste on his tongue, a dusty taste like scented flour, a different flavor than the zing from glass or aluminum. Most of all, it was touch itself which hypnotized Howard, each sensation a descent into worlds of riotous, undulating contour. He wished to have hours he might spend connected to each crafted piece, although he did have his favorites. Among these he walked, gliding from alabaster to ebony, cold-rolled steel to poured latex, feeling their distinct frequencies melt right through his skin until he simmered inside.

It took a number of years for Howard Buckram to become a student of Chinese snuff bottles. Before then he had developed his philosophy of art, and his statement of it, dictated and dutifully typed by Angela, was reprinted in numerous texts after its first appearance in *Proportion*. Buckram held that the test of true art was simple, universal and old. It was a Rosetta Stone even the least educated could decipher. Art, Buckram stated, was that thing a human wanted to be with. How badly one desired to stay near an object was an exact gauge of its quality. Once you encountered a great painting or a sculpture—or a concert or a book or a dance for that matter—you found a part of yourself which the artist had placed there for you. You regretted books' and performances' endings, you wanted to take painting and sculpture home with you. To leave these things behind amputated a part of yourself, an arm or a leg, and the sensation in that part persisted ever after. Thus, having art in your life became central and important. The patron grew by the possession of art and became, psychologically, a reunited and complete self.

Critics questioned whether this meant you should buy everything you liked, preferably from Howard Buckram. Nevertheless the theory took hold. It was recognized as the Buckram Beauty Hypothesis. The theory said, in short, that art made it hard to go home. And Chinese snuff bottles, Howard Buckram discovered soon after his theory brought fame, made it hard to get to sleep.

Howard started out on Chinese snuff bottles the way such things always begin, the first one came to him free. It was a gift a patron brought back from a political junket. The piece was three inches high and two in circumference, made of ivory. Howard's hands knew all the music of stone and of wood, knew the keening of bone and the merry trills of aluminum. Yet never before, perhaps because these hands had been busy keeping track of the inventory, did his fingers touch ivory. He would always remember the morning Senator Voight said, "Here, I brought this for you," and pressed a weighted globe of noisy tissue to his hand.

Howard peeled the paper away and felt for contents. At first touch his heart's chambers hit each other like thunder-

121

heads. He let the paper drop and closed the carved shape into his palm. All his blood pounded drums around his stomach and he leaned against a sculpture stand for fear his knees would go jello. Here at last was ivory.

He listened with pretended alertness as Senator Voight told a bit about the history of the piece. Senator Voight described the little shop where he had found it. Here at last was ivory. These five words were all Howard heard. Here at last— ivory. He fixed his lips in a pleasant smile to avoid forming the words aloud. Then Angela noticed how pale he'd grown and she rushed to his side. She made him sit down finally. Without asking for the discount on the mobile he'd come to pick up, the gift was a bribe, Voight tactfully withdrew. Once Angela brought Howard some water, he acknowledged he was feeling unusually tired that day. They would close early.

Within a year, Howard Buckram brought the sign-painter all the way out from Millford to paint five new words on the sign at the end of the drive. The painter charged him for travel and considerably extra for the gold leaf. The gallery owner was happy to pay it. Now his roadside sign matched his business cards and his new letterhead. All read BUCKRAM FARM AND SCULPTURE GALLERY—Specialist in Chinese Snuff Bottles.

Howard had placed discreet ads in classified columns throughout the world and paid postage on countless small packages. The new chrome and glass cases along the walls of the gallery opened with special locks on them, requiring both a key and a combination, and were lined with Winsome Blue velvet. They had silver-edged tag holders. In addition, Howard Buckram had changed his habitual garb.

The cutaway coat of a morning suit fit too tightly to conceal the bulging oblongs of snuff bottles, small as they were. Howard had a friend in the city, who'd made his fortune on ready-to-wear, design the distinctive loose-fitting Buckram Suit which worked for Howard but never caught on as a trend.

Concealed pockets and secret pouches allowed room for bumpy possessions, while leaving the male figure trim and elegant, if slightly in pain while adjusting to an upright chair.

Of his extensive collection, Howard selected several snuff bottles as his own and kept them on his person most of the time. He liked to gentle his fingers past the fabric of a pocket in the middle of a sale to touch his Guangxu masterpiece or, once the receipt was written up, a delicate Qianlong reign creation. Even pressing a fingertip to one of them gave him comfort, and he learned how to move so the treasures would not click together and wear out. The fall of night was a different matter.

When Angela finally went home and the rooms of the gallery glowed with only the light inside the snuff bottles' cases, Howard carried a glass of claret and moved among them. He opened all the cases at once and let the ivory breathe, giving off its redolent scent throughout the house. He closed his eyes so that he would not even imagine seeing them, and he let his fingers brush like feathers over their surfaces. Each was different. He could hold each entire in his hand.

They told of tumultuous battles and of migrations, of river journeys and floods and frozen ascents, of babies tossed onto rocks and others held close in mothers' arms. When he listened at their openings he could hear the deafening roar of history, a song so broad only a tornado could have throat enough for it. He held them close and let their barbed carving scratch his skin, he moved them slowly through his hair like combs. In their aroma he could smell the scents of oils from flesh long since desiccated in the grave, could separate the smells of gun powder and saffron, burning peat, jute and sour milk. He played among them for hours while the chimes from the stairwell struck, adding a bell for each hour. Misery only arrived when the bells shortened to one, adding to two and then three.

He gently closed the cases and let his shoulders sag as he

climbed the stairs. So little of himself remained when he left them and loneliness swept in like a curtain closing. He had known the pulsebeat of humanity. Now he was alone, one single man again. Then one night, a step short of the stairs' landing, Howard felt a soft punch on his right thigh as his robe pocket nudged it. He had forgotten to put a snuff bottle back.

No matter, he would wake up early and replace it before Angela arrived. The idea excited him. He turned from the landing and hurried back down, the heavy pocket thumping against his thigh. He opened the nearest case and swept up a handful, pressing them hard to his chest. When the case was closed, he climbed the stairs with a light step. He slept that night with five Chinese snuff bottles under his pillow.

The bed required adjustment in the months to come—a softer mattress, satin sheets, a firm rail along the edge to prevent anything, including Howard, from falling. Howard adjusted his hours of sleeping as well, requiring more sleep and rising early to get the gallery ready for Angela. Hours spent snuggled among perhaps a hundred Chinese bottles dimpled and bruised the skin, demanding at least an hour to smooth it out. Yet Howard slept better than he ever had in his life, and he rose content and refreshed, ready to take on the cares of this day in history.

Patrons felt uneasy at first when Howard's charm lost its oily patina and became more sincere. They grew used to it. Angela found his occasionally quick temper softened and no longer as cutting. Mr. Buckram had sold off all the land right up to the apple orchard to invest in Chinese snuff bottles, but he liked to walk out that way when Angela had time to watch out the window and see he did not fall. She offered to set him a chair out there, but he said no, he liked to sit on the ground in a certain location. He enjoyed the sun there at any hour. Howard was not strong in these latter years, but always rose to his feet gracefully when he heard the right kind of car turn into the drive.

There's really not much more tell, except his death, of course, an event which caused a stir in Millford as well as unsettling wider social circles. Angela Maxwell found him, or at least she pointed the way. That Monday morning she arrived at the gallery on time, turned off the alarm system and opened the door only to find the downstairs rooms stark and empty.

She'd left at 5 P.M. on Saturday. They had an exhibit of the Timson collection installed, consigned works in bronze, alabaster and marble, due to stay on hand for a month. Angela's glance swept over the front room to discover even the snuff bottle cases empty. Not one work of art remained on the whole first floor, though the silver tags stood upright and perfect in their places.

The second floor was the same, and Angela noticed, climbing from the landing up to it, that some of the risers and steps of the stairs were scuffed and broken. Mr. Buckram was usually up by now, which was odd too now that she thought of it. Suppose the gallery had been robbed and Mr. Buckram lay, possibly dead, in his bedroom on the third floor.

Angela was about to climb the stairs from the second floor, stairs whose risers were even more badly bashed up and scuffed, when she heard a noise from above. It was a sort of creak, as if the house were settling, but deeper and heavier than any sound she'd ever heard in the structure. Angela's hand froze to the banister. The sound repeated, more a groan, like wood complaining under a strain. Angela suddenly imagined the thief, or the thieves—it would have to be more than one since those sculptures weighed tons—still up there. She ripped her dress leaping over the banister, the quickest way to the flight below, and raced down the stairs.

Angela called Sheriff Dolgan from Mitch and Sally Jordan's Market, half a mile down the road. The sheriff picked her up and she rode with him back to Buckram's, but waited outside while he went in. The sheriff left with his gun drawn, but he came back out only moments later to ask a question.

"Any idea why he's got all those statues piled up on the stairs?"

Angela said they were all in the downstairs galleries when she left on Saturday.

Dolgan came back again twenty minutes later. He looked beat up and his clothes were rumpled. He said it was all right, except Angela should come back inside with him if she could handle a shock and was fairly athletic. Angela said she was.

Together they fought their way to the third floor, clambering over a piled jumble of immense art works which crowded the stairwell above where the second floor landing turned up toward the third. Angela figured that getting these sculptures up here must have bashed up the stairs, but whoever would bring them? Certainly not Howard, who lay looking lifelike between satin sheets in his third floor bedroom, but dead. Sculptures stood crowded in rows all around him, posed like sentinels in the tangerine sunlight streaming in through the curtains. The sculptures' best sides were all turned toward the bed as if they kept watch.

With so many, the sculptures filled the room and blocked the doorway. Others were left to stand in crowds on the steps. One bust of a military man perched on the post at the top of the landing.

The entire Timson collection was there, plus other assorted sculptures Howard had held onto for years, overpricing them. The funeral director had a fine time hiring a crew to move the stuff out of the way. They had to work carefully because the third floor was shifting and sagging under the extraordinary weight. It took ten men all day, and by then the body was rigid.

The coroner said Howard did not move the sculptures up there. Howard had died peacefully in his sleep, of a heart attack not brought on by extraordinary exertion. His skin was unmarked except where the snuff bottles had dimpled it.

126

When the sheets were pulled back several hundred of the small art objects were found nestled around the body.

"Heavy labor would at least have marked hands," the coroner determined. He said so at the inquest. The incident remained unexplained. The coroner had investigated the residue on the skin of the hands too, just in case, but found only oils of ivory.

Chapter Nine

*Y*es, that certainly was a strange one. That's the way it went, poor Howard. No, actually he was happy, despite dying so young. That would have been after he and Angela authenticated the Pembroke Rembrandt. Many years afterward.

Angela knew who she was by then, a regular somebody. And already in love and out of love once. You'll remember that part, with the willow tree and the minnows. Shall I tell about that? All right, some other time.

I hope you're feeling strong today. Lovely weather makes us all feel good, doesn't it? I hope you do feel better, despite staying in bed, since I really must bring up a topic. You won't appreciate this, but it's got to be said. It's about that hedge.

Yes, I know the gardener left unexpectedly. But I mentioned it, you could have asked for him to fix it long ago. It's grown thicker each day. It's grown so since my last visit, hard to believe. Look at the scratches on my hands. How do you like that?

Why, that's from trying to get through the hedge. I came early to allow time. It's all tangled and people can't get through. Do you believe me now?

Oh, the ribbon. You've put knots in it. I've upset you, haven't I? Let me untie it for you. It's like the hedge now, all tangled up like that. Yes, I'll stop about that. I am sorry.

Perhaps a story. No hedges in it, I promise. I'll never mention it again.

Now it's all unknotted and free again. Let me see. You haven't met Tom Latham yet, have you? Actually you have, but don't know it. He was standing outside Hamburgette's that day, the day Angela met Charles Madden. That was the same day Johnny Maxwell found the first photo with Nancy in it. The day Angie's friend Josephine's father tried to drown thirteen cats, and William Twelveclocks saved eleven of them, and made a hat of the last two. And Howard Buckram visited old Doctor Winthrop that day. But Tom Latham. Now it's time to tell you about him.

Thomas Latham Confounded

Tom Latham remembered the first time he saw her. He had ridden over from Ginnett with some friends, and Amzie came into Hamburgette's with her two girlfriends. It was a Saturday afternoon, after Christmas he guessed. Maybe it was in February, and definitely his sophomore year. The next summer his family moved, and the following autumn he started at Millford High. There he actually met Amzie, Angela Maxwell in those days, and he fell in love. He guessed it was love.

Tom Latham sat at the counter of Foster's Drug and Soda Fountain. He waited until it was time to drive across town. Amzie had left ten minutes ago to interview for a job. She had a job until three weeks ago, a good one in an art gallery, but then the owner died and now she needed a new job. She had told Tom about how she found the dead man, up in his bedroom with all those statues standing around. Tom listened to the sensible parts and ignored the rest. Amzie was like that sometimes, letting her imagination fly around. Girls were like that generally, but Amzie more than others. Maybe that made him love her, if this was love.

The thick soda fountain glass left from Amzie's strawberry shake sat on the counter beside his chocolate-coated one. Pink froth had dried in bubbly ribbons along the edge, making a crust on the glass lip. Even if it was pink, he liked how it looked. It was her glass. Tom wondered if, that day he saw her at Hamburgette's, she had ordered a strawberry shake. Probably not. She was three years younger then and people changed.

He could remember seeing her through the window, her shiny brown hair and dark eyes, her face like a face in a dream,

131

blurry with the window glass over it. She sat with two girl-friends. One was Josephine, they still double-dated with her and her string of boyfriends sometimes. He hadn't known who Amzie was then, did not meet her that day he saw her through the window glass. He watched her talking to her friends and drinking a soda. That was what she drank that day—a soda. He remembered it perfectly.

Tom pointed out the girl to Toby Jenkins, who had given him a ride over from Ginnett. Toby only said the girl next to her had a better shape. Toby was that way, a lot he knew. Tom guessed he fell in love with Amzie that day, instead of waiting until they met and started dating.

Falling in love was supposed to be like that. Girls talked like they knew what it was, but Tom had listened once or twice and knew they were inconsistent. For the first few months of dating, he had thought he was crazy, or getting sick, a brain tumor or something. But he didn't start falling down or keel over at basketball practice so he guessed that wasn't it. He just kept thinking of her, and they dated every weekend. He hadn't wanted to call her Angela or Angie, or even her middle name, Mona. Other people picked those names for her. Other people called her by them. Those were used names. "Amzie" came from her initials, a new name he had made for her. Now she belonged to him.

Or maybe it wasn't love. Maybe this was how criminals got started, sitting here wanting to steal a soda fountain glass because it was hers. He could tuck it under his jacket and carry it out. If he got caught he'd get arrested, lose his job, maybe lose Amzie. It was a good job, enough to support them if he asked her and she said yes. He had always been good with numbers, and figuring out insurance rates was less boring than most jobs. He had money in the bank, a car, his own apartment. Amzie still lived at home with her parents. Or maybe she would say yes because she wanted to get away from her parents and not because she really wanted to marry him.

Tom pushed the thought from his mind. Amzie loved him. She had said it—she loved him. Of course Tom asked how she knew, and she only repeated she knew, she knew. That was no answer. But anyway, Amzie liked her parents. She got along with her brother, who was moving out and going to Europe anyway. So that settled it, and it was logical: she wouldn't marry him to get away from home. Maybe love wasn't logical, but he could figure this much out. Love was different from numbers or insurance, except in some ways. It was like insurance because you had to figure the probabilities.

The probabilities counted, Tom decided, and that was why he was going to drive across Millford this afternoon. He was going to do a thing he'd never done before, never considered doing, but given that it might be love he was working with, it was best to be logical and check the probabilities. His appointment was at four o'clock. Tom Latham checked his watch.

Martin Foster, owner of Foster's Drug and Soda Fountain, leaned on the counter by the cash register. He watched the slender dark-haired young man at the fountain counter. The kid was checking his watch. Maybe he'd leave soon.

Martin lined up the toothpicks in the dispenser so all the labels read in the same direction. He was actually watching the slender, dark-haired fellow but the toothpicks were more interesting. He had been watching for ten minutes and he knew one thing. The kid had been bitten by the bug all right. That young man had a sorry case of it.

In the first place, the young fellow talked too loud while his girl was here, trying to impress her. When she left, he got the moony look in his eye. Now he looked like he wanted to slip her milkshake glass under his coat and carry it out.

Forty-nine cents, those glasses cost. Martin Foster was damned if he'd lose another one this week, not to a love-sick Romeo. He had considered going over and picking up the glass, slipping it into the dishwashing sink. The toothpicks were all lined up again. They had been twice already. Foster

133

wiggled his finger through them to make a tangle of pick-up sticks. Taking away the glass would ruin the fun.

Tom Latham sighed and checked his watch again. He had forty-five minutes. He picked up his jacket and slung it over his arm, then remembered that Amzie wasn't there. She would not notice his bravery in going without it, and the wind was cold outside. With one last look at Amzie's milkshake glass, he pulled his jacket on and went out. He would arrive early and spend the time figuring out exactly how to put the one question he needed to ask.

On the other side of Millford, Mrs. Maria Romano finished Clara Ferguson's comb-out, dropped her comb in the disinfecting solution the Health Department required, and ushered Clara and her blue hair out the door. Two more comb-outs remained. Then at four o'clock she had an appointment with a Mr. Thomas Latham. The phone call sounded like a kid, but the voice had said, "Mr. Thomas Latham."

Maria had a bad head cold and she stifled a sneeze. She took up a fresh comb, and lifted the hood of the only hair dryer that worked. She would have to allow time to change clothes before the appointment with Mr. Latham.

Maria Romano was of gypsy stock, but she owned a beauty parlor now. The sign in front of her house, across the street and four doors down from the Maxwell home on Pear Street, said MARY ROMAN, HAIRDRESSER. Below that, it said MARIA ROMANO, FORTUNES TOLD—The Answer To Your Questions About Love, Business, Marriage—Names, Dates And Facts Given. The house was a run-down two-storey structure, set back from the street with a small porch and a side entrance for the beauty parlor. Beside the porch lay a small garden. The stalks of the winter vegetables there looked stronger than the poles supporting the porch.

Maria Romano liked the house the way it was, or whatever

way it went next. Houses mattered little to her. She had accepted that the gypsy life was no longer practical, nice as it was to roam from place to place with a family tribe. During her own childhood, her family had done that and she missed it sometimes when she heard train whistles or saw travel posters. Now her daughter lived in New Lester, married to a stock broker, and her son drove a school bus in a nearby town. Occasionally Maria thought wistfully of her missing husband. At least he kept up the gypsy tradition. But it was not practical to roam for a living or wear many layers of clothes and all her jewelry at once. If one roamed a lot, wearing seven layers of clothing saved on luggage, but too many layers looked out of place on a beautician living in Millford.

Gypsy ways were passing ways. She knew of only a few families left in Europe. Even they kept permanent post office boxes these days. Maria Romano was sorry to see it pass, but she held on to the best part. The gypsy life meant uncertainty from one moment to the next, a permanent state of helplessness that only lying could cure.

The beauty parlor brought in most of the money, enough to pay the mortgage now that her husband could not squander it. The fortunetelling was just on the side. Fortunetelling had its advantages, and chief among them was lying.

Maria knew the pleasure that a well-told lie gives its teller. She had a single rule—the customer paid for the answer to only one direct question. Aside from that she was on her own. When she told a fortune, she could say whatever she liked, within limits her mother had taught her the day her ears were pierced. She kept three silver posts in each ear these days, and she knew how to make her customer listen and believe the lies. The customer was trapped, he had to listen. Lies twined together like ivy vines, each leaf covering another until a life was complete. Since this willing human wanted to believe, whatever she said would come true. And that, Maria Romano knew in the sweet taste of a lie on her tongue, was power.

Inside the beauty parlor, Maria applied a cloud of hair spray to her last comb-out. She squeezed the bottle's trigger and sneezed. Her cold was getting worse by the minute. The droplets from her sneeze mixed with the hair spray and beaded on the lacquered bouffant. A touch of tissue cleaned them up. Her last appointment was finished, and now a gawky-looking young man stood at the door. He was early, this Mr. Latham who had called. She would have to stall.

"May I help you?" Maria approached the tall young man and spoke in perfect English. She waved goodbye to her last customer. The young man stood a good three feet from the display of hairnets and brushes. He must be scared to touch ladies' things.

"I have an appointment."

"Permanent wave or color rinse?" This was going to be fun.

"I meant not for my hair. I have an appointment, I came here to consult, that is to see Maria Romano."

"Ah, my sister. Of course." Maria glanced at the wide appointment book on the counter. "You have to wait. I believe you are early." She gestured toward one of the hooded dryer chairs, the one with pink bows on the armrests. "Make yourself comfortable."

Tom Latham glanced around. He moved away from the hair dryer and sat down in a upright chair in the waiting area. He picked up a copy of *Girls' Day* and immediately let it fall. He picked up a copy of *Coif!* and opened it, frowning.

"I'll tell my sister you're here. You'll hear your name called when she is ready." Maria Romano disappeared through a fabric curtain at the back of the shop.

Maria and Mary were one and the same, shop and séance salon separated by a cloth curtain, plain on one side and sequined on the other. Only Maria's husband, driven off ten years ago at the point of a hot comb, knew of the deception. She doubted he'd come back to haunt her.

While Mary Roman turned into Maria Romano, Tom Latham looked over the faces of girls and women in *Coif!* and, having come to the end of it, studied the room. He had plenty of time to think. Getting Maria Romano ready required a complete make-over, from the skin out, and a certain spiritual fine-tuning as well.

Beyond the curtain, Maria removed the pale Caucasian make-up she wore for her beauty parlor customers and applied a coating of base and powder that brought out the olive tones in her skin. She highlighted her cheeks with rouge and her eyes with jet paint. She sprayed perfume on her neck, wrists and arms. She drew several yards of beaded jewelry from a leather pouch kept at her waist, and put these on, then layered a necklace of gold medallions over it and three silver coin chains over that. Maria had to take care to work quietly, the curtain was thin.

She unhooked her bra and let her full breasts fall to her waist. She was a plump woman, so they wedded there with her belly, the beginning mound of a pear shape which her thick hips and thighs completed. Around that shape, she wrapped several layers of fabric—first ruffled slips, then paisley and flowered skirts, and finally a purple and blue velvet which had lost its nub in places where it creased naturally. For her blouse she chose a thick cotton magenta, worn with two sweaters underneath. She would have preferred silk, but she kept sneezing and silk would be cold. She sprayed herself again with perfume. She lit the fire and set about giving the room atmosphere.

Out in the beauty parlor, Tom Latham pondered his future. He tried to ignore the hair dryers and manicure sets arrayed around him, but he was hopelessly drawn to study them. In a way, they were what he was in for. He wanted to flee from this room with its sickly pink chemical smell— permanent wave stuff he had smelled when his mother disappeared into the bathroom all afternoon. The room and its smell attracted and repelled him. It was a woman's world and if he asked Amzie to marry him he might enter it.

Tom disliked pink. Now he sat in a jungle of it. Pink dryer hoods perched like gross parrots on their aluminum stalks. Pink plastic curlers mounded in bins like strange spiny plants, and pink-handled hairbrushes and rat-tail combs clutched each other in clusters on glass shelves. Pink picture frames presented water-stained portraits of beautiful women, each proud of her hairdo. They all looked at him. He wished he knew what they wanted.

Worst of all were the pink hairnets hung like spider webs from hooks around the room. Part of Tom wanted to walk over and touch one, but he feared Mary Roman might come back through the pink curtain.

Tom reassured himself. He was here because he was logical. If this was love, and it was women's business, what better than come to a woman's place and ask a fortuneteller. After all, girls were inconsistent when they talked about love, and men were worse.

Guys talked about getting into bed with girls and how girls' breasts bounced. The married guys at work talked about the secretaries that way, but never their wives. Nobody talked about love. Tom even went so far as to ask his father about it once.

"Oh, it's a phase. You get over that," Dad said, and turned back to the pictures of naked brown women in *National Geographic* magazine.

Only girls talked about love, and their authority was tinged with pink and could not be trusted. He had touched Amzie all over, even though they had not gone all the way, and her smells and the way she moved had the same pinkness of this place. Even if they had gone all the way, Tom now admitted to himself, the sweet and slightly sickening pink mystery would have remained—that one thing he never could get at. Unless maybe married guys got to it.

138

"Thooomas!" A heavily accented voice startled Tom out of his reverie. "Thooomas Laaathaam! Pass through the curtain. Fate awaits you."

Tom guessed the voice must mean him. He left the waiting area, skirting the hair dryers and baskets of spiny rollers. He pushed through the dangling piece of cloth at the back of the shop. Bells, stitched to the bottom of the curtain, tinkled pinkly to announce him. A wall of heat hit him.

Because of her fresh head cold, Maria Romano had built a roaring fire on the hearth. Sneezing, while pretending to be spirit-possessed, would destroy the illusion. She had also turned on two small electric heaters on either side of the room. The temperature on that side of the curtain was approaching eighty. In addition, before taking her crystal ball out of the refrigerator, kept there because Maria had read that crystal kept vegetables crisp, she had taken two decongestant tablets and blown her nose until her ears popped. Now the crystal ball let off a steam vapor as its cold curvature met the warm air. Maria made a mental note to remember the niceness of the effect. She sat in a large carved chair, its polished oak shining out of the darkness around her. Her jewelry and her rings and her face and her eyes reflected the flickers of twelve candles strategically placed around the room.

"Come, and sit. Keep not the future waiting." The woman's accent was as thick as the black make-up lidding her eyes.

Tom crossed the room on tiptoe and took the seat opposite her. He sat on a small camp stool, too small for comfort. Maria preferred it because it kept the customer off balance on the edge of his seat. Tom's knees bumped the small table which held the ball of fog.

"Your one question, do you wish to ask it now?" Maria Romano's dark eyes stared into Tom's.

Tom hesitated. He had only one question figured into the fee. He had a great many suspicions about the worth of paying that fee. If he asked right away she might guess more. If she

139

were a fraud, he might figure that out first, skip the question and try getting his money back.

"I'll wait," he said.

"As you wish."

Maria Romano touched her brightly polished fingernails to her temples. Her scarf was slipping. She pulled it down to her brow, shading her eyes, then she closed them.

"Come to me now. Come to me," Maria Romano said. She began to rock back and forth on the oak chair. The old wood made a creaking sound that was eerie in the candlelight.

"I feel a spirit. Yes. It is lame. I hear it approach. A cane taps."

Tom heard only the creaking of a chair. He looked around. The candles sputtered. On the hearth, the fire hissed and spat a spark that winked out in the air. He listened closer. A low ticking, a crackly sound, came from the vicinity of the vaporous ball.

"Wait. Another spirit approaches. She comes with him. She leads him along on a golden chain."

"Are they together?" Tom blurted out. The strangeness was getting to him. The room smelled funny, but not like permanent wave solution.

"Is that your question?" The gypsy opposite him let go of her temples and glared. Her eyes glowed coals in her dim face.

"No. I guess not. I just wondered."

"About the future, we do not wonder," Maria corrected him firmly. "We listen." She resumed rocking. She swayed in silence for a full minute before speaking again.

"The man is lame. The girl wears white. Wait. Not a girl. She is a bird. Look! She takes off!"

Maria Romano's hands met each other above her lap in a sudden clap, then flew into the air, snapping and releasing a vial of popping powder toward her customer's right shoulder. The trace of powder arced in the air. As Tom spun to witness

140

it, he nearly slipped from the camp stool. The smell in the room had grown stronger.

"What was that?"

"Is that your question?"

"No, I just..."

"These things are not for curiosity. You will listen and watch. It is a powerful future you bring. Stubborn, powerful. It will go away if you do not behave." Maria Romano knew the value of keeping a customer in line.

Tom shivered. Cool air flowed from the glass ball between them and he could feel it. This place, and the low crackling noise too, were getting to him. He watched the mysterious woman take up a small shiny cloth from beside the nearest candle and use it to swab and rub the glistening globe. She shook the cloth out to her left, she shook it out to her right, she rubbed the ball again. The crystal seemed to glow in the candlelight.

"The spirits are still present. I go to meet them in the future. In this crystal they show me their faces."

The woman continued burnishing the ball, and its glow grew brighter with each stroke. To her right, Tom saw a movement, a shimmering thread of light stirring at her ankle. He blinked and a black cat appeared on the gypsy woman's thigh. It took a step and pooled like ink in her lap.

"That is good. Sinisteria wishes to join us. She will go with us though the darkness." The cat's actual name was Alex but Maria called him Sinisteria during sessions. It made no difference to the cat.

Tom debated whether to greet the cat. He decided against it. Anything he said would have begun, "Kitty, kitty," and that seemed wrong.

The crystal ball's glow pulsed and pulsed again, throwing puffs of cool vapor into the hot air. Apparently it was ready, the gypsy woman dropped her shiny cloth to the table. She curved her hands above the ball. Her fingers moved in dancing rhythm as if gentling the air and calming it. Tom studied the ball. He could see only vapor and the fireflies of candle flames dancing on its bright curvature. Its sounds had mostly quieted down, except for an occasional tick.

"Ah!" The gypsy drew back in surprise. She hunched her shoulders and approached the ball again. "They are in there!"

"Who?"

The gypsy shot Tom a look. He pressed his lips closed.

"They come through the trees. A young man. He is shackled so he walks with a cane."

Flames carved outlines in the hollows of the gypsy's cheeks. She peered up at him.

"It is you. You are lame. Shackled, a halting step. Now she appears beside you. This is downright incredible."

Tom bit his lip to keep quiet. So far everything but the popping flash in the air could have been fake. He wasn't sure about that. Yet Tom felt chilly all over and the back of his neck tickled with trickling sweat. He felt enchanted, too completely enthralled by the weirdness around him to notice how warm the room had grown. Suddenly his attention was caught and riveted to the gypsy's lap. Either the cat was watching him or the gypsy wore two jewels in her navel.

"The young girl wears white. She is beautiful. She has dark hair and dark eyes. She wears a large ring on a chain. At her neck. It swings with her steps."

That was Amzie. Tom had given her his high school ring and it was too big for her hand, even with the edge wrapped in bandaids. She wore it on a chain around her neck. Tom clutched his sides and struggled to balance on the camp stool.

"I see her now. She kneels at your feet. She struggles there. No. Wait."

Tom waited. Maria Romano waited also. She gave it a good ten seconds. She knew long pauses were good for suspense, but she was not counting the seconds this time.

"The girl knelt. She stands again now. She holds the gold

142

chain. It is the chain which shackled you. You are free. You lift your cane. Look, she is a bird again, and she lights on it. The girl is carrying your cane away."

Maria Romano paused again. She was speechless. Even though this was a poor moment for a pause, she forgot about the requirements of dramatic timing. At last she spoke.

"Twenty years, I tell fortunes," she said. "Never seen anything like this." And for once it was true.

This had never happened before. The situation was out of control. Those tiny figures actually were walking around inside the dense glow of the crystal. Imagine, she thought, a crippled young man released from his chains by a bird-girl. It was bad enough that she was too stunned to lie, but the tale itself was plain corny. The old Mrs. Romano, Maria's mother, would have smacked her across the face for a routine like that.

Yet it was all happening before her eyes. It had all happened inside the crystal globe. Two miniature figures had walked out of some trees and gone through that dance with the gold chain. Maria wondered about the decongestant tablets, but she felt normal enough. She had taken the brand before. In fact, she felt a sneeze tickling.

The sneeze broke the silence, and sprinkled moisture on the crystal.

"What happened?" Tom Latham said, unable to stand the fierce hot well of silence longer.

Maria Romano shot him a look. Tom nodded. All right, that was his question, he started to say, but she cut him off. "Okay, this one's for free. The bird flew off with the cane. She dropped it into a lake, but it didn't splash."

She looked at Tom's face. "And then?" it asked.

"And then you turned into a bird. You were a purple bird." The bird had actually been black, but Maria had suffered enough truth for one day. "And you disappeared into the sky after her." That part was true.

Sweat poured from Tom Latham's forehead and cheeks.

The air felt like molten ore and the metal edge of the camp stool was hot to his touch. The gypsy woman took up the cloth and wiped the ball, clearing away spit from the sneeze. She seemed tired now, exhausted.

"You've still got a question coming." Her shape hunched, elbows on her knees. "I don't give refunds."

Tom tried to remember the wording of his question. His mind felt soldered in the intense heat, permanently fixed on amazement. "I wanted to know, well . . . See I was thinking of doing something. And I want to know whether to do it."

"You've got to give me more to work with than that." The woman glared at him. "People do lots of things. You're not paying mind reader's prices here."

"I, sort of, I was going to ask a question. I mean of somebody else. Of a girl. She's almost a woman, really. She is a woman really."

"So?"

Tom took a deep breath. The air seared his lungs. "Should I ask Amzie to marry me?"

"Oh that."

The gypsy looked down at the crystal ball. It was making ticking noises again. She took a deep breath and blew it out heavily toward the crystal. Suddenly both of them heard a loud crack.

Maria Romano screamed and fell backward. The oak chair caught her and kept her upright. Tom Latham jerked away, teetered an instant, fell from the camp stool, one arm out to catch himself, and sprawled on the carpet near the hearth. He rolled over and looked back up at the table. The crystal ball was gone.

Maria Romano had a better perspective. The crystal ball was neatly split. A clean curve cleaved it in two, its fallen halves revealing brilliant, clear, flat faces. It had split exactly down the middle.

"Damn," Mrs. Romano said. "I got that from my mother."

And she began to cry.

Tom scrambled to his feet, saw what had happened, righted the camp stool and sat down again. Between her sobs, he managed to learn that the crystal ball had come directly from the refrigerator. At last he understood, a simple matter of physics. This heat, the cold glass coming into this hot room. He tried explaining logically, but Mrs. Romano found physics too far-fetched to believe.

She shook and rumbled with sobs. She paused for tearful apologies to her mother, directed to the ceiling. Her wig fell off, trailing the scarf after it, but in the dim light Tom did not recognize Mary Roman as her own sister. She went through all the tissues in her pockets and Tom had to run to the bathroom for more. He returned and stood in the doorway.

The fire had burned down and the candles stood low, dripping wax on the carpet. Maria Romano had almost stopped hiccuping and had the power to speak. She got up and blew the candles out, turning on the bright fluorescent light overhead.

"So now what do I do with that?"

The broken halves of the crystal ball lay fallen away from each other on a tattered ruby-red cloth.

Tom Latham stood by the door, hands and pockets full of tissues. He had seen the future split open in front of his eyes, and even if only physics counted, he had no idea what to do with the remains.

"We could try gluing it," he ventured.

Mrs. Romano's dark eyes shot a harsh look.

"Throw it away?"

Those dark eyes glittered tears. She might start crying again. Crying women made him uncomfortable, and gypsies seemed able to cry louder and longer than his mother. Or even Amzie that time he insisted they go all the way.

"I know," he said with sudden enthusiasm, "how about if we bury it?"

145

"Okay. You're right," Mrs. Romano sighed deeply. "The shovel's out by the back porch. Go start digging."

Tom hurried through the curtain, glad to get out of the room.

Out in the back yard it was beginning to get dark. Tom found the shovel and picked his way through the garden of brussels sprouts and cabbage and broccoli. He selected a spot by an old tree and began digging. The ground was hard, unwilling to break around tree roots, but he welcomed the pleasure of beating it apart.

By the time he had a two-foot hole, night had fallen. The gypsy woman's watching figure stood in the doorway outlined by light. She came down the steps and stood beside him. Her hands cradled the two halves of the ball, wrapped in its red velvet cloth.

Maria Romano knelt and slipped the ball into the hole. She patted the wrapping closed and scooped the first handful of dirt. Her open fingers let it fall. It was too dark to see, but she could hear it drizzle over the velvet.

The crystal ball was the last of her mother's possessions. She could buy one just as good in a magic store, but it would never be the same. Just this once, with this ball, magic happened. She had no idea what it might mean.

She still owed the young man an answer to his question, but she had no intention of lying. Her pocket held a check, written on the beauty parlor account, for a refund in full. When the hole was filled in and tamped down, she gave it to the young man.

It was later that evening, on his way to pick up Amzie to go to a movie, that Tom Latham remembered his question. He got a refund, he realized, but no answer. He remembered the gypsy woman's voice talking softly while they were filling in the hole. In magic, the lady said, there were symbols and clues. Supposedly symbols and clues told people what to do.

Tom pulled up in front of the Maxwells' house. Down the

146

street, the windows of the Romano house were dark. He guessed life must be even stranger than magic. There were no symbols or clues, he may as well be logical, for all the difference it made.

Late that night, parked on the bluff overlooking Cliff's Roadhouse, Thomas John Latham asked Angela Mona Zoey Maxwell to marry him.

Amzie said yes.

Chapter Ten

*Y*es, that was a lovely story. The most beautiful story we have, isn't it? I could tell it again if you like. Would you enjoy hearing it again?

Not the same words exactly, different words but the same basic story. Well, if you learned it by heart, memorized it exactly word for word, I'd probably disappoint you.

I'll take it on trust, I do believe you memorized it. Your voice is too tired to repeat it word for word. Yes, cough. Go ahead now, let the coughing clear it out. Now you understand why I'm the one who tells the stories.

I expected you'd want a story today, and I have one ready, but in a minute. First you have to answer a question.

Not about that. I did promise never to mention that nasty growing thing again. Actually I scratched my hands getting through. But let's not think about that, it upsets you. Pretend I got in a fight with a cat.

What I want to know is—how are you feeling?

Old, of course, you don't need to tell me that.

Cough it out, that's good.

Both doctors say the same thing? Being old is no picnic, I agree, but summer will come and make it warm. We can sit by the window again.

Of course we'll have stories in summer. You should lie back and listen to this one today. I worry about your strength. Lie all the way back on the pillow, please. Because it's the best way to listen to a story, that's why.

Good. I think you'll like this one.

Oh Food

Angela Mona Zoey studied her shopping list. It said:

CLEANSER
MINUTE STEAKS
WAXED PAPER

She remembered the twelve minute steaks already stored in the freezer. Angela crossed the minute steaks off.

She leaned back in her chair and glanced at the kitchen. The breakfast dishes were drying in the rack and a damp towel lay stretched over the oven door. She tried to imagine Tom in the house without her.

Each evening he came home at 5:15. He set his briefcase at the end of the green couch and he hung up his coat. He carried his briefcase to the room next to the one they had prepared for the baby, and set it between the desk and the recliner which they had brought from their old apartment. Tom came to the kitchen and washed his hands.

During dinner Tom told her the latest news from the insurance office—field agents driving into town for a convention, a new law which meant completely rewriting the flood policies. After dinner, Tom sat on the stool in the kitchen while Angela did the dishes.

Tom would do his own dishes for a few days. Angela added DISH SOAP to the list, then leaned back.

When the dishes were done, Tom read papers until 8:00. Then Angela turned on the television. While she was in the hospital Tom would not hear the television and come to sit beside her.

Angela debated whether to add SOMEONE TO TURN ON

TELEVISION on her shopping list. The pad of paper, perched at the edge of the wooden table, was a long reach off. Resting note paper on her belly made it easier to write, but the curve gave a poor writing surface. And the baby kicked. Angela settled back in her chair.

Every day for three years her feet had touched the floors of this house. Her hands had put things on shelves and dusted the doorsills. Every night for three years she had slept in the bedroom upstairs. Now, soon, very soon now, she would spend her first nights away.

The three years in this house didn't count looking down at it from her attic window since childhood. Angela had grown up next to this house. She had heard stories of the scary old lady who used to live inside it, and she remembered the day she had first seen Mrs. Madden. It was only a glimpse, the day it snowed. Then Mrs. Madden died. Angela could not remember the year.

The Madden house had stood empty. A FOR SALE sign went up in the yard and weeds overgrew it. Neat lawns and painted front porches surrounded the house, but Mrs. Madden's garden went all willy-nilly and then to weeds. Angela's father tossed some water its way when he watered their lawn and went over three times each summer to curse while mowing the tall grass.

By the time Angela and Tom were married, a tangle of morning glories and creepers had built grills over the first-floor windows. They lived in Tom's apartment downtown, but Angela saw the house each time they came home to visit. Iris splashed purple against the side of the house occasionally in spring, but the wooden stake of the FOR SALE sign rotted and fell over.

Then Tom got his promotion to Claims Agent. They wanted children, and Angela's mind was made up. Even if Mom and Dad moved, which they eventually did to be near Johnny and Nancy in Ginnett, Angela wanted this house. It was next to her parents' house. She had grown up here.

Rain and dirt had erased the FOR SALE sign. At Millford City Hall they looked up the legal owners and sent a letter. No one replied. Tom's old car was untrustworthy for the distance, so they borrowed Angela's father's car to drive three hundred miles to Pelleway. They rang a doorbell belonging to Mrs. Madden's daughter.

A tall blonde woman opened the door. Of course the old house was still for sale, she said, she simply never paid attention to selling it.

"Mother held onto both houses," the woman said, settling into a lounge chair in her overcrowded living room. "You know, Daddy died in that house on the other side of the street. Mother never would sell that. My brother took care of it. It sold fast. I'm the poky one."

Tom and Angela drank iced tea and listened. Angela thought she recognized some of the jumble of furniture in the busy room. Mixed among modern end tables and ugly floor lamps, two immense chairs stood, covered in green velvet. Dark wood scallops ran along their top edges. In a far corner, a skinny-legged table lay half in shadow. It had been refinished since Angela last saw it, but she remembered a dark winter day and a rain storm. She had met this blonde woman's father, in a way at least.

Angela wanted to ask if the woman owned a pink glass vase, a vase for roses. The woman might even own a blue and white teacup. Instead she kept quiet and let Tom do the talking.

Tom and the woman figured out the price and the terms, slightly more than they could afford. When Tom glanced at her, Angela met his gaze, hoping he could read her insistence.

"It's a deal then." Tom stood up to shake hands.

The blonde woman put her cigarette out and went to look for her attorney's business card.

Even before they moved into the old house, Angela

cleared the dead roots from around the peony. She pulled yards of vines from the rose bushes. She clipped the hedge, which had overgrown the gate, and cleaned a bed for the iris, which grew well enough without pampering. She dug and moved soil. Below the tattered lupine rows she found the remains of an old baseball mitt. Probably one of the Madden sons lost it. She tossed it onto the rising pile of morning glory vines.

When they started moving in, the rooms of the house were empty, of course. The barren, echoing spaces surprised her. She always imagined Mrs. Madden's things here—upholstered chairs with paper-thin antimacassars, gate-legged tables and dusty bowls with pale brown flowers floating in them. Instead, only faded carpets, dusty wallpaper and one broken floor lamp welcomed them.

Tom was in a hurry, of course, to put up paper and rip faded calendar prints from the walls. He attacked each floor of the three-storey structure. It was a solid house and it accepted his efforts in its own good time. It was solid of brick and wood with real hardwood floors and paneling and banisters and fixed shelving. Tom steamed and peeled wallpaper, spread paint, refinished floors, stripped varnish from the staircase posts and sanded the banister smooth. He applied linseed oil and he polished carved crevices. Angela helped and dawdled, wondering. Finally they finished the top floor, with its window overlooking the attic window next door. Angela looked around and saw that Tom and Angela Latham lived here now. Their first baby was due.

The February sun slanted cold rays through the kitchen window. Angela looked at her shopping list. If her baby were born today, that would be an Aquarius sun sign. She checked the drug store calendar over the sink. The baby was five days overdue. Tuesday's child is full of grace. Angela guessed she believed in old sayings.

Angela leaned forward and wrote the word STRENGTH

153

on her list. It was time to go, which meant the most difficult part, standing up. STRENGTH looked funny lying there below DISH SOAP. She used the sides of the chair to hoist herself and shuffled to the sink. The house around her, living room and dining room and kitchen, five bedrooms and two baths above, felt like a sleeping burden, as heavy as her own body. She tried to recall the feeling of old Mr. Madden's living room. It had to do with water, she remembered. It took years to happen. She wanted her own house to feel like that.

Angela added CHILDREN'S NOISES to her shopping list and shrugged into the one coat whose buttons still closed.

Jordan's Market was five blocks from Pear Street, catty-corner from Hamburgette's and a mile and a half from downtown. With a faded striped awning over the wide porch, and pine flooring that extended inside, Jordan's Market had not changed in thirty years. It carried the household staples neighborhood wives needed. Will Jordan, the owner, ran specials on Mondays and Thursdays.

Will ran the business now, ran it just as his mother and father had run it when they were alive, and he asked no charge for deliveries and kept the telephone on a low counter by the door. School children could use it for free.

On the morning of February 17th, Will prepared to polish the long glass of the flat butcher counter. He did this daily, shining every inch from where it began to the left of the door, down the entire five-yard length along the market's west wall. Will had apprenticed as a butcher with Full Value Foods, a supermarket chain with a downtown Millford store, and this butcher counter was his particular treasure. Will knew about trimming fat to a quarter-inch curve to show off the shape of a steak, and he could separate gristle from bone with a single, targeted whack. He could make lean ground beef with a hand grinder, as he'd shown a customer one day when the

154

electricity went out. The pink pound of beef came out in moist, lazy squiggles.

Today, beneath the glass, steaks and chops made layered rows with real parsley separating them. Will put on a clean apron before turning the sign on the front door to OPEN. He lifted the latch and saw, crossing the street behind her pear-wide shadow, his first customer.

Will Jordan stood back and held the door. "Morning, Mrs. Latham."

"Morning, Will. I'm glad the sun is warming things up."

Will nodded.

He found it hard to say anything, faced with the fact of how big Mrs. Latham was. Before she got pregnant, Mr. Latham's wife seemed a skinny string bean of a thing, moderately pretty with dark curly hair and brown eyes. She always dressed comfortably and treated him nicely. Lately she had come in buying a lot of minute steaks. Will made them up by pounding chuck steak flat and tender. He'd heard that pregnant women got cravings, so he kept a good supply on hand for her. Pregnant, Mrs. Latham looked like a school girl trying to shoplift a wheel of cheese.

Mrs. Latham reached into her basket and took out a piece of paper. She held the counter with one hand and pinched the paper open.

"Why don't you sit down today," Will said finally. He pointed to the chair by the door where ladies waited for taxis. "I'll get what you want."

Mrs. Latham flattened her list on her palm. She looked at Will, back to the list, at him again. For an instant, she blushed. "I'm okay," she said. She fingered open the buttons of her coat and began rolling from side to side, which made her move down the aisle into Household Goods.

Will Jordan returned to his work. He ran a razor along the glass edge of the butcher case to remove grime that might have collected. He checked the rims of the wooden pegs to confirm

155

they were tight. The case was long and flat, and Will remembered the day his father bought it twenty years ago. Will was a teenager then, but he remembered workmen hauling it in.

Its glass showed wavy lines, but ran straight and true to wooden edges between the sections. The case had a metal bottom to hold ice, but the year Mother died Will had installed a refrigeration unit. Best of all, Will liked the broad slanted glass along the side and the thick glass countertop. He washed it with hot water and vinegar, then wiped it with newspaper. Beneath the glass, meats glistened, arranged in rows and a few pinwheels, each piece chosen and carved to display its best side.

Will Jordan liked food. He had grown up around it and learned to appreciate its beauty. Even during bad years, when people bought only cheap cuts, his parents' house overflowed with boxes and sacks—cereals and slightly bruised fruits, cakes and store-bought cookies, pot roasts and corn bread and cans of condensed milk. Will sometimes wondered if he ever had a chance of being a thinner man. At forty-eight, two hundred and thirteen pounds, he often thought of his father, taken by a heart attack at sixty, and he admired thinner men, like old Lamar Pembroke before that skinny fellow died. But Will guessed he had been born to be big.

Born to be big and never to marry, he supposed. Born to shoulder the side of a cow and carry it five steps to let it fall on the cutting block. He'd been born to wrap a palm around the wide handle of a cleaver and bring it down solidly. He had proposed to a girl once at Full Value Foods, but she turned him down.

When he thought about his size, Will liked it. Just that morning he had helped his delivery boy load the truck. He liked the red and white bread wrappers and shiny rinds of oranges and bananas. He liked the bulky packets of red kidney beans and tan macaroni wedged softly between neat packages of meats. He could enjoy the fine marbling of a steak before

156

he curled it into a white paper blanket. He liked curling sausages into swami's hats, watching them rise coil by coil, or rolling rump roasts in parsley to put green sweaters on their fat. He could even enjoy the thump-thump-thump of pounding minute steaks, in case Mrs. Latham wanted any this morning.

Will Jordan paused to listen. Mrs. Latham had disappeared into Household Goods a while ago, and he could hear no sound of her moving on the soft wooden floor. He wiped his hands on his apron and stepped from behind the counter.

"Mrs. Latham?" he called. He felt silly. "Did you want me to make up some minute steaks?"

Her voice came from near Paper Products. "No, Will, I don't think so today."

Her voice sounded funny. Will hurried down the aisle, and saw Mrs. Latham braced against the paper towel display. She looked pale. Her shopping basket had fallen at her feet and a can of cleanser rolled away along the floor. She looked like she had stooped for her basket, but couldn't straighten again. Will scooped the cleanser up as he loped toward her.

"Are you okay?" He wanted to put a hand on her shoulder but decided not to.

"Fine. Fine. I dropped my basket."

Will put it back in her hand. Mrs. Latham managed to stand straight and let go of the paper towels.

"You better let me shop." Will collected her shopping list from the floor. "Do you need help walking up to the chair?"

"No, really." Her brown eyes were dazed and she stared at the paper towels as if they were someone she recognized. She tried a step, but swayed.

"You wait here."

Will Jordan hurried to the front of the store and pulled a shopping cart loose from the row. He pushed it toward Household Goods. Mrs. Latham still swayed, studying paper towels. Will rolled the cart next to her and unhitched the metal front flap.

"Can you sit up on this? Here, let me help."

Her weight, when his arms closed above her middle, was light but poorly balanced. The cheese wheel of her belly made her shift like a tumbling fifty-pound sack of potatoes. He steadied the cart with his foot, situated her in it, then grabbed several rolls of paper towels to pad the sides. He wheeled the cart, its wheels complaining about the weight, to the front of the store. When he got there, he hoisted her from the cart. She was set solidly in the chair before he realized he had not asked permission. Now a new question rang in his mind.

"Are you having your baby, Mrs. Latham?"

"I don't think so," Angela Latham replied. She smiled up at him, her lips barely parting and that dreamy look deep in her eyes. "But you could help me finish my shopping. I'll take a taxi cab home."

Will studied the woman in the chair. He realized his hand still held her shopping list. He read the half dozen items, examining them one by one.

A new can of CLEANSER gleamed up from the wicker basket by her chair. WAXED PAPER was there too. He saw the MINUTE STEAKS, crossed out, and then STRENGTH.

"Strength?" Will stared at Mrs. Latham. "Extra-strength something? The dish-soap maybe?"

"Oh, that's for the baby," Mrs. Latham said. She exhaled deeply. "I need strength for the baby. Do you have that?"

"Huh?" Will Jordan said. "Mrs. Latham, are you sure you're not having your baby?"

"We have to finish my shopping first," the pale woman in the chair said. "This chair feels wonderful, by the way."

Will Jordan studied the woman sitting in the old wooden chair. The chair used to be part of his mother's dining room set and after Mother died Will had brought it down to the store. Will hoped Mrs. Latham was not having her baby.

Will studied the list. The next item said CHILDREN'S NOISES, which was just as crazy as STRENGTH, and the fol-

158

lowing items, the next three in fact, said FLOWERS.

During her five-block walk to Jordan's Market that morning, Angela Latham had paused several times. At each pausing she reflected over a new necessity, then noted it down on her list. Will Jordan read to the end of the list, then shook his head slowly. He returned to FLOWERS FLOWERS FLOWERS.

"What kind of flowers do you want?"

The woman in the chair shrugged "I don't know. I meant to look it up on a calendar. I need flowers for this month, and some for Tom's birthday month, that's March, and for mine. Do you have a calendar?"

"No."

"It's all right then. Later I'll go to the florist. What's next? Oh dear."

Mrs. Latham leaned forward and wrapped her hands around her shoulders. She seemed interested in the floor. Then she repeated, "What's next?"

"Clouds," Will read from the list. "Clouds, Whispering Leaf Noises and . . ." he paused and studied the handwriting. "I can't read this last word."

"Beethoven." Mrs. Latham leaned back in the chair. Her hands gripped her shoulders. At last, taking a deep breath, she relaxed. "A baby needs beautiful music," she said.

Will Jordan stared. "Mrs. Latham, you are having your baby, aren't you? I just know you are."

"Yes I am," Angela Latham said. "Call my husband, then find me a place to lie down."

Will Jordan grabbed the telephone from the low counter. He called for an ambulance. The voice at the other end of the line said they'd come as soon as they could. There'd been a fire over in Ginnett, everyone was tied up for a while. Then he dialed the number Mrs. Latham repeated. She managed to get it out in spite of leaning way back and breathing, leaning forward and breathing. Mr. Thomas Latham's office said he was away at the moment, but he would get the message as soon as he returned. Will Jordan hung up.

The woman sitting in his mother's dining room chair was having a baby. Bright tears trembled in her eyes and her face was red and perspiring. She rocked backward and forward, alternately crying out and huffing.

"Find me a place to lie down," the woman said. Will Jordan looked around.

The delivery boy had taken the truck and would not return until noon. Aside from the floor, mopped this morning but still sixty years dirty, he saw only one choice. Hurrying behind the counter, Will pulled five yards of white paper from the roll and spread it over the glass. He wished he knew how to make glass warm, but this would have to do. He pulled the blinds over the front window and turned the OPEN sign to CLOSED.

Will Jordan reached beneath Mrs. Latham and closed his strength around her shoulders and legs. With the weight of the baby in the middle, she was easier to move. She was light in fact. For an instant, hovering over the meat counter, she reminded him of a sack of bran meal. His muscles thrummed, remembering a moment when he worked back at Full Value Foods. He had lifted a sack of bran from the freight elevator, then turned to reach and lift a young woman, light as a feather, onto it. He had stood her higher than himself so he could propose.

Will Jordan blushed. This was no time to be thinking of marriage proposals. He tightened his muscles and eased Mrs. Latham's weight smoothly onto the butcher counter.

Mrs. Latham leaned back. She took a big breath. Tears rolled down her cheeks, so Will pulled a paper towel from the roll and dabbed at them.

"Are you having the baby really soon, Mrs. Latham?"

She finished whimpering her way out of another huffing cry.

"Right now I think," Angela Latham said. "You have to

160

deliver it. Would you please call me Angela?"

"Right now," Will Jordan repeated. His hand lifted to his lips and he tasted paper towel, salty with tears.

"Right now," he said again. Her legs were lifting and her skirt fell back from her thighs. They were smooth and as pink as fresh veal. He was supposed to call her Angela.

"Unhook my garters and take my underpants off. Oh, just a minute."

Another contraction arched her back. She came puffing out of it.

"Okay, do it now."

Will Jordan fumbled at the strange hooks and loosened them. He pulled the slippery white fabric of her underwear past them. So this was what they looked like, Will thought, or maybe they only looked this big when they were having babies. In the opening he saw a dark smooth shape.

"I have to wash my hands," Will said.

Too soon his hands were pink and clean from disinfecting soap. Mrs. Latham had screamed twice more while he was gone and when he got back, the dark shape between her pink legs looked bigger. The butcher paper had gotten rumpled and pushed around. Now below her bowed thighs, rows of pork chops and rolled roasts glistened. Will tried looking up again.

In a way, he persuaded himself, the vision between her thighs looked like a small pot roast set neatly between two filet mignons. She was having a baby.

"Remember those things on my shopping list?" Angela Latham said. "I tried to think of all the things a baby needs, and there were a lot more than those."

Will Jordan nodded. She was breathing twice as hard and her voice was high. Her wide eyes stared up at him. He wondered what his fat jowly face must look like. A pale leg of lamb gleamed in the case beneath her. Food, he thought, I look just like food.

161

"A baby needs clouds." Mrs. Latham stopped for a breath. "Whispery noises leaves make. The wind blows." She stopped and huffed three breaths in a row. "A big bright sun. I forgot to put that on the list. Moon."

"Should I write that down?" Will said.

She shook her head.

"What do I do?"

Her eyes got wider, then pain pierced them. A frightened spasm darkened them as her mouth opened a pink rose on her face.

"Tell me," she whispered between the sobs that let her back release its arch inch by inch. "Tell me.

"Tell me all the things a baby needs.

"Help the baby come out."

Will wondered what he could say. What words helped a baby be born? He didn't know them. He didn't think they'd be STRENGTH or BEETHOVEN. Mrs. Latham did. Mrs. Latham seemed to like those words, but they were hers. What words did he have?

"A baby needs milk." Will said at last. He liked the word and placed his wide red hand on the lady's skin. It felt soft, like veal too, only warmer. "A baby needs wheat," he added.

"Yes. Yes. Tell me. Help the baby come out. Use your hands. You have to help."

Will stepped along the counter to get a better view. The dark shape down there had turned into a head. He reached his hand, the hand that had touched her belly, and felt. It felt spongy, like angel food.

"Angel food cake," he said.

"That's good. That's beautiful. Tell more things."

Gently, Will slipped his fingers around the dark head. He felt neck and then shoulders. The thing was slippery and smooth. He was afraid his hands would pull back, and then he remembered how fresh sausage links looked, smooth and clean in their wrappers, ribboning out from the sausage

162

machine nozzle.

"Jello." He slipped his hands further along and massaged the shape toward him.

"What else?!" the woman's voice cried out from above him. "What else? A baby needs Beethoven!"

"A baby needs cereal," Will Jordan said. He massaged the warm, moist lump. "A baby needs pudding."

"Bananas," the woman's voice cried. "Yes. Yes."

"A baby needs bread. Cheese. Evaporated milk."

"Sugar!"

"A baby needs cottage cheese. Peanut butter. Raisins. Rice."

"Cinnamon!"

"And malted milk balls and apple juice, cornbread, muffins, peaches, licorice."

The slippery pink shape moved further and further onto the butcher paper.

"Custard," Will said. "Gingerbread." Then he remembered lemon sauce drizzled over gingerbread. "Mayonnaise."

"Brussels sprouts, artichokes." Angela had finished the family of grains and was starting on vegetables. "Snow peas."

"With white sauce," Will added, working the hot shape closer. "Mustard greens."

"Boiled down with a ham hock."

Will told the baby about Christmas cakes, currants, raisins, "Cardamom frosting."

Angela sang the family of vegetables—broccoli, cauliflower, snap peas, spinach, and squash.

Will lost track of time. It seemed to go on forever. Every time he got stuck, he glanced up at the shelves of food. His big voice sang the labels and the brands.

"Rigatoni-lasagna-spumoni," he said. His big voice was the first Baby Latham heard. She heard, "Tomato sauce. Onions. Walla Walla sweets," in a man's voice cut with sobs. With huge arms pulling her in against the big chest, she felt, more than

163

heard, a deep rumble that moved through her skin.

"Biscotti," it said.

"Butter lettuce," Angela cried.

And the baby, red as a radish, cried.

It was a cry that turned Will Jordan's spine to a popsicle of shivers, and hot tears, big as bell peppers, rolled from his eyes. The warm bundle in his arms fought and squalled, tied to the woman by a licorice whip of umbilical. Then the length loosened and he held the baby free. He thought all at once of the food the baby would need, tons and tons probably in all the years it stayed alive. He leaned forward to where Mrs. Latham had loosened the front of her dress, and lowered the baby onto her. Small red fingers squashed the white pudding of her breast.

According to the scale at the end of the butcher case at Jordan's Market, Angela Maxwell Latham's first baby weighed, after feeding, seven pounds and six ounces. The ambulance arrived five minutes after the weighing, and the father, Tom Latham pulled up only seconds later.

When Tom got inside, the ambulance attendant handed him a wailing bundle. Elizabeth Latham was wrapped in a clean apron, strong white butcher paper tucked around her for appearances.

Chapter Eleven

She certainly was a lovely baby. Quiet and good, as you say. You'd know better than I would.

None of my own, I'm sorry to say, but I visit children now and again. I tell them stories. Different ones, naturally. Stories always depend on the person listening.

What about the ribbon? I suppose it could have been tied to the butcher paper. We could go back and change the story. That's right, then the story would not be quite as true, and true stories are a lot better than the real kind, aren't they? I think so too.

I did put the ribbon in the story. The ribbon was there, if you listened closely enough. I put the ribbon in every story, that's what you asked me to do. I keep my promises.

There is one promise I made to you, perhaps you remember, a promise I'd like to break. You remember which one. I know what I said, but did you see how it grows even faster in the summer? July must be that plant's growing season. July and the rest of the year. I started wearing gloves, see there in my coat pocket. I wear those gloves just so I can push my way through.

You are right, I did promise. Enough about that, what else is on your mind on a lovely summer afternoon?

More stories. Honestly, some people are never satisfied. That's good, smile but don't laugh. A laugh will only get the cough going again.

Another story, all right. Andy deserves to have a story, doesn't he? He was a good child too, of course, but different from Betsy. You'll recall that he was born under more ordinary circumstances. Andy grew up for a few years. Here's what happened once.

In the Tick of Time

Andy's big sister Betsy was born at the grocery store. Everybody knew that. Andy's mom and dad laughed when they talked about it. One day Andy went with his mother to the grocery store. Andy Latham was six then, and his big sister Betsy was ten. The butcher was a big man. He stood behind the meat counter, only a cabbage head over the shining glass, and Andy's mother said something about fresh meat. The butcher said something back. Then they both looked at each other and Andy's mother laughed. The grocery man's face got as red as the meat in his butcher case.

Today, an April morning three days after his seventh birthday, Andy sat alone on the low end of the see-saw outside Millford Elementary School. It was Saturday. Andy sat watching the clouds and trying to figure out why he had been adopted. It looked like no one else was coming to school to play.

Andy shifted on the seat and the see-saw's board creaked. His older sister Betsy had helped him discover that he was adopted. During their talk this morning Betsy had explained that she was three years old when Andy got there, and Andy came home wrapped in a blanket. Betsy came from Jordan's Market, but Andy had come from an "adoptspital." Andy guessed it was like toys his mother got for him. The lady at the store wrapped them in brown paper bags, and his mother had to pay money before the bag was ready to go.

"What color was the blanket?"

Betsy couldn't remember.

"Brown?"

Yes, brown, Betsy said. Some babies were born, Betsy

explained, and others were only adopted. In her class, they had an adopted girl who had lived in three different houses already. Andy had heard of this girl, but never considered that he might be like her. Then Betsy left to go over to Marcia's, her friend's, to draw pictures.

The word "adoptspital," a big word coming clear like that, rang like a dropped penny. Andy repeated it over, it sounded like "spit." Why had Betsy come from the market, but they got him at the adoptspital? Andy wandered into the kitchen.

Andy's mother stood by the counter. For the first time, standing in the doorway and watching her make sandwiches, Andy saw who she really was. Her hair was brown and silky, soft if he touched it. His hair was red. Everyone said Andy looked like Uncle John Maxwell, his mother's big brother. Uncle John probably came from the same adoptspital.

His mother knew how to do things. His mother could sew, and Betsy sewed too. Betsy could turn a stick into a puppet and make tissue paper flowers and dip their petals in food coloring. His mother, standing there by the window with sun making her hair glow, could fix things. She fixed sandwiches and broken plates and the hinge on the cabinet. His father fixed tires on the car, the garage door, a broken faucet and a book that broke in half. For the first time Andy understood why he could not draw, or add up numbers as fast as his father, or fix things. He could not get anyone to talk to him when he answered the telephone.

Andy could sing. The music lady at school said he had a good voice. Andy began humming "Fishes Under the Sea."

"Would you like your lunch now?"

His mother turned so the other half of her hair glowed.

"I don't know."

"You're not feeling sick are you?"

Andy decided not to tell her he knew about being adopted. "I feel okay." The worried look stayed in her eyes. "I don't know what to do today."

168

"Where are your friends?"

Andy shrugged. Friends were at school on the weekdays, but this was Saturday.

"I know, I bet somebody's playing at the schoolyard." Her eyes stopped worrying. "You could go, and come back if nobody's there."

"Okay."

She folded two sandwiches into waxed paper and slid them into a bag. "Here." She held out the bag. "Take a sandwich for yourself and another sandwich too. You can meet a friend and have a picnic." He took the bag and walked to school.

Now Andy shifted sideways on the see-saw after sitting for awhile. The wood creaked, but all around him the schoolyard lay quiet. The sandwich bag, sitting on the ground now, was made of brown paper. He guessed his mother had saved it from something bought at the store. They probably saved his blanket too.

He wished he had been born at Jordan's Market. He wished Betsy was adopted. He knew that wishing, no matter how deep it went, was only good for more wishing, so he wished his mother had given him three sandwiches.

The first baloney sandwich had tasted good, but he was saving the second. He might need it. The adopted girl in Betsy's class had lived in three people's houses already. He was not going home. He had better get started.

On the far side of the schoolyard, along the edge where yellow weeds tangled into the fence wire, a big tall man was walking but watching the ground as he walked. The man stooped. He picked something up. He put what he had found in his pocket, and pulled out a watch and looked at it. He put the watch back. The man turned at the end of the fence and entered the schoolyard. Even from the distance of the see-saw, Andy could hear ticking.

Mr. Twelveclocks was an interesting man. All children in

169

Millford knew him. He wore old green clothes and a sock cap pulled low so he could see the pavement where he walked. He didn't seem to work. At least he didn't go to the same place every day, like fathers did. Nor did he go home at a certain time, again unlike fathers. Mr. Twelveclocks might be anywhere, any time, and wherever he went he was working.

Mr. Twelveclocks brought things back. If you left your books at the schoolyard and your name was written in front of them, Mr. Twelveclocks waited for you when you left for school the next morning. Mr. Twelveclocks returned your books. If your sister left your skate key on a sidewalk, Mr. Twelveclocks, if he knew it was yours because he'd seen you skating and using it, put it on your front porch. If you dropped a silver gum wrapper, Mr. Twelveclocks could be counted on to pick it up. A boy at school said that he had been out to Mr. Twelveclocks' cabin and seen a million silver wrappers. They were rolled into a ball even bigger than the cabin.

The most interesting thing about Mr. Twelveclocks was that he ticked. If you were sitting outside reading, or playing in the alley behind Pear Street, and if you heard ticking, Mr. Twelveclocks would come around the corner. If you stayed too late and fell asleep on a swing at the schoolyard, Mr. Twelveclocks might wake you up when he came past ticking. Mr. Twelveclocks wore watches and clocks, lots of them, and he wore them all over. He wore two watches on each wrist, and one watch on each ankle. In every pocket and fold of his green clothes, he had watches that had no bands. He pulled them out, looked at them, put them back. It was no use asking Mr. Twelveclocks what time it was, though, because each watch told a different time. Once in a while he'd get the right time, but Mr. Twelveclocks didn't seem to care.

The tall man was crossing the baseball diamond toward the see-saw. The ticking grew louder. His sock cap almost covered his eyes, but it left enough room for him to study the sidewalk. Now he pushed the cap back. A stub of gray, like the end of a whisk broom, grew on either side of his bald head.

"Hello." Mr. Twelveclocks' whole body ticked. "How're you doing?"

"Okay," Andy said. It was a lie. "Maybe not quite okay."

The big man pulled his cap loose of his ears. His face was wide and round, and it looked like the face on the moon looked—interested. He pulled a watch from the pocket of his green pants and studied it. He put it back. His big body bent and he sat on the metal bar in the middle of the see-saw.

"What seems to be the problem?"

Andy wondered what to say. Everybody liked Mr. Twelveclocks. His mother said Mr. Twelveclocks brought back her flannel sheet when the wind carried it down to Mrs. Roman's lawn. His father said that when the muffler fell off the car, Mr. Twelveclocks was the one who left it sitting on the hood the next day, even if it was wrecked to junk. Mr. Twelveclocks brought things back all over Millford, so Andy guessed it was okay to talk to him.

"I'm adopted," he said finally. He hoped the man knew the word. "I have to find a new place to live."

"How's that?" The man's gray eyes studied Andy. "You better tell me about it. Aren't you Tom Latham's boy?"

Andy agreed, he was. But only in a way. He explained about his sister being born at the grocery store.

"I heard about that." Mr. Twelveclocks nodded.

Andy told where he had come from, the adoptspital. He told about the girl in his sister's class and about how he had to find a new home. He could not go back to the house where the Lathams lived.

"I see." Mr. Twelveclocks patted his pockets. "You're running away."

"I'm not running," Andy answered, "I'm sitting down."

Suddenly a thought jumped into words before Andy could completely hear it in his head. "Can I come and live with you?"

A wrinkle drew a line across Mr. Twelveclocks' forehead.

171

The wrinkle moved and rewrinkled. He no longer looked like the concerned, contented face of the moon. Mr. Twelveclocks pulled his cap completely off and rubbed the bald top of his head with it. On either side, the gray bristles bent, then stood up. Mr. Twelveclocks finally spoke. "On one condition, I suppose. Do you think you could help me straighten out a story?"

Andy stared. "What's wrong with it?"

"Don't know the end."

Andy guessed he could figure out the end of a story. His mother had read to him before he started school. He could read for himself now, and he knew lots of stories. His favorite book was *Wind in the Willows*.

"Sure."

Mr. Twelveclocks checked a watch from a pocket he hadn't checked lately, and put it back. He stood up. He walked slowly to the other end of the see-saw.

"Of course, you have to hear the whole story first. And not go wandering off in the middle. I wouldn't like that." Mr. Twelveclocks reached up and touched the far end of the see-saw.

Andy felt himself rising. He could see a map in the window of the school building. Then the map rolled right past and he saw empty desks in the room. When the end of the see-saw reached Mr. Twelveclocks' waist, Andy saw the beginning of the school roof. He kept rising.

Finally Mr. Twelveclocks pushed the other end of the board to the ground. He sat on it.

Andy was up in the air.

Birds in the trees around the fence chattered and jumped between branches. Clouds were far away, but closer. He guessed he was higher than he had ever sat before. Usually only kids his own size sat at the other end of the board, but Mr. Twelveclocks was a big heavy man. This had to be higher.

Straight ahead, all the way down, Mr. Twelveclocks' big shape sat. His gray eyes looked straight up the board.

172

"Now that I have your attention," a faraway voice spoke, "I can tell you my story. It's about a boy. And the boy grows up."

Mr. Twelveclocks checked to see that Andy was listening. Andy nodded.

"You probably want to know the boy's name. We'll call him Billy. Yes, Billy Oneclock. That's his name."

Mr. Twelveclocks settled his arms across this chest, and began talking. The boy called Billy Oneclock lived in a town called East Junction, he explained. East Junction was far away, over a thousand miles west and with a far worse climate. Billy Oneclock got born and was christened by Methodists. Mr. Twelveclocks guessed Andy knew what a Methodist was.

Andy nodded, not quite sure.

"Billy Oneclock was the son of a man who owned a shoe store. Billy was a good student and he graduated just like all the other children." Mr. Twelveclocks leaned forward to get more comfortable. The board creaked, making another tick among the sound of many watches ticking. "But the same year he graduated school, a war broke out."

Billy's older brother already worked in the shoe store, Mr. Twelveclocks said, and the shop was too small for three. The family was patriotic—Billy's father donated two dozen pairs of slippers to the Hospital Needs Drive—so Billy decided to go into the army.

For some reason only the army understood, Mr. Twelveclocks did not know why, Billy Oneclock got special training. "He learned to pretend he was lots of different people. He lived in towns the army picked for him. He watched out for the enemy's troops nearby."

Billy Oneclock was very good at what he did. He belonged wherever he lived, and he was smart and learned languages fast. He could sound exactly like the people he lived by. He won medals, but he also had a problem.

A message came back to the army that Billy Oneclock was in trouble. The enemy suspected that a spy was hiding out near them, hiding exactly where Billy Oneclock hid. The enemy had a secret method for figuring out who the spy was.

"The army was worried," said the voice from the other end of the board. "But they didn't know the enemy's secret method."

The army sent somebody to save Billy's life. Enemy troops were searching for the spy all around the town and they used dogs. By the time the army's rescue man found Billy, it was almost too late.

As the rescue man got closer, the secret method the enemy had became clear. A shape crouched under some straw in the hayloft inside a barn. The shape was ticking.

"You see, Andy Latham, Billy Oneclock liked clocks." Mr. Twelveclocks paused and refolded his arms the other way. "He more than liked them, really. He bought a watch in every town where he lived."

Down at the end of the board, Mr. Twelveclocks was no longer looking at Andy. He stared over to where jumping birds made the tree leaves move.

"Billy wore one watch for Borgen and another for Fusillorn. He had a watch he had bought and set in East Auslingon and one for West Auslingon. He had watches from Lengenhead and Mendelstang and South Stromen."

Andy was having trouble following the words, but Mr. Twelveclocks did not appear to be paying attention.

"He wound each watch every day and wore them all. He would not give them up, not even after the rescue man, who got into the barn without being seen, said a patrol was coming. The enemy was listening for them. They must leave their watches in the hay and escape."

Mr. Twelveclocks looked around. His big bald head suddenly shook itself. He looked then back up the see-saw at Andy. "Billy Oneclock said no. He said no even when the officer said, okay, that was it then."

Billy Oneclock wanted to stay in the barn. The army man

dropped his own wristwatch into the straw and lifted a board and slipped out. Billy Oneclock listened to the stirring of the grasses outside. He listened all day, burrowed deep to muffle the ticking of his clocks. Late that night he crawled out and over the ground, using touch to find the road. He moved along it at night. He hid in ditches in daytime. He wound his watches every day, plus the extra watch, the one the army man left.

"It took a couple of weeks." Mr. Twelveclocks paused to sigh. Somehow Billy found his way back to his own side. He got lost, but he remembered a few landmarks, and when he got back he was okay.

"Still ticking." The face at the other end of the see-saw smiled. Andy guessed there was a joke and smiled too.

"And that's the end of the story?"

Mr. Twelveclocks shook his head. "That's half. You have to help me find the ending, remember? That is, if you still want to come live at my cabin."

Andy considered his choices. He had eaten his first lunch early, and he was hungry. The bag held another sandwich, but it was down on the ground. He remembered his mother. She had made that sandwich. He began to hope Mr. Twelveclocks' story had a happy ending. For some reason the story was making him sad. Then he remembered. It was up to him.

"Go ahead," Andy said and settled himself more securely on the narrow wooden seat of the see-saw. He decided the ending would be a happy one.

"Well, here the story gets interesting." Mr. Twelveclocks rested his elbows on the board and got comfortable all over again. "You see, Billy Oneclock got back, but he could not remember who he was."

Andy looked to see if Mr. Twelveclocks was kidding. The man's big moon face looked pale.

"It can happen, Andy. When he was out in those towns, pretending to be somebody else all the time, Billy caught a

175

disease. The doctors called it amnesia."

"Did he remember his name?"

"The doctors told him. The name didn't sound right."

Andy nodded. He guessed it really did happen.

"The doctors tried reading Billy Oneclock's army papers to him," Mr. Twelveclocks went on. "Billy listened. He said the papers didn't sound like anybody he knew." The doctors tried giving him a rest. The doctors made him memorize a name and address. At last they gave Billy a thick packet of papers. Then, even though the war was not over, they sent him to Mr. and Mrs. Thomas Oneclock living at 128 Creek Lane in the town of Lortonborough.

"Unfortunately the army had made a mistake." Mr. Twelveclocks stared up at the see-saw board and shook his head.

"Oh no," Andy said.

"Billy knew." Mr. Twelveclocks nodded. "But at first he thought he was wrong."

So Billy Oneclock went back to his country. He wandered around for a while, then on a late summer evening he found the address.

"He knocked on the door. A woman opened it. She did not recognize Billy so she got her husband." Billy Oneclock showed them the wrinkled paper from the army. The husband explained that their son had already come home the week before. The people were very nice and they shook Billy's hand and wished him good luck. Then Billy put on his hat and walked downtown to find a hotel.

"The army found Billy the next day. They were real sorry." Billy got two days' extra pay for the time the army had lost him, and he got a new piece of paper with the address 174 Oxford Lane, East Junction printed on it. He got a train ticket to that place.

"Billy felt pretty bad by now." Mr. Twelveclocks looked up the see-saw toward Andy. "He guessed it was his fault in a way.

A man ought to know where he lived." Mr. Twelveclocks paused as if waiting for the answer to a question. He went on. "But Billy rode the train to East Junction."

The train station in East Junction, unfortunately for Billy, looked just like the train station in Lortonborough. The stationmaster was an old man. He looked like he'd seen many young men in uniform, and they'd all asked him how to get home. He was counting yellow tissue papers, snapping them up from the stack, when Billy asked about the address. The stationmaster gave directions and went right on counting.

Billy went across the street to the dime store and bought a new watch.

"He liked to keep the old ones on Fusillorn and Auslingon time," Mr. Twelveclocks explained.

He still carried the young officer's watch, and it still ticked all the hours since that man said goodbye. Billy had a new watch from Lortonborough, eleven watches in all by now, and each watch ticked safely in a pocket as he walked to the address.

Billy Oneclock walked a long time before he reached the corner across from 174 Oxford Lane. It was dusk. Billy stopped in front of a blue two-storey house. The windows were dark. The garage door was closed.

Mr. Twelveclocks' voice was getting softer and he was looking up into the trees again. Andy had to lean down the see-saw to hear.

"He guessed this might be the house, his home, but he felt no certainty of it. Night fell and the streetlamps came on." After a while a shiny car came along and pulled into the drive. A man and a woman got out.

The woman went ahead of the man through the door, carrying a bag of groceries. The man held a bunch of shoe boxes. Billy guessed these people might be his parents. He had been told his father owned a shoe store. But then there were so many shoe stores. Billy had seen hundreds passing

177

the windows of the train over the past several days.

"There are even more parents than shoe stores," Mr. Twelveclocks explained softly. "There are brothers. Billy had been told he had one of these. There were soldiers named Billy." There were not many Oneclocks, but some, obviously. There were towns called East Junction and Lortonborough, Fusillorn and Auslingon, Middlebrighton, Gap, and Blue Whistle.

Lights came on in the windows of the house. Billy tried to remember getting letters, knowing any people like these. The woman closed the blinds. She was middle-aged but pretty with dark brown hair.

"Billy Oneclock stood there wishing. He wished he'd kept just one picture from home when he'd gone to those towns. He'd been so many people since he left home. The only way he could remember all those people was to listen to a watch from each place he'd pretended to be somebody."

Mr. Twelveclocks had begun tilting sideways toward the trees as he talked. Andy worried that if the big man fell off, the see-saw would drop fast and pound him into the ground. All of a sudden Mr. Twelveclocks seemed to remember where he was. He straightened and patted his pockets.

"So Billy didn't knock on that door at 174 Oxford Lane," he said quickly. "He was afraid. He was a lot of afraids." The people might have a son who died in the war, Mr. Twelveclocks explained. Or their Billy might be lost too. Or they might have no son at all. "Anyway, how could anybody be sure he was their Billy? He'd seen a lot of the world and some of it washed off on him. He knew he looked different."

Andy looked down the see-saw at the big grown-up sitting there. From this high in the air the ticking was faint, but he could hear it. He also heard cars far away, and the sound of the fan that blew all the time on top of the school roof. It went tick-rat-tick, like one more clock.

"By the time Billy got back to the train station, the station-

178

master had a new stack of yellow tissues."

The next train was in four hours, the stationmaster told him, at 11 P.M. Billy checked all his watches. That meant sixteen hours by Borgen time and seventeen by the young officer's watch. It was only five hours by Lortonborough Standard Time, but twenty-two hours by East Auslingon. Billy asked the stationmaster to sell him a ticket that would carry him to another time zone.

Andy thought of his mother looking at a clock, wondering why he did not come home. He thought of Betsy. Betsy's hair got red in the summer when they went swimming a lot. She could draw. But Andy could sing. Andy noticed that Mr. Twelveclocks was not talking anymore.

"So then what?"

The big moon face looked up the see-saw toward Andy. Mr. Twelveclocks shrugged. "You tell me. You have to finish the story."

Andy thought about it. Stories he read had happy endings, but this was a story about a grown-up. It could be different then. "I think he got a ticket," Andy said at last. "I think he went to live in a new place. That was a happy place."

Mr. Twelveclocks studied Andy. "Could be. Let's see what happens if that happens. Things always do."

Mr. Twelveclocks paused. "So Billy went to a new place. He bought a watch in that place. He thought if he knew what time it was there, he would live there. It was a nice watch, but kind of strange. Old now." Mr. Twelveclocks pulled a silver watch out of his pocket and held it up for Andy to see.

The sunlight caught on the watch face and made it look like bright water. Andy squinted, but the watch was too far away to tell time.

"I guess that's the story." Mr. Twelveclocks pushed his feet against the ground.

The clouds and birds got suddenly smaller. Despite being so high, coming down went remarkably quickly. The map

179

went past in the window. Mr. Twelveclocks eased the other end of the board into the sky gently and Andy did not bounce on landing. Then Mr. Twelveclocks walked past the middle bar and held his hand out.

The watch did not have a wrist band. It was a silver circle with a thin loop at the top. Its face was white and round with fancy numbers on the outside. On a thin ribbon of silver in the face of the watch the shapes of people danced. They were men and women holding hands, and they seemed to be chasing each other to get around the circle. Mr. Twelveclocks' hand wouldn't hold quite still, so sunlight shook on the shapes and made them run faster.

The face of the watch had no hands. Millford time, Andy thought. That's what time it is here—always. That's what time it was for his mother, and for his father, and for Betsy. It was always-time, even for Mrs. Roman who lived down the street.

Andy thought about going home. He thought about not going home. If he went someplace else it would be a different time, a real time. He might have new parents, but he would be alone. It would be a new time, but only for him.

"Did he ever remember where he lived?" Andy asked.

"I'm not sure."

Andy felt disappointed.

"I guess he did," Mr. Twelveclocks changed his mind.

"It was 174 Oxford Lane, wasn't it?"

"You're a smart one," Mr. Twelveclocks said.

Andy thought. A question had been bothering him, but he guessed it might not be a fair question to ask a grown-up. He decided to risk it.

"Mr. Twelveclocks, is your first name Billy?"

"Certainly not." Mr. Twelveclocks' hand closed quickly over the silver circle and pushed it back in his pocket. "My first name is William."

Andy guessed he'd made a mistake.

"Would you like a baloney sandwich?" he said to apologize.

"That would be nice. If you're sure you won't need it."

Andy took the sandwich out of the bag and put it in Mr. Twelveclocks' big hand.

"Thanks," the man said, "and thanks for helping me figure out that story. I'll bring your skate key back if I ever see it."

"Sure." Andy started walking away. He turned and looked back. "And thanks for making up that story."

Mr. Twelveclocks waved and took a bite of the sandwich. Andy turned to go home. In his back pocket, the brown paper bag, which he had decided to fold up and save forever, gave a little push and tick with each step.

Chapter Twelve

We got talking about baloney sandwiches last time, and that's why I brought it. The lunch meat is for me, tea and cookies for you. Your stomach can't take these meats.

I'll just have one, the chocolate chip, thank you. The sandwich filled me up. Maybe another, only one. I stopped by the bakery to get them.

Does the agency pay for the treats I bring? Well, not exactly. They did pay me well. It was a very fine job while it lasted.

I didn't tell you? Certainly, they closed several months ago. I saved enough to get by, and I enjoy visiting. I keep up with a few people, you and a couple of others. I lost one last week.

I should take that back. Forget what I just said, won't you?

If you want to ask questions, that's fine, but I can't talk about it very well. It hurts me when I lose one. You? Never. Your color is good today, and look how tightly you pull the ribbon. I expect talking about these things must upset you.

You're certainly firm about that. If it does not upset you then it does not. I understand. Actually, I don't understand how you can talk about it so easily. The whole idea makes me sad. I'll try to understand, but don't expect I'll ever get used to the idea of death. Most people aren't like you. They never mention it.

All right, you're old and I come to visit because I want to. The delivery boy brings the essentials, but I like to enjoy a snack and sit with you. Your stories are my favorites. You are old, yes, but healthy, all considered.

If you want me to, I'll say it. It might hurt me less to admit it could happen—which I don't think it will, by the way—but I never talk about it with those I visit. I've lost five in the last year. It hurts every time.

Of course I'll say it if you insist. Not everyone likes pretending, that's true.

Let me say it in my words—I may lose you.

There. Does that feel better? I'm not sure if admitting it beforehand will help. Would help, I mean, because it won't happen. Anyway it does hurt every time.

Curl the ribbon, that's good. A fine length of green ribbon, very old probably. It's a wonder it's never gotten broken or lost. You keep it on the nightstand, that's good.

If I'm changing the subject it's only because I have a story to tell. And here I am forgetting it, imagine. It is a story about memory, after all. And the ribbon is in it.

Do we lose anyone in this story? I suppose, if you insist that's how the world really is. But if we must lose someone, I'll do it in my own way, thank you very much.

Do you still want to hear it? Good. Then let's talk about what happened one autumn.

Sheriff Dolgan Gets His Man
and Catches a Cold Too

It took a couple of weeks for the suspicions about William Twelveclocks to come together. The story took shape at Bissell's Restaurant over flapjacks and Mildred Bissell's famous raspberry syrup, delicious stuff which everyone poured generously over the flapjacks. Only Sheriff Dolgan ordered oatmeal, saying raspberry syrup bothered a filling he meant to get fixed. To this, Morton Larchman, D.D.S., gave a snort and raved about the syrup.

No single member of Bissell's Unofficial Breakfast Club—seven in all once word got around that people gathered there to talk about Mr. Thomas Latham's disappearance—had all the details. Dolgan had done some checking. His first morning at the restaurant he ordered oatmeal and let it cool while he filled them in on William Twelveclocks' early years.

The Department of the Army had sent him Twelveclocks' service record. Pages of carbon paper copies told about Fusillorn and Lengenhead, and about a disturbing incident in a hayloft in Borgen. Twelveclocks was suspected of having taken the watch from a dead man. The report said Twelveclocks' real name was Oneclock, and that the reasons for his medical discharge could only be released with stronger justification than Dolgan's suspicions. The army sent Twelveclocks a pension every month. It was all the man lived on. Dolgan had been in the army himself, so he translated. Twelveclocks was screwball and the army knew who had caused it.

Sheriff Dolgan repeated all this slowly, over his cooling oatmeal, to those who knew William Twelveclocks in Millford. The faces around the table took Dolgan's account with quiet watching. There was an occasional nod. Dolgan added that it was kind of a shame, to have to suspect a war hero and all, and Dee Anna Martin agreed. But she pointed out that William Twelveclocks lived out by Millford's culvert pool. That was beyond West Brooke on the edge of town. The news from the army fit with suspicions the breakfast club had already put together, and with how Twelveclocks had been asking nosy questions ever since Tom Latham disappeared. Only the mystery of dating Twelveclocks' arrival in Millford remained.

Frank Bicker insisted it must have been a decade ago. Mort Larchman said that it was twelve years, "Twelve almost to the day." There'd been that awful wind storm. "I came out the next morning, and there were all nineteen missing shingles. Twelveclocks stacked them up on the porch. Unless you think the wind rounded all nineteen up and put them there."

Gradually, counting back, a muddled consensus emerged. William Twelveclocks might have lived in Millford a long time before anyone actually noticed him. It was nice how Twelveclocks brought things people in Millford had lost back to them, Dolgan said, blowing on his oatmeal, "But that doesn't mean he isn't involved in this Latham business."

Mort Larchman agreed, "That's as good as true." Millford's dentist lifted the steaming pitcher of raspberry syrup. "That's as good, why as good as this delicious syrup Mildred made for us."

Dolgan leaned back in his chair. "Sure wish I could go out there to investigate."

The faces around the table stared. "We thought you already had," Dee Anna Martin said.

"The widow's the problem. I mean Mrs. Latham's the problem." Dolgan's usually pink face went to raspberry. "Sorry about that."

Nobody blamed Sheriff Dolgan for assuming Angela Latham's husband was dead. Tom Latham, Angela Latham's husband and a man well-liked as an insurance salesman, had gone hunting in the woods out past the culvert. He had been missing ten days and the local scouts' search of the woods had only brought back Wilderness Badges. Donald Winks, who had worked alongside Tom Latham at Millford Insurance, shook his head slowly.

"I know what you mean. Every morning, 8:15 on the dot, Mrs. Latham calls. Says Tom's sick. Won't be in today. I worked across the room from Tom Latham fifteen years now. Never was sick one day."

"He's not at the house either," Dolgan added. "First she calls me up and says he's missing. I tell her three days, that's the law, before I file a report."

"It's been ten," Dee Anna Martin burst out. "Hasn't she filed one yet?"

"No she hasn't." Dolgan looked at his watch. "Yipes, I'm late."

The breakfast club had lingered late. Skim was forming on pools of raspberry syrup and Mildred Bissell had stopped bothering to serve free cups of coffee. Dolgan wasn't a young man anymore, but it was reassuring to see how fast the blocky sheriff could move. He grabbed his jacket from the back of his chair and his hat from the rack.

"I'll be by tomorrow," he said over his shoulder.

The patrol car sat out front. He plopped into the driver's seat and slammed the door. The car took off with lights and siren going. The members of the breakfast club guessed he must be awfully late.

By Friday morning, two days after Sheriff Dolgan had filled them in on William Twelveclocks' army record, a gloom settled over Bissell's Breakfast Club. The coming weekend meant two days when they would not meet to consider the mystery of Thomas Latham's disappearance. They wished anybody had more news. They asked little questions. Dee Anna Martin, who ran the floral shop where Tom Latham

187

regularly bought flowers for his wife, poked her first finger into the growing hole in Mildred Bissell's oilcloth table covering. Sheriff Dolgan's tongue worried the hole a missing filling had left on his back molar. Mort Larchman speculated on whether Latham might have run off with another woman.

"Too steady," Donald Winks said.

Several heads nodded.

"Picture of that wife, Angela, on his desk, and it's the first thing to get dusted every day. Besides, he's not a man for a whole lot of imagination, if you ask me."

No one had. For fifteen years, Tom Latham had sold them insurance and kept them posted on changes in the tax laws. He drove his daughter to her high school in the mornings, and he could shop for what Angela wanted at Jordan's Market without needing a list. He painted the shutters of their big old house every spring, always the same green color, and mowed the lawn Saturday afternoons in the summer. When autumn came he went hunting Sunday afternoons after services at Millford Presbyterian. He had attended services every week but last Sunday.

"Anything else?" Dee Anna Martin looked up from the hole in the tablecloth. "Any questions Twelveclocks has been asking? Questions we haven't heard about? The smallest thing might give us a clue."

Dolgan wished Dee Anna would stop playing detective. That was his job, if only he'd be allowed to perform it. "Okay, Mort, you heard him over at the library. What was he wanting to know?"

"Just asked what books Tom checked out. That librarian girl looked it up on a card. Then Twelveclocks went over by the shelves and started looking at signatures in the back of books."

It was the same at the drug store. Twelveclocks had gone there to ask if Mr. Thomas Latham's prescription was ready. It was a trick question, but Dolgan had figured it out. When the druggist went to look on the shelf, Twelveclocks peeked at Latham's medical record. There had been no prescription.

"Just like the office," Donald Winks put in again, since no one was offering anything new. "Asking me what time Tom went to lunch, what he ate, what he joked around about. I told him like I told you, Sheriff. Tom Latham was strictly business, best agent we had. I mean, we have."

"We heard you the first time, Don," Mort Larchman snapped. "Want to go back over how Twelveclocks got into my dental charts?"

No one answered.

"Somebody, anyway, slipped back there and rearranged my files."

Gloom returned to the breakfast table. Steam fogged the plate-glass window, but they could hear the swish of cars on wet streets outside. The weatherman said it would rain all weekend. If they took walks past the big old house on Pear Street, as each had done several times in the past eleven days, they would catch only colds. Their shoes would squish if they walked slow enough to peer in the windows.

"All right, I've been holding back one thing," Dolgan said finally. "We're stuck at this point, even though this is none of your business." He glanced at Dee Anna Martin. "That Twelveclocks is spending too much time with a certain Mrs. Angela Latham. If you know what I mean."

Dolgan enjoyed the ensuing silence. He counted seconds to measure the impact of his words. He counted to two before Mort Larchman laughed out loud.

"Hell, Dolgan, we knew that."

Dee Anna Martin's salt-and-pepper curls shook with her giggling. "When did you finally figure that out?"

"Why, all along," Dolgan answered with vigor. "I noticed it right away. First a woman reports her husband missing. Then she says he's not missing, only sick. Then Twelveclocks' truck starts leaving an oil spot in her driveway, parked there so

189

much. Tom Latham's car never dripped a spot of oil. Anybody notice that oil spot?"

Several heads nodded.

"And Twelveclocks starts asking questions, wanting to know anything and everything about Mr. Thomas Latham. Like he wants to turn into him or something. And we all find out Twelveclocks is not what he appears to..."

"That's it." Dee Anna Martin turned so fast that curls bounced on her forehead. "Impersonation."

"That's what?" Dolgan snapped.

"Don't you see?" Dee Anna glanced around the table. Apparently Mort Larchman saw. His jaw dropped to show rows of perfect teeth.

"Impersonation." Donald Winks nodded rapidly.

"Twelveclocks is studying up to impersonate somebody?" Dolgan asked.

"Somebody? Tom Latham." Dee Anna Martin's eyes beamed. "It might have to do with insurance. Or maybe Latham's already dead. Or they're finding out all about him before they kill him."

Dolgan looked mildly confused.

"And Angela Latham's in love with William Twelveclocks," Mort cut in. "She always was strange."

"Dee Anna," Dolgan tried to interrupt.

"Or Twelveclocks has got something on her. Maybe for the insurance money."

"Tom had a heap of coverage," Don Winks said.

"And maybe they got him out at Twelveclocks' cabin," Dee Anna went on. "Torturing him to unravel every stitch of his life..."

She trailed off. Sheriff Dolgan was on his feet. He stood slowly, with a deliberate stretch, and took his jacket from the back of his chair. A steaming bowl of oatmeal lay untouched on the table.

"Just remembered. I promised to stop by Will Jordan's

Market. Kids been shoplifting him crazy."

Dolgan took his hat from the rack and stood in the open doorway. He slowly put his hat on. "What hooey! Complete hooey." He shook his head and went out.

The members of the breakfast club sat in silence. Behind the counter, Mildred Bissell was washing dishes, but she looked up at the sound of scraping chairs. Flapjacks steamed on the plates and the pitcher of raspberry syrup stood untouched. She had never seen the breakfast club break up so fast, and she glanced at the clock. That was odd too. Dolgan had left with his siren on. Dolgan never ran his siren unless he was late.

The woods around William Twelveclocks' cabin were glossy with rain. Clumps of moss glistened on the oak bark, and droplets ran down the north sides of trees, making the moss into ribbons and soft weeping sponges. Fallen branches and trunks of birch, ash and maple gave off the decrepit breath of age and damp and decay. Small animals huddled in burrows, their usual stirrings replaced by the skitter-plop of drops descending leaf by leaf down the overweighted trees.

Above, around, among the animals' homes, footsteps moved. Twigs broke and steps squeezed pools from sodden books of leaves. Shadows faded and reappeared, human shapes slipping in and out between trees. Shadows caught like rags on the old spiny stumps.

Beyond the trees, in clear spots and beneath overhanging canopies, cars were parked. The cars stood empty. It had been twenty minutes since Sheriff Dolgan's siren let out its first whip as he turned onto Elmwood.

Dolgan, broad and round in a khaki coat the rain had polka-dotted, took up position at the edge of the clearing. The clearing's center was broad and a cabin stood in it. Light spilled from its windows and tossed dappled rectangles on the rusted metal sides of a car parked out front. Dolgan recognized it as the old beater Tom Latham had bought for his wife. Beside it, on the cabin side, Twelveclocks' own truck sat.

Dolgan began his slow glide away from the trees. He moved toward the cabin, a khaki shadow in the green darkness. Suddenly he stopped. A movement caught his eye. In the dim light on the far side of the clearing, another shadow stirred. Its features gave off an infrared glare. The face was Dee Anna Martin's.

Dolgan felt mad enough to stamp, but he stood in a puddle. Several yards to his right, another shadow moved. Dolgan turned to study a peculiar-looking tree. When it moved, he caught a gleam from white teeth. Mort Larchman. There were Sally and Paul Burford to the left, separated from each other across the clearing. That was probably Margie Pearson looking like she grew sideways out of that tree, and Donald Winks, in his tartan wool raincoat, looked like a cross between a ghost and a bagpiper.

The shadows swayed. A sound of female laughter came from the cabin.

Dolgan took a deep breath and squared his shoulders. The shadows stiffened and leaned inward. He shot a hard look at each, then took a step. The shadows drew inward like a net.

Dolgan gave them each another look, took a step. The net drew closer. Dolgan shrugged and gave up. Three more steps and the shadows shrank to crawl the few last feet before they swelled again to lean on windowsills. Dolgan approached the cabin. The others already hung, seven small sleeping bats, against the walls.

Dolgan crouched and raised his eyes to peer over the sill. Beyond the window lay a square, snug room, paneled with rough wooden boards in odd sizes and shades. No piece of the plaid, flowered, and striped furniture seemed to match any other. In a plaid arm chair, a man sat. Another man, standing by a broad oak table, sorted through a pile of papers. Angela

192

Latham leaned against the arm of her husband's chair. It was her laughter they had heard. She still laughed.

Folded into the plaid armchair, Tom Latham looked his usual self. The rose light from the fireplace caught on the handsome height of his cheekbones and his features looked healthy, if concentrated, his brow furrowing as he studied the fire.

He paused, and then spoke. "An A in Chemistry. C in Literature. B in Physical Education."

"Breaking your nose playing tennis." Angela Latham laughed, leaning further over her husband's chair. She tousled his hair. "How could you do that?"

Tom Latham's head shook. The fine black strands of his hair fell back into place. "Amzie, now we're almost done."

"His school record says so, Mrs. Latham." William Twelveclocks ran a finger down the sheet of paper his hand. "Now tell the year you graduated."

Twelveclocks was a tall man, a full hand bigger than Tom Latham, and heavier. He wore his usual old green clothes, the two bristles on his balding head standing up like matched whisk broom stubs. His back was turned to the window, his shoulders hunched in concentration, and his big frame swayed from side to side like the pendulum of a clock.

"Graduated high school, eighteen years ago," Tom Latham said. "Amzie graduated a year later. We got married in July."

Angela Latham nodded approvingly. Twelveclocks selected a new sheet of paper from the pile to the left of his hand. He resumed swaying.

"Here's stuff we started on the first day you wandered in." He turned toward Tom Latham. "What month is it now?" Dolgan could now see William Twelveclocks' weathered face.

"February," Tom Latham said quickly, "can't remember the date today."

"That's normal." Twelveclocks smiled.

"But Betsy was born on the seventeenth, on Will Jordan's meat counter. She's fifteen now. And Andy was born the third of September. He's thirteen."

Twelveclocks picked up another sheet. "Last book you read from the library?"

"Fundamental Principles of Tax Accounting. Bundling, third edition."

"Good," Twelveclocks said. He placed the paper carefully on the pile to his right.

"This is all old stuff," Angela Latham said. She had left her husband's chair to crouch in front of the hearth, warming her hands. Now she rose and crossed the room to where Twelveclocks stood, glancing over his shoulder. "Can't we go on to anything new?"

"That's it. There isn't anything more." Twelveclocks handed a tablet to Angela. She turned its pages. "We put everything back in its place. We got it all."

It was Tom Latham's turn to stand and walk to the fire. He stood washing his hands in the heat, closing his palms around his fingers to twist and wring them. When he turned toward the window from which Dolgan watched, the gesture seemed more nervousness than cold. Tom Latham's face looked frightened.

"You mean that's it? That's everything?"

The whisk broom bristles and Twelveclocks' large head nodded. Sheriff Dolgan could see that Twelveclocks looked even more tired than usual.

Dolgan could also see Dee Anna's white face. It stared into the window straight across the cabin. Other faces shone faintly in windows nearby, but Dee Anna's nose looked like squashed bubble gum.

Dolgan wished he could unravel this mess. Latham looked scared, but his wife and Twelveclocks, who grew even bigger when a man considered he might have to arrest him, appeared pleased as punch. They'd been up to something in that cabin,

194

no question, and it tied into the business at the library. Probably that trick at the drugstore too. Dolgan guessed he'd have to go in.

He glanced across the cabin to see if Dee Anna had pushed herself through the glass yet. The window was dark. He checked other windows. They were empty too. He turned to begin easing his way to the cabin door, wedging steps between snappable twigs, and saw his worst suspicions confirmed. A clump of wet, dark shapes approached the door at a rapid creep. Dee Anna Martin led them.

Careless of noise, Dolgan strode through shoe-sucking mud. The clump caught sight of him and Dee Anna speeded up.

Dolgan lengthened his strides and made the door in three. Shapes closed around him. "I'll handle this," he commanded. The words broke the hush and released a volley of voices.

"They'll kill him."

"They're ready to do it."

White teeth shone in the dim light. "Dee Anna was right. They've got what they want now."

"It'll be murder."

Dolgan didn't want them busting in the door, all hysterical, but as he opened his mouth to speak, it was too late. A widening band of light washed the shock-white faces. He heard ticking at his back.

William Twelveclocks, huge, ticking and smiling, threw a shadow band across the lighted doorway.

"Morning, Sheriff," Twelveclocks spoke slowly, calmly. His voice was deep and comfortable. "It's warm and dry inside by the fire. Would you like to come in?"

Twelveclocks stepped back from the door. His gaze lifted and took in the crowd at Dolgan's back. "I hope there's room for all of you."

"I've come on police business." Dolgan's face was red, but his voice and his stride snapped with authority. "I'm here

195

investigating the disappearance of Thomas Latham. These folks..." He paused and cleared his throat. "Maybe they just happened past. Let them leave safely."

Dolgan heard a murmur at his back. He did not turn. Once inside, he stripped his sopping raincoat from his arms. Twelveclocks' hands took it. Meanwhile the others had followed. They struggled free of their coats with Twelveclocks' help. Dolgan went to stand by the fire.

At last, when the coat rack by the cabin door stood as humped and dripping as a movie monster, Twelveclocks turned and faced the room. Angela Latham, a yellow tablet clutched to her chest, stood smiling and nodding, exchanging pleasantries. Tom Latham had finished shaking hands all around and now moved toward his seat. He moved with a slight limp on his left side, and the others had thoughtfully left the plaid chair empty for him.

The members of Bissell's Breakfast Club leaned against tables, windowsills and rough wooden walls, a motley crowd that made the room's furniture look store-bought. Tom settled into the armchair. Dee Anna Martin was asking how he hurt his leg.

"Sure to clear up in a week or two," he told Dee Anna. "No big problem."

"Now then." Dolgan braced himself in a wide stance in front of the fire. "I've come to investigate the disappearance of Thomas Latham. Exactly what's been going on here?"

Angela Latham, her voice high, continued chatting with Mort Larchman. "I told Sheriff Dolgan my husband wasn't missing." She looked from Mort to her husband and back. "It's like I told Don. Every day last week, I called and said he was sick."

"That's true." Don Winks had made himself comfortable by the bookcase and was examining Twelveclocks' fly-tying equipment. "Angela called every day. Didn't I tell you that?" he asked the sheriff.

Dolgan could see the tide was turning.

"That's not the point," Dolgan went on alone. "I want to hear from Tom himself, in front of witnesses here, exactly where's he been for the last eleven days."

William Twelveclocks turned at last to face Sheriff Dolgan. His long arms spread to take in the cabin. "Tom's been right here. The whole time. I even drove into town to pick up a prescription for him."

"Of course," Angela Latham echoed. She nodded rapidly. "I drove out to bring Tom back this afternoon."

A voice spoke from the group gathered near Latham's chair. "Can't a man visit?"

Dolgan did not turn to identify the speaker. He saw enough in Dee Anna Martin's eyes, targeting his from across the room. "Honestly, Sheriff Dolgan." She was shaking her head. "What seems to be the problem?"

"The problem is," Dolgan said sternly, and he wished a plague of aphids on Dee Anna Martin's flower shop, "the problem is, I haven't heard word-one from Tom Latham. If this is Tom Latham." He paused and surveyed the crowd. "Now I'd like to hear what he has to say."

Faces turned toward Dolgan. Conversations trailed off. Margie Pearson's voice was left alone to ask, "Mr. Twelveclocks, is it true you've got a big ball of silver gum wrappers?"

The question hung in the air. Tom Latham had begun massaging his leg where it rested on a hassock. At last he shrugged and looked up.

"It's like they said, Sheriff. I've been out here all week. Or two weeks, right?" He glanced at Angela, who nodded.

"See I was out hunting. Stupid to go by myself. Anyway I fell over a root, banged up my leg, and hit my head. When I came to, I had amnes..."

"A-knock-on-the-head, bad one," Twelveclocks interrupted. "Wandered in here. I put him to bed. I haven't got a phone, you know, Sheriff, and he was hurt pretty bad. Two days went by before I could go tell Mrs. Latham."

Dolgan cut Twelveclocks off. "I said Tom was doing the talking. And that's who I want to hear from."

Tom Latham settled back in his chair. "That's all there is to tell, I guess. Head's fine now, of course, but I'll have Winthrop look at the leg when I get back into town. A knock on the head," he repeated slowly. "That's all."

Dolgan considered his options. The man sitting in the plaid armchair looked like Tom Latham. Don Winks, who'd worked in the same office for fifteen years, recognized him. Dolgan still felt something was wrong.

"How do I know you're really Tom Latham? Got any I.D.?"

Tom leaned back in his chair. He began laughing. "Sheriff, a man doesn't take his wallet when he goes hunting. Deer don't take checks. That was why I couldn't remember where I liv..."

Angela cut him off this time. "Tom couldn't remember where he left his wallet at home."

William Twelveclocks chimed in, nodding, "Tom wanted to pay me for picking up food. Said he felt bad not having his wallet."

Dolgan looked around the room. Conversations were starting up again, several faces smiling and nodding. Mort Larchman stood by the coat rack, separating Don Winks' sodden wool coat, a tartan fungus, from his own. Red dye dripped from the tartan onto the floor, and Don moved to take the coat off Larchman's hands.

"Guess I'd better go too," he said.

Mort mumbled something about having to pick up a set of dentures on his way to the clinic.

"See you at Bissell's," Tom Latham called in farewell. "Save me some syrup."

As it happened, Don Winks walked down the path in a distracted daze. He missed his car by ten yards. He was remembering that Latham had joined them at Bissell's only once, and that time Tom skipped the raspberry syrup. Don forgot the matter during a twenty-minute search for his car.

Meanwhile Dee Anna Martin was wringing out the last bit of pleasure, and her raincoat. She put the raincoat on. "Honestly, Sheriff Dolgan," she said, joining the others at the door. "Where do you come up with these ideas?"

Paul Burford held the door open. "What a bunch of hooey," he said. "Complete hooey."

And so Sheriff Dolgan backed down. He might have tested this Tom Latham to make sure he was the original article, asking questions about his life history, his salary, and his mother's maiden name. But he guessed that if what he'd heard through the window had gone on for eleven days, any impostor would know Tom Latham's life backward and forward, every word of it true.

About this last item, Millford's sheriff was wrong. William Twelveclocks had drilled memories into Tom Latham for eleven days, but Dolgan overlooked the source of those memories.

William Twelveclocks had resurrected Tom Latham's life from the mists of amnesia. He had researched slowly, patiently, and taught every item he learned to Tom Latham. Angela Latham supplied most of the memories. Angela provided facts, but facts and Angela Latham had a special relationship. She knew they were wedded to truth, but she considered the marriage one of convenience.

Tom's life had taken on interesting hues. He now remembered, from when he was ten years old, being able to swim free style in a strong wind. He had lifted off from the ground and simply flown free style in the air. He also remembered listening to a long conversation between two trees in the back yard of his childhood home, and he remembered every word each tree had said. The subject was leaves. Tom Latham did have difficulty believing a few of the events he could recite from his life, but he had no choice but to remember them. If

Twelveclocks had suspected what Mrs. Latham was up to, he did not care. His job was to bring back what people in Millford had lost. In this case Millford had lost Tom Latham.

Now Tom was returned, complete with remembered telephone numbers and high school girlfriends' names and a preferred method for opening the tight lids on a jar. Tom Latham was complete.

Dolgan saw this. "All right," he said after a long pause. "I guess I'll let it go this time. Just don't let it happen again."

People got used to minor changes in Tom Latham after that. He laughed more often and told better jokes. He painted the shutters on his house blue one year, but went back to green. He no longer hunted alone.

Sheriff Dolgan noted all of this down. He kept a file and included the carbon copies of the report from the army. He also noted that every year, once a year, the entire Latham family went out to William Twelveclocks' cabin for dinner. Dolgan put two and two together. He figured out that this always happened on Tom Latham's birthday.

Chapter Thirteen

No snacks for you today, that's fine. I'll just have a bite or two myself. You lie back. I'll pull the covers up, since it's cold outside. Miserable with that rain today. You should keep warm.

I wasn't planning on mentioning it, but all right, since you brought it up—you do look unusually tired. More tired than I've ever seen you. Did the delivery boy come from the market? Then you had to go down the stairs and let him in. That tires you, doesn't it? There, lie back.

He's one to complain about the hedge, a young fellow like that. He's skinny and strong from working hard at the market. I manage to get through the hedge. You know my opinion about how it grows, and about what ought to be done, but I get through every visit. It's not as easy for me, but am I complaining? He's complaining, not me.

You'd better lie back. I bet that pillow feels comfortable, just enjoy it. The chore woman lifted you over to the chair yesterday. That's tiring too. But feel the lovely clean sheets. Isn't that better? You have to rest.

I don't think we need a story today. Enough of them, those stories probably wear you out. And to think that last one was sort of a mystery thing. Too exciting, now that I think about it. No story today. We'll just sit and hold the ribbon.

Please, you should not talk. My hearing's not so good anyway, and I have a slight sore throat. Suppose I lean close to hear, because I have to when your voice is so weak, and suppose you caught this little sore throat? How would we like that?

Look at you, hardly strong enough to hold up the ribbon. Why lift it out of the covers? What? Here, if I have to listen I'll turn my head.

I did put the ribbon in every story. I did, absolutely. You just don't remember. Well, that's age. After what we talked about last time, you know, about losing you, I feel I can be frank.

You are old and you are sick and you are tired. You're too tired for a story today. No sense shaking the ribbon at me. I won't tell one. I'll sit here and eat cookies all by myself.

My, that was good. Another good one, almond flavor, I think. You usually get those. I'm not looking at you. You can shake that ribbon all you like. I won't look.

Oh please, put your arm down, stop. I'll listen. I will.

All right, I have to do what you want or else leave you all upset. So that's how it is. I'll tell a story. And this time I promise you'll notice that the ribbon is in it.

Put your arm under the covers. We'll keep the tail end of the ribbon out on the pillow so we both see it.

But I'll only begin on one condition. You must close your eyes. Close them before I even start. Close them, keep them closed. That's good. I've got you all tucked in again.

Now you have to listen because this will be a very short story. And it will end the minute you fall asleep. That's the way, snug your head down. Your cheek is paler than the pillow.

A very short story to put you to sleep.

Listen now.

A Story with the Ribbon
in Its Title

Several years passed.

Chapter Fourteen

Of course you can't remember the story, but you do remember the title, don't you? Our old friend the ribbon, you got that part. I'm certainly thankful you heard. For once. I do put it in every story, you know. Only because you ask me to.

Never mind, you hardly missed a thing. Several years passed, that's all. You fell asleep as soon as you heard a certain word in the title.

Quite a few things did happen actually, but it would wear me out to go over each one again. If I told that story again, we wouldn't get to today's story, would we? Well, all right, just the high points.

Will Jordan—you'll recall he owned Jordan's Market—he got married. Too bad about how that marriage worked out. Angela's son Andy grew up and married a pretty girl from East End. They had twins, but I don't think we've come to that part yet. Sheriff Dolgan retired. The retirement party was at Bissell's Restaurant and Dee Anna Martin brought lots of flowers from her shop. Until then no one knew what difficulty Sheriff Dolgan had with hay fever. And there were more day-to-day events like that, et cetera and et cetera. You should know stories are no fun if we hit only the high points.

You can have a story today if you like. If you're feeling up to it. You do look better, your eyes are clear and not too tired today. Is that a new quilted robe? Your daughter made it, I'd never have guessed. It looks ready-made from a store. She's a talented one, all right. She made another with the left-over cloth? Nice, if this one ever wears out, I suppose. Two new robes exactly alike, that's interesting.

Deep blue looks good on you, and your color's good, even if the voice hasn't come back completely. The cough's not quite as deep. Lean forward, that makes it easier. I'll hold you. Cough it loose. Spit it into the cup.

That's better, take a few deep breaths.

What's that? Your voice is soft, I can hardly hear. Try pointing.

The window seat? The window, maybe? Something outside. Let's see, tell it like in charades. Your finger's moving and it's something outside. The wind? It's a nasty October wind, but nothing special.

Oh—the hedge. Don't strain your voice, I got it when your fingers tangled up. Yes, the hedge is still out there, count on it. I hardly expected you to ask about that.

The hedge does look a little like the ribbon, now that you hold it up. Well, I get through. I use a stick to poke, the delivery boy leaves the stick on the planter strip for me. It's a long, strong stick and I poke for a thin spot and work my way through.

You know what I think ought to be done about the hedge. I've said it often enough, I'll gladly call someone. Easy for you to like it the way it is. You're not the one that has to get through every time I visit.

I will get to the story, you're the one who brought up the hedge. I imagine you would like to change the subject. All at once now it's time to come around to the story, isn't it? Then we will.

That bathrobe is pretty on you. Pull the collar up to keep your neck warm. There, a nice cozy robe. You know, it almost gives me an idea. How about this?

Betsy Betsy

One summer morning Betsy Latham, the unmarried artist daughter of Thomas and Angela Latham, saw sunlight fall across a wooden table in her studio. It was a humid morning in mid-July and the table was a hand-me-down, scratched from years spent in Angela Latham's basement. Betsy usually mixed her pottery glazes on it, and clay dust covered the surface.

Betsy Latham had no particular plans for the day. She owed an order of ceramic soup pots and a woven wall hanging to Marshall and Morton Department Store, for the Home Craft Shop. On the east window, near the door of her studio, plaid cotton curtains stood apart and a rectangular band of sunshine slanted between them. The sunlight made a ribbon across the table. Betsy watched the strip of light edge gradually northward.

It took the better part of an hour to see it actually move, and Betsy stood trembling at the sudden, terrible beauty of sunlight crossing a table. Betsy ignored the unglazed soup pots stacked near the north wall's kiln, and she made up her mind, or, as some say, she lost it. The ribbon of sunlight on the table was the most beautiful sight she had ever seen.

Betsy knew she could not mix sunshine or scrub the air to make it shine pure gold like that. Yet others needed to see this beauty. She could build a table, an exact duplicate of the beat-up one in the center of her studio. She would carve its scars not by accident, as time had done, but by deliberate, patient art. When the table was finished, she would put it on display. Betsy studied the vision a moment longer. The idea meant a lot of work, but the work was worth it.

Betsy hurried out the door and across the yard. From a

woodpile at the rear of the shack where she lived, she collected scraps and carried them back to the studio. She dumped them on the floor beside the sunlit table. Then she began to piece sizes and shapes, pulling tools from the cluttered shelves on the studio's east wall and clearing a space for the new table. She made scratches in the wood and carved scrapes and gouges and blemishes that would eventually fit together beside the real table.

Betsy worked all that day, as history would remember the story, and quit only when light failed her at dusk. The day's work, combined with the labor of three more, became Studio Table Replica One. More work would be needed before Betsy finished Studio Table Seven, the one she finally found acceptable. She spent most of her twenty-fifth year making a kitchen table.

Betsy Latham was a Millford girl, born and bred. She grew up on Pear Street in a huge old house owned by Thomas and Angela Latham. The house had carved mahogany banisters and intricately cast brass plates around the door knobs, and the iron hinges on the doors had tiny figures cast into them. The ancient wood frames were lapped with decorative ridges, waves spreading away from the opening of the door, and as a child, Betsy often contented herself with staring.

Betsy's teachers said Betsy was bright. In fifth grade one noticed that the girl might forget her vocabulary words if her teacher wore much jewelry. Betsy's mother said this was normal. Betsy's father insisted on taking his daughter to doctors, including a specialist in East End. The doctor reported his findings in Betsy's own words, she simply liked looking at things.

After high school, Betsy went to college in Wilburton, ninety miles north of Millford, and she returned on weekends to be with her mother. They baked pies and invented lattice patterns to weave complex crusts, and they went for walks, their forward progress seldom equal to the length of their pauses. Angela Latham would point out the curlicues from a snail trail, or Betsy might remark how Mrs. Mary Roman's FORTUNETELLING/BEAUTY SALON sign weathered more on the fortunetelling side. They stopped long and thoughtfully.

Betsy finished her art degree and began supporting herself. Her student work in ceramic dishes and bowls sold well in the campus bookstore and she eventually sold to department stores in downtown Millford. Her wall hangings softened the walls of dentists' offices. Her pie-lattice wall screens kept children interested during talks their parents attended in the church basement. The year Betsy began patching quilts from her mother's sewing scraps, Millford winters grew harsh and everyone wanted one.

Betsy never settled on any single medium, although her father, who had finally checked out a library book about art and artists, thought she should. Tom Latham was happy to see his daughter making her way in the world while his son, Andrew, had settled in as a clerk at an accounting firm and married a young woman named Elizabeth. Tom Latham knew his daughter was unlikely to marry. She was pretty, with her mother's willowy limbs and immense brown eyes, but no man could live long under the slow scrutiny Betsy's eyes turned on each object and face. Tom loaned his daughter money to buy land and set up a studio out where the Buckram property used to end, a mile west of William Twelveclocks' place. In that studio Betsy Latham first saw sunlight cross a table.

The house itself was little more than a shack. The studio was somewhat less. Both perched on ungraded ground two miles west of the Millford culvert pool, land too rocky to add a patch to the quiltwork of farms on nearby hills. Betsy wove rag rugs for the floors of the house, collected a woodstove and used furniture. She put up unmatched curtains, fringed lampshades, old brass lamps, and shiny mirrors to bring the light to dark corners. Betsy worked in her studio every day, and when she wasn't finishing orders for department stores, she took long pausing walks.

Betsy looked at things. Occasionally customers recognized what she saw—a tapestry woven like green water and twigs rushing toward the culvert pool, a flash of blue from a bird against a winter sky. Once in a while Betsy walked past William Twelveclocks' place, and if he was out in the yard, at work on his sway-backed cabin, both would look up and wave. Most of all, Betsy liked looking at things. She found it annoying to recognize or remember them.

By the time the artist finished Studio Table Seven, winter had returned to Millford. Betsy Latham had pounded and fitted and glued wood through the long heat of summer, making Tables Two and Three, and had overlooked the crunch of autumn leaves underfoot, somewhere between Replicas Four and Five. Now, in January, Studio Table Replica Seven stood complete.

Betsy nudged its corner and it squeaked sideways into position beside the real one. She had listened to a lot of wood to get that squeak. She brushed sawdust from her palms and walked around the table, slowly, 360 degrees. Then she let her shoulders settle and slid her hands into her overall pockets. The replica was exact.

It was identical, from the knothole her brother Andy had picked smooth the summer he was ten to the scrape from the trunk lid of the car when her father brought the table out from town. Sighting along the surface, she saw the slight rise of the wood's warp which began two palm-widths to the side of the burned circle. She could follow the warp along a split board until it ended in a bent nail at the far corner. The leg beneath that nail had thirty-seven cat scratches.

Betsy smiled. She heard rain rattle on the corrugated tin roof overhead. No sun shone between the plaid cotton curtains today, but the beauty of both tables was as eerie as what she had seen back in July. The tables were plain and used, scarred by hand and mind and neglect. If she kept the original and sent the duplicate back to her mother, the substitution would never be noted. And that, Betsy thought with a sigh, meant Studio Table Replica was ready to exhibit.

Betsy's sigh caught in her throat. She shook her head and looked at the table. She tried to imagine Studio Table Replica in the showroom at Marshall and Morton. She looked away and looked back.

M&M would display any piece Betsy offered, she knew that. She had kept up with the orders for ceramic pots and woven wall hangings, so they would be happy to hear she had a new big sculpture. They would set the table up in M&M's spacious fifth-floor showroom, and when Betsy came, she would see it standing there, a set jewel shining with wonderful ordinariness. If her mother came to visit, Angela would see it instantly—a table serene in being exactly what it was. But visitors would come to the showroom too. Neighbors and patrons from Millford would visit. Strangers would drive in from nearby towns. They would see a beat-up kitchen table in the middle of a fancy art gallery.

Betsy pulled her hands from her pockets and slumped to a chair. Most people would walk past an old broken table. Others would ask questions. They would try thinking about it, which was all wrong. They would say it was "Interesting." Perhaps one stranger, maybe not even one, would truly see it. She had made this thing for them all.

Betsy rubbed her eyes with her palms. Bright stars exploded behind them and the gritty sawdust rubbed into them. Betsy leaned back and let the hot tears flow. Her shoulders beat a slow rhythm against the back of the old wooden chair.

The seat of the old wooden chair creaked. Raindrops rapped impatient fingers on the tin roof. Betsy's breath came in stabbing, stunted gasps and the wind outside the thin studio walls rattled loose window panes. She had failed. She had tried and she had failed. She accepted that. Then a thought, as clear as a ribbon of light, rode up the wave of pain.

Betsy stood. She looked at the chair. Betsy sat down. The chair creaked. Its worn seat fit the thump of her collapse into it, and when she rocked, the weight of her body made the wood sing like cries held in her chest. The chair felt solid beneath her spine. Betsy pushed herself to her feet and stared at where she'd been sitting. An uncast shadow held her shape in the air.

A crooked leather strip mended the chair's seat, and one leg was stronger because a stranger, somewhere long ago, had mended it. Around the chair a cluttered room watched the beauty of failure slam home again. Betsy Latham nearly banged her hip on the corner of Studio Table Replica Seven in her rush to reach the door.

She stopped, her hand trembling on the cold knob, and willed herself to slow down. She must begin work slowly, patiently. It would take a long time to perfect Studio Chair Replica, but the work would be worth it. Others needed to know about this beauty too.

Five years later, William Twelveclocks arrived on the scene, and was the first to discover what Betsy Latham was up to. He stumbled upon it by accident and, predictably, thanks to a clock.

In those years, as Twelveclocks recalled them, he had not seen his neighbor passing his cabin on her usual pausing walks. Angela and Tom Latham still came to his home for dinner on Tom's birthdays, and William gathered that Betsy was busy making pots and wall hangings. Her work was selling well. Twelveclocks himself had been finding lost possessions and returning them, an especially challenging job since Millford had grown more populous. Thus, at first anyway, Twelveclocks did not even connect the ringing alarm clock outside his cabin to Betsy Latham, his neighbor.

Twelveclocks owned many timepieces, but never set one

to wake himself. He slept soundly and let his early morning snores pull him awake. One morning he jolted alert, dazed, mistaking the buzzing in the air for the echo of a dream.

Twelveclocks shook his head. The sound went on. He stumbled from bed and to a nearby window. He grabbed his wool robe and ran down the hall and out the back door. A wind-up alarm clock, sitting on an old tree stump, croaked faint, metallic growling. It had a bell on top and was dented. The alarm had almost wound down.

William pushed the button to make the alarm stop. A piece of string was knotted to it and draped down the stump to trail over the ground. A yellow slip of paper was taped three feet down the string. It was damp, but large black letters said, "Follow Me," and William Twelveclocks did.

The string wound between trees and around rocky outcroppings for nearly a mile. The March morning was frosty, and brittle ice cracked underfoot, so before he left the cabin, Twelveclocks paused to pull on boots, pants and a jacket. He was not ready to give up his p.j.'s, so he wore them underneath. He followed the string and plunged through underbrush, winding it into a ball. When the string ball had grown to nearly the size of his palm, he recognized landmarks approaching Betsy Latham's place.

The way he'd come seemed odd. Betsy's place felt more west and north of here. The peak of Log Mountain, if he remembered right, formed a backdrop to the right of the house. Now Log Mountain lay to the left. Lights burned in the house and the studio. In fact, lights burned in the windows of two houses and two studios. William walked clear of the trees and saw two of everything.

The Latham place had two run-down houses, two studios, two woodpiles by the back steps, both exactly alike, two rutted paths to the road, each identical, and two fields of weedy grass around everything. William Twelveclocks scooped a skim of ice from a puddle and washed his face. It felt cold, he was not

dreaming double. A hundred yards of weed-choked field separated the house-studio sets, and William let the ball of string
roll from his hand and followed its trail to the end.

Where he stood, tall grass parted as if a comb had run
through it. On either side, identical weed fields stretched toward identical houses. The fields were matched, down to the
many ways grass knotted itself on twin hillocks. Twelveclocks
looked left and right. From the still center of a mirror, he
wondered where to begin.

At last he approached the lighted windows of the eastern
house, trying to avoid disturbing the grass since it looked arranged with great care. He came to a window and looked in.

Betsy Latham's living room appeared normal. It looked
much as it had the one time he'd visited when he had returned
a lost glove. Twelveclocks moved to the next window. In the
kitchen, rag rugs made colorful circles on the floor. Drying
dishes lay neatly stacked on the drainboard. William hesitated
to keep peeping since Betsy might at that moment be getting
dressed in the bedroom. He retraced his steps to the comb-
part in the grass and stood a moment. Then he approached
the kitchen window of the western house.

Twelveclocks stared through it. The kitchen looked like
the one he had already seen. Neatly stacked dishes dried on
the drainboard. On the floor colorful circles were made by
rag rugs. Twelveclocks moved along the wall to where the next
window showed an identical living room. Only one detail of
the room was different—Betsy Latham.

Betsy sat at a table working. Her hands held a fringed silk
lampshade, and its edge looked exactly like the torn fringe of
a lampshade in the other living room. The lamp stood to her
right, a replica of the brass lamp in the twin house. That
morning Betsy Latham was pulling a few last threads from
the silk she had carefully frayed. She had worked all night and
had no idea it was morning, or that Mr. Twelveclocks had
obeyed her instructions.

214

In the five years since Betsy completed Studio Chair Four, the one which perfected that series, she had learned a great deal about making replicas. She worked more quickly these days, knowing that the secret lay in staring at an object a very long time, then letting her hands discover how to make it. She seldom planned projects anymore. This new skill allowed her to complete the Studio Replica in detail, to shift soil and scatter seeds to duplicate the field outside and, in only a few years, to almost finish the house.

Betsy had also learned that the weather played copy-cat tricks around real structures and their replicas. During more than one winter storm she had run back and forth between the houses, studying how the rain matched splashes on identical wainscoting and windows. Wind rearranged weeds in the yards in mirror patterns and, as her visitor this morning had noted, spring wildflowers sprouted randomly in matched sets.

Betsy had also learned that she had plenty of land. At first she'd feared that another house and studio would crowd her small plot, but gradually she came to understand that the ground itself was expanding. She guessed a fault line began at the culvert and ran right through her property. In any event, measurements taken on mornings several months apart confirmed that work on the exterior of a replica made the ground around it grow. Buildings found the right distance from one another overnight. It happened only while Betsy slept, and that was why she set the alarm clock.

Betsy enjoyed the way the weather and the land replicated. It made excellent sense without the drawback of being logical. It helped her efforts too, and made her job easier. She now also understood her own need to replicate.

No object stood complete if it stood alone. The beautiful everyday things—trees, plants, and stones—were always together. Loveliness shone through them and onto each other. Their beauty took wild turns and popped out unexpectedly— in sunlight, shadow shapes, and accidents the wind left lying around like advertising. Betsy knew that few people would see this, assuming, that is, anyone ever came by to visit. She no longer cared. Her responsibility was to complete replicas, and it gave her plenty to wonder about.

Betsy pulled the last unnecessary thread from the fringed lampshade. She set it over the lamp and looked. It cast a glow on the threadbare carpet, the exact same glow that the original cast. Betsy glanced out the window and mistakenly concluded that she had finished by sunset. She felt relief. She would go home to sleep in the original house while the ground grew around her. In that instant a knock sounded at the door.

Betsy went to open it. William Twelveclocks stood on the top porch step, shivering, his jacket clutched around his pajama shirt. Betsy stared, unbelieving. Her amazement doubled. For the first time in her life, Mr. Twelveclocks was not ticking. She had gotten him out of bed.

"I worked all night. Oh no." She invited Mr. Twelveclocks in. "I am so sorry."

It took several minutes for William Twelveclocks to still his shivering enough to sit down. During that time Betsy brewed her visitor a cup of tea, in Teapot Replica Three. She served it steaming in Mug With Six Chips. Meanwhile she hurried to explain.

"The last couple years, I work so late. I get afraid sometimes I'll forget to stop."

Sitting beside by Woodstove Replica, welcoming the warmth from its sides, William Twelveclocks nodded.

"So I started setting the clock, over by your place, you see. At first once in a while, then every day. I set it out twelve hours before I planned to stop."

Twelveclocks nodded. He wanted to speak but he was shaking too much with cold.

"So I'd have to stop, isn't that right? To bring back the clock. Or else the alarm might wake you. Which I didn't want. Which happened, I'm so sorry. But every night for two years

216

now I've run over to bring the clock back. Really."

Silence fell. William Twelveclocks' teeth chattered.

"Except I worked right through last night. Did it ring a long time?"

Her visitor nodded.

"Oh dear. It rang all the way down."

Betsy folded her hands and stared at them. Back when she was a child, Mr. Twelveclocks was already a grown man, and he looked very old now. The wrinkles on his face went right up to his sock cap and his body seemed too tired to still go looking for lost things. He had enough to do without being called out to check on her. Yet she had to rely on someone.

Too many times she had worked through several nights, not just one, and found mail stacked layers deep in her mailbox. She occasionally lost track of hours, or days, or weeks, then the exhaustion would hit. She'd lose days in sleep. It was bad for her health, and she wondered what would happen if she fell sick or injured herself, perhaps welding the sides of Woodstove Replica. So she devised the clock with the string on it. Now she faced the visitor she dreaded.

Mr. Twelveclocks shivered more slowly. His hands, their skin ripply with age, cradled the mug. He took several sips. Betsy wanted to say more, but guessed it was his turn. He was bound to be angry. When his eyes finally left the mug to look up, only a patient sort of wonder lit them.

"It's all right. But I guess I was wondering." He spoke softly, his gaze averted to the stove. "How come you have two of everything?"

"Oh dear," Betsy said. "I forgot."

What followed gave William Twelveclocks plenty of time to calm down and begin getting warm. Betsy searched for words, stumbling over the few that came to her mind. She had never much liked words. She found searching for the right ones rather like trying to shake hands with a fish. The fish wouldn't.

217

"I like everything so much," she began, then stopped. That approach sounded silly.

"In art school we learned," she began again, "that the emotion's objective correlative might or might not be a facsimile of the concrete perceptible image of the object . . ." She abandoned that approach quickly too.

"Well, I do like everything so much," she began again. "Every single thing, you know, not just one or two."

Mr. Twelveclocks settled back in his chair. He got comfortable in Green Upholstered Chair By The Fire Replica Two, the warm mug resting on his paunch.

Betsy talked for a long time. William Twelveclocks dozed in and out of listening. He enjoyed the young woman's voice and he liked the comments the woodstove put in occasionally. Betsy told about Table Replica Seven, and about the long hours spent getting thirty-seven cat scratches right. She spoke of dents in old teapots and how the planks for the porch had to be hollowed out where people stepped most. In her way, she tried explaining how her heart felt when she wanted to show everyone how beautiful things were, how if you stopped and looked at anything, why, it walloped you from right inside your head. Mostly she managed to list how she had reconstructed every detail. "People need to know how beautiful things are. If it means duplicating all of Millford," she said, then paused and gave a helpless shrug, "Why, I guess I will."

Betsy finished. William Twelveclocks opened his eyes slowly, sleepily. Her face was a pale circle indistinguishable from the dawn in the window.

The big man stood, using the arms of Green Upholstered Chair By The Fire Replica Two. "Well now," he said. "I'd better go home and get dressed."

The shivers seemed to have drained down his body and out his boots. He walked to the door and paused. "Then I'll come back and you can tell me how to help." He went out the door.

From that day, Betsy Latham's work on the Millford replica gained ground. For the first few years, Betsy and Mr. Twelveclocks worked alone. They perfected Twelveclocks' Cabin Replica, and when William saw how beautiful it was, he wanted to show it off. He began telling people about what he was doing.

People came from miles around to admire the replica. They followed William Twelveclocks through the almost finished Replica Of The Woods to see Betsy's place. They walked slower than usual, and Twelveclocks liked to watch them pause and look at things. Generally by the time they reached Betsy's Studio Replica, they were silent with awe. A few babbled or chattered, not many.

It got so people came to gape and stayed to marvel. Many brought a favorite table or chair and asked for a copy of it. Some brought old clothing they wanted to appreciate just as it was, and they begged Betsy to make replicas of it. Unless they insisted on paying, Betsy put them to work. Marshall and Morton sold imperfect replicas, advertising GENUINE FACSIMILES OF REAL BETSY LATHAM REPLICAS. Lots of people from out of town bought those.

Eventually neighbors from Millford had to take turns working shifts on weekends, the intersection between the real Millford and its replica got too crowded with volunteers heading out that way. As the replica expanded, growing with the work of many hands, Betsy tried to keep track of the stories.

She occasionally grieved the many wonderful memories of Millford's homes and its people that got left out. There is little time to tell them all here, but they are many. No matter how busy or overworked she was, Betsy always went home to sleep every night.

William Twelveclocks did the same. He especially helped put Millford's memories into the things people made. William Twelveclocks died before the work was complete, but he will always be remembered. He is part of the reason there is a real Millford and a Replica.

Chapter Fifteen

William Twelveclocks was a dear and special man, I agree. Everyone missed him. Things got lost the usual way after he went. These days he's no longer traipsing around Millford returning people's lost possessions. I lost an earring last week. Maybe it'll turn up.

No cookies for me today, thank you. Weight is one thing I'm not losing. It is a pleasure to see your appetite's back. I brought a few extra groceries, and I'll put them in the nightstand before I go. Nothing perishable, and it's such trouble to go down the stairs, isn't it? The groceries will be here in the nightstand if you get hungry and the delivery boy is late, or whatever.

It would be nice to sit by the window, but too cold for you today. Even if you did wear both bathrobes, it would still be too cold, I'm sorry. Let me go and look out. You stay under the covers.

So that's how it looks from up here.

Nothing, only the hedge. When I fight my way through, I see only the low part. I had no idea it grew so high, looks like it wants to climb to the windows. It has a ways to go yet, you won't see it from the bed any time soon.

What else is there to see? The vacant lot across the street, hardly attractive. That old boarded-up house by the bus stop, but the other homes are nice.

Which painted sign? At the other end, you say. That probably came down long ago, it's not there. That house, if I'm looking at the one you mean, certainly does need painting. Wait, there is a sign. It's a FOR SALE sign, not the one you described. Families come and go in old neighborhoods like this.

That's true, it all depends on how we look at it. Every town has attractions, special places. Let me come back by the bed. Your voice isn't strong enough to keep calling across the room.

There, we can each hold an end of the ribbon while the story begins. You do want a story, don't you? Truth be told, I'm glad to hear it because this is a special story.

I've been saving it. Today's just the day. Remember how you liked the story about Tom and the gypsy? Tom's stories are your favorites, I know. Tom's in this one too. Hold the ribbon, here we go.

A Journey Everywhere

The future was a real thing for Tom Latham. When he came from his den in the evening, to sit with his wife, Amzie, and watch television, Tom would say, "We'll pay off the house next year." He meant it and they did. When he and Amzie drove past Millford Flats on their way to East End, Tom said, "Five years from now, that land will be covered with houses." He was right. Another time Tom remarked, "Andy is going to propose to the Knecht girl." His son was married now, and the Knecht girl's last name was Latham.

Tom's wife Amzie agreed, while differing, about the future. About owning the house, she said, "We just might." As Amzie watched the expanse of Millford Flats flow past the car, she said, "It's certainly possible." About Elizabeth Knecht she said, "It could be. Two Betsys, a daughter-Betsy and a Betsy-in-law."

To Tom, Amzie's answers seldom made good, hard sense.

This occasionally annoyed Tom because matters usually turned out as he expected. They owned the house on Pear Street free and clear, and he had set aside a sum so taxes would always be paid, even if, as insurance policies put it, he predeceased Amzie. The flats out by the cemetery went to a housing development years ago. Those houses were cheaply built, as Tom expected, and his company refused to insure them. From time to time, Tom tried explaining the future to Amzie.

"It's consequences, that's all. A man simply has to consider things as they are, then face the future."

Amzie looked past him with a gaze which, he wished, looked ahead through the years. "I suppose," she said. "It's easier for you. You know how to consider things as they are."

223

Amzie never looked into the future. Tom Latham finally accepted that. He did not know where her gaze looked, but he took out another policy to pay the taxes on the house.

Yet the year Tom Latham retired, he began to wonder what lay in the distance his wife's gaze studied. He had watched that stare for many years, looking off for miles from a twenty-foot room. It definitely saw something.

Tom had planned for retirement, and they would live on a pension nearly equal to his paychecks. Doctor Paul Martin, who'd bought old Doctor Foster's practice before Foster retired, seemed capable of keeping track of the usual problems of aging. If the unexpected came up, the city of Ginnett, half an hour away, had two big hospitals. Their son, Andy, was getting on well as a tax accountant, and Andy's wife, Betsy-in-law, was pregnant with their first child. As for daughter-Betsy— there was no accounting for daughter-Betsy.

Tom Latham sat in Doctor Paul Martin's waiting room and thought about these things. He sighed and let the magazine he'd been reading fall to the table. There were consequences a man simply had to face, and today he felt moderately ready to face up to one of them.

He had not told Amzie about the three previous appointments with Doctor Martin. He had also avoided mentioning the occasional shortness of breath and the tightness along the breastbone that prompted his pre-retirement exam. He had run on a treadmill for Martin, and given more blood to Martin's nurse than he thought necessary, and he had breathed deeply and wheezed and coughed and spit when Martin told him to.

Martin had promised to mail the results in an envelope that looked like a bill. Amzie never opened bills. It was odd, alarming in fact, that instead Martin's nurse called the office to set this appointment today.

Tom picked up a magazine. Doctors and wives, he thought. Neither gave answers straight out. He opened to an article on contract bridge and read the first three paragraphs. He let the pages fall closed. He'd been reading the same article a moment ago.

Martin's nurse stood in the doorway. "Mr. Latham, Doctor Martin is ready in his office."

Tom stood and followed her, turning right automatically down the hall that opened into examining rooms.

"In his office," the nurse repeated. He turned and followed her the other direction. She stepped aside at a doorway near the end of the hall.

Inside, Paul Martin sat at a glass-topped desk. He was in shirt sleeves, without his usual white coat, and a stethoscope hung over the telephone.

"Sorry you had to wait, Tom." Martin stood and extended his hand. He was wearing reading glasses.

Tom settled into the chair across the desk. He tried reading the look in the doctor's eyes, but Martin sat down and glanced at a file he'd been studying. He eased the folder closed and looked up, his eyes dim behind his glasses.

"I expect you're wondering about the test results." Martin smiled but his eyes were not smiling.

"You were going to mail them."

"Yes, but I decided we'd better talk, go over these results together." Martin's clean white fingers turned the file sideways on the glass. He swiveled it back to vertical. "When you came in you said you were feeling, how did you put it—aimless. I think that was your word. You wanted to know—my word now—if ennui was a natural consequence of the aging."

Tom's thoughts backtracked rapidly. He recalled that he had lied.

Sitting in the waiting room before the first appointment, he had remembered Maria Romano. He recalled the day he'd asked her crystal ball whether he should propose to Amzie. The woman had come up with a story, gypsies were notorious for such tricks. Doctors were probably in a class close to

225

fortunetellers, discovering only what the patient already admitted to. Instead of telling Paul Martin about the painful spasms of breathing, Tom had left a few things out.

Martin was watching him now, fingers tented above the file folder.

"Aimless, right," Tom repeated. "Ever since retirement came up. Finished last week, by the way." He wished he knew how to put a good light on his last afternoon at Millford Insurance. "Left with a nice bonus."

"Congratulations." Paul Martin smiled and his eyes smiled too. He opened the file and studied it.

In a way, Tom persuaded himself, the symptom was not entirely untrue. He had been feeling aimlessness. The last few years, each time he looked straight at the future, it had a way of curving out of sight. He tried to follow the curve, but it twirled away without features or plans. He could see himself living in the big house with Amzie. Grandchildren would visit. He would be happy. He would do things. But what those things were, he could not guess. Gradually he came to envy Amzie because apparently she lived without a future. She did not have to peer down that endless curve.

Martin let the file fall shut. His eyes, when they met Tom's, no longer smiled. "I can't account for the ennui, Tom." Martin shrugged and let his hands fall open. "Maybe one of my colleagues in those therapy fields can help."

Tom shook his head. He'd heard of what Don Winks, back at the office, called the Sigh Doctors. Psychia-this, Psycho-that. People went to them and sighed a lot, not much of an improvement.

"But I did find something else." Paul Martin paused. "I'm not sure quite how to put this."

"Heart, right?"

Paul Martin looked pensive. "A non-medical way of putting it." He nodded. "But to the point."

A flash of sunlight, from a car passing beyond the window,

226

caught on Paul Martin's reading glasses. Tom blinked. He saw a light, as bright as that, flashing at the end of the curve which led into the future.

"I'm a man who likes to think ahead," Tom said firmly. "About consequences." In the instant of that flash, he knew he was lying. His arms pushed up on the arms of the chair and his body stood. Paul Martin watched him rise, and Tom tried to figure out what he was doing. He had better say something.

"But today's a particularly busy day, Paul." Tom's voice had the ring of confidence he used before closing a policy sale. Perhaps he did know what he was doing. "How about a game of golf sometime?"

Tom paused, disbelieving the easy way his voice had spoken. "Not that this isn't important. I appreciate that you've gone over this thoroughly, figured it out for certain. You have done that."

"Well, yes, but there are things you should know." Paul Martin was on his feet now. His hand reached automatically to meet the hand Tom Latham extended.

"Then it's settled. Thanks for your help. I'll call you next week about that golf." Tom's hand released Paul Martin's. He felt pride and an ache of nostalgia. He had always had a good handshake.

With his heart pounding, Tom expected his legs to feel like putty. His legs felt fine. They got him as far as the door. For a panicked moment he saw a vision—the end would come right here in Martin's office. He would never tell Amzie good-bye. He turned the knob.

Paul Martin's voice pulled him back. "Don't get me wrong, you've got nothing to worry about. Just slow down."

"Sure thing." Tom managed a smile. It pulled at the muscles in his neck.

Martin's voice followed him past the nurse's desk. "You should get annual check-ups." Tom did not turn back.

Walking to his car, Tom felt glad he'd parked near the

building. The heart could go at any time. He drove from the lot, but instead of taking the right which would lead him to Pear Street, he turned left. He drove east down Brooke and followed it all the way to the turn-off for Millford Flats. He parked by the side of the road above the Flats subdivision.

Tom Latham stared at the windshield of his car. He saw dirt spots and studied them. Passing cars slowed to go around him, and faces glanced back in rearview mirrors. Tom ignored them. He wanted to look into the future, but he studied the windshield a long time.

Beyond it, he saw single-family dwellings laid out on a geometric grid. The houses were cheaply built and he knew it. To the east, dark clouds collected over Millford's downtown. To the west, the blinking lights of a car dealership were visible. Tom had heard Bud Dolgan, Sheriff Dolgan's second son, bought that dealership a while back.

Tom tried looking past the houses, past the clouds and the ricocheting neon of the car lot. He saw an airplane descending to land at Ginnett Field. Beyond it, radio towers blinked back red eyes.

"Things as they are," Tom said aloud. There were things as they were and there was Amzie. He was probably going to suffer and he was surely going to die. That was. And then there was Amzie.

Suddenly a thought struck him. Tom's heart raced with it, and he started the car, took a U-turn across the road, and drove quickly back toward downtown Millford. The nearest parking place was a block away, so he had to run. His heart accelerated but he did not care. He had to get to the bank before it closed.

When her husband left that day, Angela Latham had set down her pen beside the Easter note she'd been writing to Andy and Betsy-in-law and gone to the front hall closet. She looked inside. Tom's golf clubs leaned in the corner, behind five winter coats and the archery set Tom gave Andy the year he turned fifteen. Angela Latham wondered if her husband was going to die.

Tom Latham was right when he said his wife could not figure out the future, but Angela had perfect pitch for the present. She also knew her husband was a healthy man in his mid-sixties, and that he had left a few details out when he said he was going downtown to ask Paul Martin if he wanted to play a few rounds of golf.

Tom would clean and check his clubs before asking Paul Martin, or anybody, to play golf. The clubs in the corner were dull and dusty.

Angela pulled a thin sweater from a hanger in the closet, and went out to sit by the apple tree in the back yard. It was a warm spring afternoon, but the breeze could turn cool in late afternoon and she did not know how long she would have to sit. Angela had sensed her husband's uneasiness lately, and had seen him return, more anxious each time, from three previous trips downtown on Wednesday afternoons. Tom was not asking Dr. Martin about golf. She lay the sweater on the bench that ringed the tree and sat down. She began to wait until she knew an answer.

Tom had built this wooden bench the year Betsy turned twelve. He had cut five planks, sanded them, painted them, and rounded their edges until splinters dissolved. The planks were wide and Angela leaned back, feeling the rough bark of the apple tree against her shoulders. She looked up at the house.

Tom painted the shutters on their big house every year. He always did it in July. The shutters hardly weathered, but Tom enjoyed driving to the hardware store and taking time with the decision, picking out the same color green every year, then driving home to unload the paint and the ladder onto the back porch. Angela tried looking into the future and

229

imagining Tom painting the shutters this July.

She visualized her husband climbing the ladder, the eaves of the big house above him. The can of paint in his hand had green drips down the side, like always, but somehow the picture looked wrong. The sky was deeper blue than a July morning haze. Below the ladder, the branches of the apple tree hung full and low with fat fruit. Apples never ripened until August.

This year Tom would paint the shutters in August. Angela could not figure why the chore would begin so late, but at least it would be done. Tom always enjoyed it.

Angela shifted her back against the tree and looked at the walkway that led toward the front of the house. Tulips and daffodils bordered the cracked pavement, catching the last hour of sunlight. Behind them, the hedge began. They would trim the hedge this year. She imagined Tom standing beside the hedge with his clippers, chrysanthemums and marigolds, late August flowers, blooming around his ankles.

As he cut back leaves and stray branches Tom would be talking about laying a new walkway. The old stones were broken. He'd suggest flagstones, but because it was August, he'd say that the job had to wait until the following summer. He would get an early start the following summer and use pale gray flagstones. Angela could see the fine walkway. Tom would build a new walkway two years from now. He was not going to die.

It was a shame how everything was going to get started so late for this summer, Angela thought. She listened to the first breezes of sunset rustle leaves overhead, and she picked up her sweater.

Angela was never sure how she knew what was going to happen. Sitting by the apple tree helped. She had been sitting here when she learned that William Twelveclocks would die in his cabin in the Millford Replica, instead of his cabin in the real one. She simply knew how it would happen. In this spot she had foreseen that Mary Roman's supposedly dead husband would return, then disappear after mowing the lawn once. From here she had watched her daughter Betsy get famous and move away. Angela began missing Betsy that day, even though twenty years would pass before Betsy left. Angela saw things in places other than below the apple tree, but being under its branches worked best.

Angela watched shadows take bites out of the house and the garden and the bench beside her. Dark was beginning to fall and the house was only a hulking black shape. She knew a number of things now. They were disconnected and they fell apart when she tried to touch them, like the tissue paper flower little Andy made once. Yet left untouched with questions, each was perfectly obvious.

Her husband would walk with a cane one day. Once Tom accepted that his left leg would never feel right again, he would buy a good cane in Ginnett. Andy and Betsy-in-law would have five children. Tom would buy archery sets for the three boys. One year, far into the future, Tom's leg would get so bad he'd admit he could not climb the ladder anymore. He would put off hiring help until Betsy took a few weeks off from the Millford Replica. Betsy painted the shutters that year. Every year, Tom would complain she used the wrong green.

Angela knew these things, but there was one thing she did not know, and she felt excited and curious about it. For all her listening, for all the stream of memories flowing toward her from the future, not one clue told what would happen next week. Angela smiled in the darkness. It was exciting not to know what would happen this summer.

Headlights swept past the tulips and daffodils, coming around the side of the house. Tom was home. The future was about to start and Angela hurried into the house.

Tom came through the door as she turned on a light and began unbuttoning her cardigan.

231

"Leave your sweater on, Amzie."

Tom left the front door standing open. He kept his jacket on too. He went to sit on the sofa and motioned his wife from where she stood in the living room doorway. "We're going back out in a minute. But first you have to sit down."

Angela turned on the floor lamp and crossed the room to join him on the sofa. Tom looked different. He wore the same clothes he'd worn when he left at noon, but he looked as different as if he had tried a new barber. He had not gotten a haircut. His eyes were bright. His face was ruddy and flushed, and he looked as happy to see her as if he'd been away all week instead of a few hours.

"Are you ready?" Tom asked.

"I think so. Is there something I need to be ready for?"

"You're right. I'm the one that's never ready. You've been ready for years."

Angela looked at him. Tom was not making much sense. Usually if he came home with a plan—they would drive to Ginnett for a better price on lumber, or he would once and for all explain to Betsy that she should charge admission to Replica Millford—his plan made sense. He was sounding nonsensical, and Angela liked the change.

"Okay, then we're both ready," she said. "Tell me."

Her husband took a deep breath. His cheeks grew even redder. "You've never been out of Millford," he said. "You're going to show me what's out there."

"I've been to Ginnett and East End," Angela pointed out.

"Yes, but every time I go, every time I went on a business trip, you told me what the place would be like. And it was always like that."

"You said it wasn't."

"It was. It always was. And every time business got bad you said it would get better. And when I had amnesia, you remembered things you couldn't possibly have known. Remember that?"

232

Angela nodded.

"You know things, Amzie. You always know things I never knew, I'll never know. I don't have enough time left to know them all." He paused, and suddenly the reddened flush paled. The words stopped tumbling out and Tom looked away.

For an instant Angela wondered again if he was going to die. Then she remembered. He would watch Betsy painting shutters and complain the whole time.

"Never mind that," Tom's voice hurried on. "I know a lot of things, but not the things you know. And I'm ready to know them. I have to know them. Amzie, please, I need to understand how you think about things."

Angela bit her lip. Tears welled in her eyes, making them sting. Tom looked happy. He felt hopeful. He was standing on the edge of a new future, and he believed she could tell him what it was going to be like.

Angela stared down at her hands. They were old, she saw. If she tried to explain, it would be all wrong. If she said she could not explain, Tom would give up believing. Her hands were old and she could not tell her husband what he needed to know. Through the springs of the couch, she felt his weight trembling.

"But wait." The couch bounced. "I forgot. I bought maps. I got a compass, out in the car, and suitcases." Tom's hands dug into his pockets. Maps and shiny folders tumbled onto the couch between them. The maps' covers named places she had heard of—Webster and Drosserville and East Junction—but others had unfamiliar names—Milkweed River Basin, Innisglen and The Flying Caverns of Moss Lake. The travel folders had glossy pictures of mountains and rivers and towering trees. Half-hidden in the pile, a large pink receipt said "BUD DOLGAN AUTOS—Your Millford Dealer."

"We're going on a trip," Tom said, pushing the maps and folders to spread them in front of her. "I know you can't tell me what I want to know, but show me. I bought a car." Tom's

233

fingers quickly snapped the receipt from the pile and tucked it back in his pocket. "We'll go on a trip and you can show me."

At last, Angela smiled. Now she knew what would happen this summer.

"When do we leave?" she said, but Tom was halfway to the door.

"Wait until you see this car," his voice finished saying after he was already gone.

It took several days to make the arrangements. The newspaper had to be stopped and a neighborhood girl appointed to pick up the mail. Suitcases had to be packed, and since Tom and Angela had no clear idea where they were going, Angie threw in two of everything, then took one of each out. Daughter-Betsy promised to cut the lawn regularly.

Tom spent time going over the car. It was a brand-new Lancombe Fleet Sedan, dark blue with all the options. Even though Bud Dolgan personally guaranteed it, Tom checked every system for himself. He measured tire pressure, checked water and tested the battery. He put bricks in the trunk to equal what the suitcases might weigh, then checked the tires again. He constructed a luggage carrier, while his wife read aloud to him.

"Place Rib B on Strut A," she would tell him, and he seemed to know what she meant.

He counted the money he'd withdrawn from the bank, his full retirement bonus. Even after the cost of the car, they had plenty. He spread maps on the dining room table and said to Amzie, "How about if we start by going north, a few hundred miles, maybe to Bricker Plains, then east as far as Colbo. We could go south from there, make a complete circle. What would you think of that?"

"That could happen," Amzie said distantly, "or something else."

Tom quietly folded the maps and put them back in the glove compartment of the car. Amzie was right, of course. If

234

he made up the future, it would have already happened.

For Angela's part, there was one item of the future that might need to be planned. One day when Tom was out buying auto supplies, she dialed the number of Dr. Paul Martin's office. She asked the nurse if there was any medication Tom should have along on a trip.

"Medication?" The voice at the other end of the line sounded uncertain. "Nothing I know of."

"Would you check?"

A moment later, the nurse returned to the line. "Let's see, advise to slow down, the doctor's notes say." Paper rattled in the background. "Heart rate normal. Respiration normal. Muscle tone adequate."

Angela waited out a pause.

"Here we go. Prescribe relaxant. There's a question mark after that. Recommend increased activity. Anxiety associated with retirement." Another pause. "That's it. Did Doctor say Mr. Latham should have the relaxant?"

"That's okay," Angela said, and she was smiling. "I'll take some extra aspirin along."

Paul Martin's nurse wished them a good trip and asked where they were going. Angela said that the trip was all planned except for that part.

Yet that first morning, when Tom backed the blue Lancombe Fleet Sedan from the driveway—its sides gleaming from a wash and wax the day before and its windshield spotless—disaster almost struck. The trunk was weighted with suitcases instead of bricks. Amzie's back, which bothered her when she sat too long, was supported with a special cushion Tom had bought at the auto supply store. His wallet was firm with traveler's checks, and several were hidden under the seat. Tom had planned every detail he could think of except what to do next. The Fleet Sedan's hood faced the drive and its trunk hung in the street. He did not know which way to turn.

Tom glanced at Angela. He shrugged. His wife stared for

a moment, uncertain what was wrong.

"Look," she said, pointing past him. "Mary Roman's cherry tree is blooming early this year. Let's drive past." And Tom turned left, which was south.

Angela Latham had never been out of Millford, except to Ginnett, East End and Pelleway, so their route was a wild one. They went south past Brockton, Meridian and Mouth Creek, then took a turn to follow another Fleet Sedan exactly like theirs and went west for several days.

They turned off and let the twin Fleet Sedan go because a sign said "Scenic Attraction—Don't Miss The . . . ," and the rest was broken. They did not want to miss it without even knowing what it was, so that night they stayed in a motel overlooking a lake which the sun turned purple at sunrise. The motel was called The Purple Isle, and its neon sign was burned out. The next morning they decided to go east, because it was a direction they had not tried yet.

If a town had a pretty name they stopped at it. If a place had an ugly name, they turned off the highway and went to see what was wrong. If a lake lay in warm sunlight, Tom and Angela waded a few feet out. If ice water trickled from a glacier, they dipped their fingertips and tasted. Gas station attendants looked at their license plates and remarked that they were a long way from home. Waitresses served strangely named specialties, which were sometimes good, but often not. Deer leapt across the road in their headlights and small animals stared at their taillights.

After a few days, Tom figured out how to suggest new destinations. He picked the route along the Millituckkawappta River because it had the longest name so far. They followed it for two days, seeing signs naming its name all along the way. When Tom finally said, "I've actually learned how to spell it," they turned south.

Angela's suggestions took them to battleground museums and five-foot-wide cottages and several bowling alleys. Tom took them to gorges and wide city streets, and into the Caverns of Mystery and over suspension bridges.

"Let's see snow," Angela said one day. The Lancombe Fleet Sedan turned north.

Of landforms they saw mountains, deltas, glacial plains, buttes, dunes, deserts, capes, slopes, isthmuses, plateaus, cliffs and coastlines. Of bodies of water—channels, shoals, creeks, rivers, brooks, lakes, ponds, marshes, swamps and one ocean. Three days out they bought a flower book and a box of gold stars. They put a star beside each flower they could name. Tom began learning the names of birds, and Angela learned many new ones. Tom remembered he'd forgotten to bring a calendar. He wanted to buy one until Amzie asked him why, and he could not remember. They read newspapers in small towns they'd never heard of. They got remarried twice, because they wanted to see their names in the *Amberville Breeze* and the *Saint Frog Courier*.

At last one day, a day whose heat made Tom guess the middle of summer had passed, he noticed something strange. Amzie had been making most of the suggestions for the past several days, so he had no idea where they were. Yet the terrain looked familiar. Tom liked the forested hillsides they were driving through, liked the small farms he could see dotting the plain ahead. He felt at peace and at home, as if whatever the future brought would be interesting, as interesting as the small-town landscape which now came into view as the Fleet Sedan topped a rise.

"Amzie." His wife dozed in the summer heat beside him on the car seat. "Where do you think we are?"

Angela slowly opened her eyes. It was a question they had often asked in the last three months, and she always enjoyed answering it.

A sign by the side of the road said, SEE THE REPLICA! AN AMAZING WORK OF ART!

"We might be coming back to Millford," Angela said.

Then she thought a moment. "Or maybe not."

Tom Latham smiled. He reached across the seat and gripped his wife's hand. "Let's go see if that town up ahead has a Pear Street," he said. "If it does, let's live there." Amzie's hand returned his grip.

Late that evening, Tom and Angela Latham sat in the back yard until night fell. Angela was tired and went up to bed, but Tom remained on the bench below the apple tree to watch the light on the second floor go on, then off. He listened to insect songs, and the distant murmur of traffic drifted to silence. He would go to bed soon. He knew that much of the future. About the rest, he no longer cared. He would sleep and maybe wake. If he woke, hot coffee would taste delicious in the morning.

"So that was it," Tom Latham said aloud to the darkness. He went up to bed.

Chapter Sixteen

*I*f you insist on sitting by the window, you'll have to have a blanket around you. Imagine, January, I come and find you by the window. Don't talk, you argued enough already. Your voice is too weak to keep that up. You can stay and look out the window, but we want the blanket tucked under your chin. I put it there because it falls open if it's not tucked in.

How about this for a compromise—you get into bed and I'll tell you a story. But only if you're in bed.

Don't look at me like that. You know. I'm not fooling you and you're not fooling me either. I'd tell you a story anyway. I'm an old softie, coming to visit every day, letting you do what you want. Did you see I brought groceries? Too bad you're not hungry, I stopped at the bakery. Maybe later. We'll save the treats for later.

Would you tell me absolutely truly about one thing? You can nod, I don't want you talking. This is important, please, I'm not joking. With your eyes sad like that, I guess you hear what I'm thinking.

I'm the only one who comes anymore, aren't I? Go on, nod if it's true. I'll tuck the blanket back up.

I thought so. The only one.

You're welcome, but please don't talk. No, not even to say a "thank you." I understand.

Only one visitor anymore. That smart-aleck delivery boy wouldn't bother with the hedge. I found the stick in the same spot I left it. Don't shrug, it loosens the blanket. You may as well know I talked to your doctor. He said he'd call and tell you. A nod means he did? That's good.

The nice young doctor can't figure out what you've got against hospitals. Easy for him. The older one said he understands. He said it was all right, as long as I came every day.

That's right, I was here yesterday. You just don't recall. And the day before too. Remember I told you all about Henry getting lost in the corn field, and about that song he made up? This one.

Don't hum along, just nod your head. You're too tired, I'll just hum a few bars. Remember that pretty song? And the preacher let him sing it in church too.

You don't remember, do you? I see it in your eyes when you try. I don't want you to hum, let the song go for now. How about the ribbon? Let's look at that.

That's right, the ribbon ran through the song. The ribbon coils into each of our stories, doesn't it? Let me just tuck the blanket back. You can keep the ribbon in your hands inside.

I'll tell you another story in a minute, but I have to make sure you're warm first. Are you cold? Your skin does look the wrong color, maybe only blue with the blanket reflecting the sun. I still say you'd be better cuddled up in bed. Think how warm the pillow would feel.

All right, we'll stay in the sun. If you shake your head it only loosens the blanket.

Another story? I promised one a moment ago. I did say I would tell one.

No more than a minute ago. "I'll tell you another story," I said. Another story after that? We'll see. Maybe another day.

I'm the only one, aren't I? The only one who gets through anymore.

I know, I know, the others come too. We remember each of them—Sheriff Dolgan and Mildred Bissell, Johnny with a sunburn from playing baseball all day, little Betsy making a tissue paper flower. They do all come to visit us.

What's that about Tom? The chair in his den, that would be his favorite chair, I think. Naturally you can see his face.

240

I dust the picture by the bed every day before I go. I dust it every time.

I did dust it yesterday. I was here, you'll remember in a minute. I promise I'll dust the picture today. Don't worry. I was here yesterday, you just don't quite remember.

That's true, you would remember exactly how Tom looked. Better than any picture, I agree. On which day? The day he came home with the new car, that's a good one. His face must have looked very happy that day.

Which chair? No, Tom's not sitting in a chair now. He's not here now, you just don't remember. No, he won't be impatient if you're late.

I promised and I keep my promises. We will tell a story today. It's almost ready to begin. Don't worry, another story after that too, but another day. I promise. I do. If only I can get through the hedge.

One day Angela Mona Zoey Maxwell Latham woke up and she was old. It was a Tuesday morning, the 15th of January, at about a quarter past seven. It was winter—a cold clear day just like this one—and Angela Mona Zoey wondered if her visitor would come today. She decided to get out of bed, to use the bathroom, and then to sit by the window and watch.

To the left of the bed, an oak and marble nightstand, which she and Tom had bought as part of a set several beds ago, offered a firm handhold so Angela could lever herself to a seated position. Two steps away, the clothes horse, where Tom used to hang his trousers so their creases would hold overnight, supported only a brief touch while Angela's other hand reached to the side of the dresser. The dresser's six drawers held sweaters Angela had not worn in years, slips and panties tucked into corners, and a girdle bought for Andy and Elizabeth's wedding and washed only once. Angela edged along the side of the dresser.

To its left, she reached for the clothes hamper, an unsteady structure of white wicker. She leaned there and, curious, lifted the lid. Many times she had bent to pull the last sock from the bottom, but now a tangle of flowered nightgowns filled the hamper halfway up. Apparently the chore woman had not come in a long time to do the washing.

The gap between the hamper and the bathroom door posed a problem. One leg of the hamper was broken and it wobbled, and the lining under the carpet was bunched at the edge. Angela paused and caught her breath, steadying herself with a hand on the wall.

A broad smudged scar marked the wallpaper at the height

242

of her hand. The worn place moved along the pale pink paper for two feet like a gray thunderhead. At the thunderhead's edge, the trailing rose pattern began again and continued along until the next place Angela planned to rest her palm. Angela guessed she must actually be old.

The mark on the wallpaper was worn through to the plaster. She could not have made this mark from touching it only today. She had come this way many times. The carved metal knob of the bathroom door felt cool when she grasped it.

From behind the bathroom door, an old woman was creeping into the mirror. White shoulder-length hair hung like corn silk over her face. A hand brushed the hair back. The hand had blue veins and white bones, and the skin covering it looked like a hankie caught on a tree stump. The face in the mirror came closer.

If an invisible hand had pinched the bridge of her nose, it could not have pulled the skin forward in more lines. Angela leaned on the sink and studied them—straight lines and wrinkly lines, lines that looked like scribbling and others that could be a poem written in shaky handwriting. One cheek might be a map of Millford. The other cheek mapped Millford's replica.

The nose of the woman in the mirror had no wrinkles, which was interesting. And the lips were pale and smooth above the hinge of jaw, like a marionette's chin. The lips were slightly parted, and Angela raised her eyes to meet the eyes in the mirror. The woman looked surprised.

How could this have happened? And overnight too, a remarkable thing. Terrible in its way. Angela thought of calling her daughter to tell her about it, then remembered that Betsy must be somewhere in Europe. Betsy had been invited on a tour to talk about the Millford replica. Angela thought of her son Andy, but he would be at work, and his wife Betsy-in-law needed all of her time to take care of the babies. The face of the woman in the mirror wrinkled a new way.

243

Doubt crossed her eyes. It was something about Betsy-in-law. The babies had grown up and moved away. Betsy-in-law's babies had their own homes now in places with new names, like Lancaster. That was one of the names. Angela realized she had grandchildren living in places she could not remember. She did recall that one of the grandchildren had his own children now, and that meant she must be the great-grandmother of great-grandchildren. Angela Mona Zoey began to wonder exactly how old she was.

Looking down, she saw that the old woman's body was wrapped in a long flannel nightgown, and the gown had faded violets printed on it. She worked her body free of the cloth and took a splash bath in the sink. Then she eased the muscles of the body down until the toilet seat supported them. The body gurgled and sensations probed it, a pain here, an ache lower down. The food she had eaten was moving through the parts that still worked.

For an instant, a memory clenched her heart. Long ago she had rested on the cool glass of a butcher counter, and a baby tugged at one nipple. Andy or Betsy, she could not remember. But the tug pulled a memory—a baby's body was nothing more than a tube for food. She felt like that now.

The cabinet to the right of the toilet held three fresh nightgowns. Angela chose the flannel one on top, the one with big blue irises overlapped on it like pond ripples. She worked it over her shoulders before she stood. As she managed the movements to push it down past her calves, she tried figuring out what had happened.

She remembered being eighty. The children had given her a birthday party. The grandchildren had come, or else the great-grandchildren. There were a lot, they were hard to keep track of. If the party happened, that meant she was more than eighty. Possibly eighty-five. No, the eighty-fifth birthday party definitely had great-grandchildren. So eighty-six, and probably older.

Tom had trusted numbers and could keep track of them. Tom would have known how old he was when he died, seventy-six and of a lung infection. Tom remembered every place they had gone on their trip, and he repeated them to her the day he died. Tom remembered everything, once he got over amnesia. He even remembered the untrue stories she had made up to replace missing memories. Angela leaned against the bath-room cabinet and thought of William Twelveclocks. It was nice of him to keep silent while she told Tom those stories.

William Twelveclocks had died in his cabin in Replica Millford. Angela guessed she must have been more than sixty then. William Twelveclocks went to the replica cabin to sit in the Plaid Armchair Replica and watch a fire in the fireplace until it burned out. It was night and when the last coal took a bite of darkness and swallowed it, the room fell silent. When they found him, only one of his watches still ticked. It was the old one made of silver with figures dancing on the face.

Betsy took William Twelveclocks' death hard. He had willed all his replicas to her, but Andy Latham got the watch that still ticked. Angela remembered asking her son about it once, and Andy said he had no idea why it came to him.

Angela leaned her weight against the wall and tried to remember what had happened after that. The Millford rep-lica made Betsy famous. Soon they would want her to come to Europe and talk about it. No, that was wrong. Betsy was in Europe already. Betsy was in Europe today.

Someone else had been to Europe, Angela remembered. She tried to recall who it was. Her mother, her father? They had lived in only Millford and Ginnett, and they were gone many years now. William Twelveclocks had been to Europe in the war, but there was someone else too, a man.

Johnny—that was it—her brother, Johnny. Johnny had gone to Europe twice, but the first time in a new way. The story came back gradually. Her brother had told her a secret once. He said that in another life he had led tours in Europe and he met his wife Nancy there. It was in another life, Johnny said. He asked her to keep it secret and she had. Johnny was gone now, dead at least a few years. And Nancy died too, maybe last year. Angela guessed she'd done okay with the secret.

But how had she managed to get old? That was the mystery, and today was as good a day as any to solve it. If she could find the pieces, they might fit together for an answer. She let her weight slide sideways along the wall until the edge of the sink supported it.

She remembered one day when she was seventy. The doctor had told her she should not drive. She remembered sitting in the car outside his office and wondering what, on the average, old people did. They could not drive. They played bridge and canasta and pinochle. She had never learned the rules of those games, but she tried reading the articles about them in the newspaper. Cards and their numbers never made sense. That day she had decided she would not grow old or play cards, but she stopped driving.

Old people gardened and played with cards. She enjoyed the garden, but gave up on cards long ago. There were the faces of playing cards, each one different and interesting. She loved to imagine a big hand, standing somewhere above her, gently tossing cards on a pile. Cards would land on the carpet, face up and face down, a few separate, but most overlapping. She always wanted to figure out what each card meant. They had actual names, like king, queen, electricity, map and oboe.

That was it.

Angela stood and pushed herself free of the sink. The fresh nightgown felt cool and smooth on her skin.

That was what had happened. She had been busy watching the cards fall, forgetting to watch herself grow old. How long had it taken to figure that out? Beyond the door of the bathroom, the sun had moved along the bedroom carpet.

Angela gripped the edge of the sink, braced herself and moved to the door. Sunlight had filled the bedroom, and it was filled with many things too. She knew the names of them all. There was carpet, with its red twining background and the sunlight woven into it. There was dresser, drawer pull, antimacassar, jewelry box. Inside the box were pearls, tourmaline, silver and turquoise. There was a china dish on the dresser with postcards in it, and paper clips, and a plumber's business card and a graduation tassel. She could remember them all now without looking. There was a window seat and a bed. There was a nightstand. There was a length of green ribbon fallen on the marble top of the nightstand and coiled there.

Angela noticed that she was standing by the nightstand, and she wondered how she had gotten there. Cards were falling from a deck perhaps and the dream was still going on. Cards fell from above her. One card had the name Lancaster. It had the picture of a great-grandchild on it. Another card was called William Twelveclocks, and another with a beautiful face when she turned it over was called Tom. That was how she had gotten old. Angela leaned on the nightstand and let her relief go. Getting old was a way of turning over cards. She wondered how many were left.

A length of green grosgrain ribbon, twisted into figure eights and curled over itself, lay on the marble top of the nightstand. Angela took it and let it uncoil over her fingers. The ribbon was important, she could not remember why.

She hoped her visitor would come today. If her visitor came, there would be a story and the ribbon would be in the story. This might be the day the visitor came. Or it might not. She decided to sit by the window and watch. Her hand closed around the ribbon. She had known once why the ribbon was important, but she could not remember it now.

A leaning touch on the clothes horse brought her to the edge of the dresser, and she shifted along it to reach the wall by the window. The rose-patterned paper on this wall was ruined by handprints too, but not so many. This is a good day, Angela thought, and she would sit by the window. She settled

247

onto the window seat and spread the ribbon on her lap.

If her visitor came today there would be a new story. Beyond the window, Pear Street shone, flat and gray as if baked by the winter sun. At the end of the street, where Mrs. Roman's BEAUTY PARLOR/FORTUNETELLING sign used to hang, workers were erecting scaffolding. Several large black canisters stood on the front walk, paint possibly. A big blue van was parked at the corner, and young men called to each other in laughter, carrying tall cartons toward the house. Angela hoped they would start putting on the paint while she sat by the window because if they painted today she would know what color to remember the house.

New people were moving in. They had names she would never know. It was odd how Mary Roman and Maria Romano had died on the same day, twin sisters apparently. Tom had told her so.

Mary Roman's husband came back once. Angela remembered that. She had been sitting under the apple tree and dreamed it would happen, and she had wanted to tell Mary Roman before he came. She told the gypsy twin sister instead. Maria Romano probably never told Mary. The husband was dark and swarthy and dressed in dirty clothes, but he had mowed the lawn once. Angela saw him kiss Mary Roman on the lips, and then he left again.

A week later, passing where Mary Roman was hanging out laundry, Angela mentioned him. Politely, she thought.

"You saw nothing," Mrs. Roman snapped. "My sister casts spells and people imagine things. You imagined it." And she stepped behind a wet bedsheet to end the conversation.

Angela smiled and wondered. The sisters were dead many years now. A swarthy man had come to the funeral, but he was dressed differently. He wore a suit.

At the other end of the street, Mr. Pembroke's house had weathered boards nailed to the windows. Angela leaned on the cold window glass and studied the house where Lamar

248

Pembroke had painted a Rembrandt.

Angela guessed she and Tom might have stopped at a town with such a house. But they would have stopped in any town that advertised its own replica, they would definitely have turned off the road to see that. The replica brought tourists, and visitors got confused, mistaking the real Millford for the Replica. Millford residents knew how to tell which was which. If you got lost, you went to the library and if the main room did not smell of mutton and rising bread, you were lost in the replica. Not even Betsy Latham had been able to make a perfect copy of the Lamar Pembroke Rembrandt.

The sunlight cast a shadow in the shape of Lamar Pembroke's house. Angela studied the shadow a long time until she could see a lovely young woman's face in it, and then she looked away.

Now that she thought about it, Angela supposed, this might have been a nice day to sit at the other bedroom window. That window overlooked the house next door, and the dormer window where she had once seen snow. They were all gone now, her mother, her father, Mary Roman, and nieces and nephews moved to towns with their names hidden on the faces of overturned cards. Johnny gone, Nancy gone, only Angela left to remember Johnny in his baseball cap. His team said he was a hero one night, but she could not remember why.

Angela forced her eyes to focus nearer to her own house. She would have to face it, after all, sooner or later. She wished her visitor would come so she would not have to look at her own garden, at the hedge, and then upward across the street toward the bare field where a house used to stand. Old Mr. Madden had died in the house that once stood there. The bare field looked dry, no place for him to sit without a house built around him. But he was gone, Mrs. Madden gone with him. Mr. Madden had waited in that house until Elinor came to meet him.

For a moment, Angela wondered what chair Tom would choose to sit in and wait for her. He liked the living room sofa well enough, but would probably sit in his den, in the potato brown leather chair. He wore his plaid Saturday shirt, visible enough if she closed her eyes and looked carefully. His red shirt with the gray squares. His eyes were calm and he watched the door. Angela hoped he did not mind waiting. Tom was the one to arrive early for appointments, but in those last few years he never minded when she arrived late. He only asked what she had seen in the meantime.

Angela opened her eyes. Below the third-storey window, her own lawn lay overgrown. Trailing grass covered the walk and the dead heads of last summer's flowers fell at injured angles. She tried to imagine the lawn banked high with daffodils.

The house had seemed huge and frightening back then, when Mrs. Madden lived in it, then one day daffodils appeared on the lawn. Angela wished Mrs. Madden had not raked them up the next morning.

Angela paused and gripped the edge of the windowsill. There was another memory, and it was trying to get through. The gardener was standing in the doorway downstairs.

"I can't keep up with how fast it grows, Mrs. Latham," he had said. Grass stains made patches on the knees of his overalls. "You'll have to hire someone else."

How long ago had that been? She managed to get down the stairs that day and to answer the door. The gardener helped her back upstairs before he went away that last time. Now the gardener could not get through. When the hedge had finally knitted itself over the gate, he had stopped coming. No one came now except the visitor. The visitor was the only one who came anymore. That was why the laundry was not done. The chore woman could not get through.

Angela doubled the ribbon and coiled loose knots of the twin lengths. The ribbon twirled over itself, green and tan-

250

gled. It grew new shapes when her fingers played with it. She looked down at the hedge.

It was wide and green, circling the front yard and disappearing around the side of the house. From above it looked like a broad bumpy wall, but by squinting she could make out branches and leaves. They wove a path as wide as the sidewalk, twining shoots that sprung out and curled back with their own weight, tendrils joining and twisting with others until the hedge clamped every leaf into itself for a solid barrier. The gardener used to cut it back, but the vines grew too fast. They got ahead of him. It seemed he had stopped coming. She could not remember when.

If the visitor came today, the hedge would grow thicker. Already shoots flared from the top to reach the height across from the third-floor window. Below them, vines wove nets that twisted thicker to curl deep into the green wall. It grew so fast. Deep in, leaves grew which had probably seen light for only an hour before other leaves covered them. Vines twisted and knotted. There was no gate anymore. The hedge surrounded the house completely and every one of the stories made it grow.

That was what the visitor had missed, Angela decided. The visitor came because the people she worked for said an old woman needed company. The visitor could not understand about the hedge. The woman complained but her talk made it grow and grow.

Angela looked down at the ribbon. It was knotted into a ball. She let it roll on her lap and her fingers probed it. "Tell me a story," she remembered saying, and the hedge grew.

There were so many stories. There were happy stories and tragic ones. Joyful stories coiled into the sad ones and found their ways back out. Stories doubled and knotted over themselves and the hedge grew and it grew thicker again. Each face rose up like a leaf, each life a branch, every word shot strength into a vine.

251

Angela herself had only understood it when her memories began to go like the hedge. She kept getting lost and following paths that button-hooked back, and time and again she found herself enclosed in lovely turning torture, unable to find a way out. She tried reciting the leaves from wherever she stood. There were leaves for Howard Buckram and Josephine Gimetta, for Coach Sobella, and for Clara Ferguson. There were leaves for William Marshall and Edgar Morton—who had started a department store—and leaves for Mrs. Winnellton and her daughter, and there was one leaf for each of the eleven cats William Twelveclocks had saved from drowning.

If she followed the vines, things went other ways. The vines twisted and turned, showing leaves and hiding them. Following vines, she got lost easily. Johnny Maxwell married Nancy Gibson and the twins were born. One twin, Sandra, married a boy named Jonathan and the other twin, Mona, died during a war. To Jonathan and Sandra were born two sons—Henry, who lived in East End, and Mitchell, who lived in Bockworth. To Henry, Lawrence was born, son of Martha; to Mitchell, the daughter Cecilia, of Ruth. Of those last two boys, one lived in a place called Lancaster.

There were tendrils on each of the vines, and on the branches too. She could begin at any point and find her way along smooth turning growth to all the other places. Stories twirled and twisted from them. There was the day Henry lost his way in a corn field and made up a song with words that rustled like corn stalks in wind. There was the day Will Jordan finally got married. He wanted his wedding music played on the ocarinas he had made of ears of corn. His bride disagreed. And then his bride of only a year ran away with the magazine salesman who stocked the rack at Jordan's Market, but they got no further than Replica Millford and set up shop there. Only tourists shopped at the Jordan's Market Replica, no Millford resident ever spent a penny in it. Then Will Jordan died of a heart attack, fallen over his butcher block. And the children came to buy candy after school. The biggest child called home on the phone Will Jordan always let them use for free.

Angela made herself stop. With each remembering, the hedge grew thicker. She lifted her hands into the sunlight that spilled onto the window seat. Between them, the green ribbon caught the light. Below, the hedge looked thick, perhaps not even the thin coiling ribbon could pass through anymore.

It was only a bit of ribbon. She had found it one day tangled into the hedge. Long ago, she could not remember. Maybe trimming back the new growth when she was seventy. Maybe weeding the flower bed before the hedge overran that part.

The ribbon looked like the greenest leaf until she touched it. The soft length began to uncoil, pulling broken twigs and brown leaves along until it caught and came free with a tug. The last edge tore and a thread unraveled.

But it was good ribbon. It was a strong length of fine green grosgrain, practically new, ingrown into the hedge for years probably. It was too pretty to throw away, and she had brought it upstairs. It stayed in the white dish on the dresser for too long to remember. No dress quite matched the color to wear it. No Christmas package needed closing with it. No pair of shoes needed kelly green laces. What use was an old ribbon anyway? Except to hold in your hand.

Angela looked up. A blue and yellow bus rattled to the curb by Lamar Pembroke's house and she remembered hearing the noise. A figure, loaded down the groceries, was slowly descending the bus' steps.

Angela felt glad. The groceries were a good thought, she decided. The visitor was kind to bring them. The delivery boy from the New Jordan's Market could no longer get through the hedge and she hoped the visitor would manage somehow. The hedge had grown so thick.

The visitor wore a dark blue winter jacket and thick red

gloves. She set the groceries down on Lamar Pembroke's weedy lawn to stop and pull her neck scarf over her chin. She looked up the street toward Angela's house, shielding her eyes against the sun. Angela wanted to wave, but the ribbon felt too heavy. She could not lift her hand.

The woman picked up the two bags and began to move along the street. When she reached the hedge, it hid her from Angela's view. She went first to the place where the gate used to be. Tangled vines covered it completely now, no getting through that way.

A stick lay on the planter strip. She picked it up and began poking the hedge for weak spots. The branches were thick and difficult to the right of the gate, but a few yards to the left the stick wiggled through. The woman picked up the two heavy bags, ducked her face and began pushing her shoulders into the vines.

From above, leaves and vines fluttered sideways into new patterns. Something was moving among them. The hedge swayed when weight plunged forward, then shivered with movement stirring the thinner reaches nearer the edge.

The visitor was getting through, Angela thought. She wound the ribbon tight between her hands, holding on. She pulled the bright green edges until they were tight enough to hurt her hands. The ribbon was strong and did not break. She wondered what story had a ribbon running through it today.

So the visitor got through the hedge. She told a story which is ending. And when it was done, Angela Mona Zoey let the ribbon go.

About the Author

Carol Orlock's critically acclaimed first novel, *The Goddess Letters* (St. Martin's, 1987), won the Pacific Northwest Booksellers Award and the Washington State Governor's Award. Her stories and poems have appeared in *Ms.*, *CALYX*, *Women Of Darkness* (Tor Books), and *Fine Madness*, among other publications, and she has frequently published nonfiction in *Lear's* and elsewhere. In addition, she serves as fiction editor of *Crab Creek Review* and teaches writing at Shoreline Community College, where she is faculty advisor for *Spindrift* literary and art magazine. Her first book of nonfiction, *Inner Time*, is forthcoming from Birch Lane Press. She makes her home in Seattle, Washington.

Design by Ken Sánchez.

Text set in Baskerville with Ballé Initials
by Blue Fescue Typography and Design,
Seattle, Washington.

Broken Moon Press books are printed
on acid-free, recycled paper
exclusively by
Malloy Lithographing, Inc.
5411 Jackson Road
Ann Arbor, Michigan 48106.